Rose Tattoo
Marisa Haartz

Contents

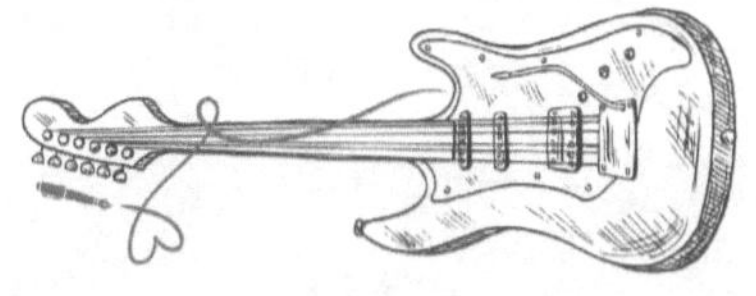

For those who find themselves in music.
And for my parents who believed in me.

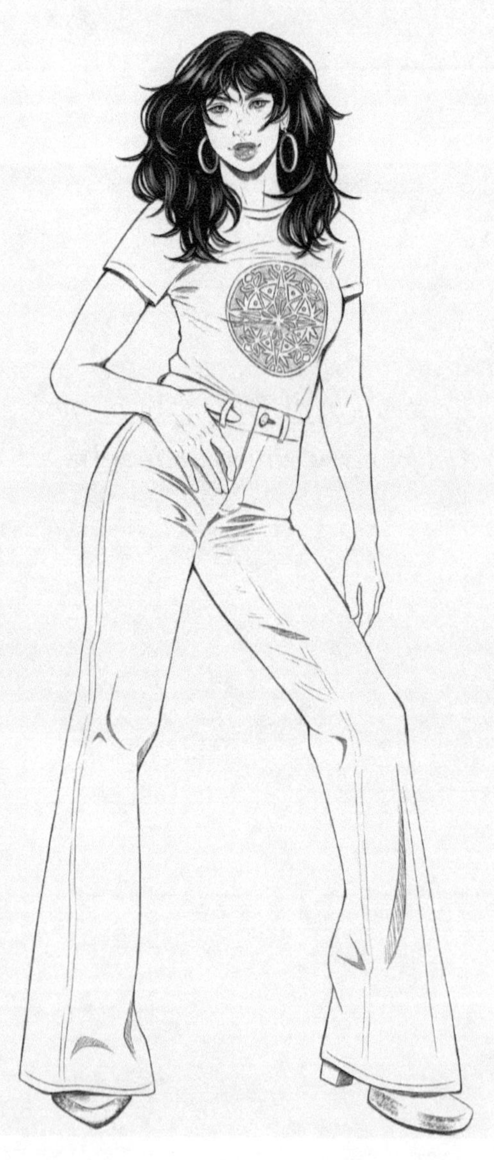

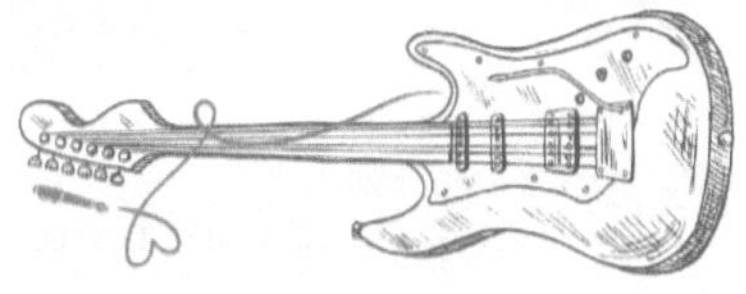

One
Atlas

Smells Like Teen Spirit-Stevie Howie Cover

There she is.

She doesn't look like she belongs at a punk rock concert in the South Bay. She looks like she stepped out of the 1970s and right into my life like some retro goddess granting wishes. Oak-brown hair parted down the middle with bangs that make her doe eyes look like saucers. A red halter top that hugs her narrow waist and striped flare pants that make her round hips look voluptuous. She's a vision that captivates my attention from the second I lift my gaze over the microphone, clearing the sweat from my vision to focus on the fair skinned angel standing in the center of a roaring crowd.

There's no way a rowdy grunge concert is her scene, so what the hell is she doing here?

I'll make it my mission to find out.

As we sing through our cover of "Smells Like Teen Spirit," I hold her gaze, not knowing if she can tell I have my sights set on her from the platform. The mysterious outsider that's going to make my night.

Our version of the song is a tad slower than the way Cobain intended, but with a heavy beat and a lot more bass, it still carries the same energy. Enough for people to dance on the floor and move their bodies with the rhythm.

Of the hundreds of reasons I love being a musician, seeing the control our instruments and voices have over a crowd is intoxicating. Better than any drug, we are gods with the ability to make people move the way we want, feel the way we feel, do whatever we desire for the sake of our craft. That kind of power sends adrenaline through every vein in my body. I don't think the other guys feel quite the same way, but they enjoy the rush of performing nonetheless.

But at the end of the day, we're in this for the love of music, that has to remain our foundation for us to work. For *this* to work.

We close out the set with an original piece that has everyone headbanging and a mosh pit starts in front of the stage. The chaos continues even after we say our farewell and thank everyone for coming out.

The second I say our closing line: "Thanks for coming. We are Broken Compass. Goodnight." I set my guitar on its stand and leap off the stage to track down the flower child through the sea of distressed denim and black t-shirts, shirking out of reach from any of the groupies trying to score a night with a musician. Blonde bimbos in band tees they got at Walmart are easy to find, seduce, and dispose of. I need to find the mystery siren.

And there she is, leaning a curved hip against the bar waiting for a drink, looking at something on her phone. Perfect. That probably means she's here alone.

Putting on my most charming facade, I approach her by inserting myself between her and the couple facing each other one spot over at the bar. They get the hint and slide over a little to make room.

Her deep chocolate eyes flick up to mine. With her chin still angled toward her phone, she peers through thick lashes to make eye contact. Even though I'm the one with the height, I can't help but feel like she's the one sizing me up. Evaluating whether I'm worth her time or not.

"Did you enjoy the show?" My voice is carefully crafted, girls love the mysterious allure of a musician, but they also want the charm.

She slides her phone into her pocket before laying her bent elbow on the bar top, leaning even more to amplify the effect her curves have on me.

"It was a good show," she says. Though I sense a *but* coming. "But you were a little stiff on stage. Not much fun to watch a live band unless they put on a show."

Ouch. She's ruthless. "I could argue that people should be here for the music, not a dance recital."

That's when the bartender slides her the seltzer she ordered and her card. She takes a leisurely sip before replying, making me wait for a response.

"You make a good point. But music is one of the few things in life where people are encouraged to feel every ounce of emotion. Where you're allowed to feel everything to the fullest instead of stifling it. So put a little movement in your hips and give yourself permission to *feel*."

Thinking this girl would be an easy target was my greatest mistake and greatest reward. Because her keen, confident mind and wicked tongue might be just as enticing as her curves.

Although we're already standing inches apart, I take half a step forward so her face is all I can see in my line of sight, so I can smell her fresh perfume over the scent of beer and adrenaline.

"Maybe you could show me how you'd like me to move." I swear she stops breathing for a second. Then she blinks herself out of the momentary trance. Flashing her a playful smile I follow it up with, "How to move on stage, I mean."

Suppressing a grin, she shakes her head in disbelief. "How many times has that worked before?"

"Well, if you give me your number, I'll be one-for-one."

This close, I hear the ping of her phone just as her lips part to answer me. Distracted by the damn electronic, she ignores my play and looks at her phone only to crush my heart.

"My ride's here." And there goes my shot.

In a move that shouldn't be hot, she chugs a good portion of her drink before laying a hand on my chest. Her touch is electrifying. If I thought playing live music was a drug, her touch is downright intoxicating.

"I guess you'll have to get creative and learn to move on your own. Best of luck, Atlas."

Ugh, my name on her lips would be so divine if it wasn't a farewell.

I feel no shame in watching her walk away. The view is perfection. But apparently I'm a glutton for punishment because the sight of her walking away is pure torture.

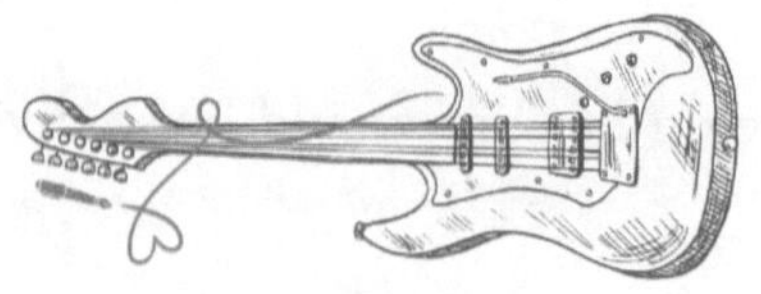

Two
Layla

9 TO 5-DOLLY PARTON

My editor wanted more connection in my pieces. She wanted me to humanize my subjects and make them relatable, not just superstars on their way to fame. Apparently, and I quote, my "work holds a tone of formality and distances the readers from the subjects."

I mean, I'm the pop culture columnist. I'm not writing pieces about how to find love and happiness. I'm writing about what's current, what's trending, and the underdogs I predict will make it big in this world. I predict trends and popularity, I'm not Howard Stern.

But if I don't deliver an article that makes her swoon over a heart-throb musician and fall in love with a local theater company, Mira will send me back to writing articles about university parking rates.

I've worked too damn hard to get to where I am just to fall back down the ladder, especially this close to graduation. I need all the printed material I can get for my portfolio.

Luckily, I stumbled into a club the other night and found my next subject: Broken Compass. Cheesy name but it has the potential to be a household name, if they play their cards right.

I won't say I set the trends, I'm just a small university newspaper journalist, but I have a habit of spotting the greats before the rest of the world.

And I spotted something incendiary in those four guys on stage.

I don't have a car so I had to walk from campus to the smoothie place McKenzie loves so much to meet her for a study session. Finals are only a month away. Praise the Lord, cause I'm so ready to be done with college, done with school.

I know, logically, that the workforce will still entail many of the same rudimentary tasks such as making deadlines and research for articles, etcetera, but performing said tasks for a job I love instead of for professors who barely take the time to read our work seems more rewarding.

If I never have to take a pop quiz ever again, it will still be too soon.

McKenzie is sitting at a table in the corner that's meant for six, yet her coursework blankets every inch of the tabletop.

"Thanks for leaving room for me," I say as I pull a chair out and slide into it. This place is so crunchy the chairs are supposed to be ergonomic but they just feel downright uncomfortable. Between the two of us, I'm the one who looks like she's supposed to be vegan and use reusable paper towels. But I love bacon and I hate cleaning.

McKenzie, on the other hand, looks like she has four rambunctious kids. Yet she and I are both childless. Blonde hair in a messy bun, bags under her eyes, the same black leggings she wore yesterday and a pale blue tank top. Studying for the LSATs has consumed her entire existence.

"Oh, sorry," she shoves a few pieces of paper to clear a spot big enough for my laptop. "I'm a little frazzled. I only have another two weeks before the LSATs."

Reaching my hand across the space between us to clasp hers, I steal two seconds of Mckenzie's attention. "I love you. And I support you. And as soon as your LSATs are done, we are going to celebrate with loud music, food that will rot our insides, and enough alcohol to kill an elephant. Ok?"

The tension slips from her shoulders for just a second as she agrees, "Ok." Then the air returns to its stiff state of being in her presence as she cram as much information into her brain as she possibly can.

"How'd your meeting with Mira go?" My considerate friend takes a short break to check in with me.

Rolling my eyes, I inhale deeply and exhale a harsh breath through my nostrils to control my tongue before I let it get the better of me.

"She said I need to humanize my subjects more. She said my writing comes off as distant and clinical. I have to write in a more approachable manner if I want to continue being the arts and music columnist."

"What?" McKenzie gasps without looking up from her textbook, highlighter in hand. "You're writing is extremely approachable. I mean, I personally like that you don't glamorize everyone. Whether you're writing about a nobody or Taylor Swift, these people aren't our BFFs. You're supposed to be objective."

"Apparently she wants more of the nitty gritty about people. I need to learn what I can and write about their favorite food as well as their artistic approach."

"Maybe you should find a local band or something and ask for a more in depth interview. Maybe shadow them for a bit to really get a sense of who they are and how they work."

Seed planted.

An idea starts to form, a vision of how I can not only accomplish this mission, but blow Mira's twisted pantyhose right off.

Pulling out my phone, I open the Instagram app and search for the Broken Compass account. Sliding into their DMs makes me feel a little too much like a groupie, but with a polite and formal message inquiring about an interview, I hope I come off as a respectable journalist, not just another fangirl.

They were a good band. I see lots of potential with them. Their lead singer has the mysterious charisma of Kurt Cobain while looking like bronzed Jim Morrison, and the voice to match. But he also gives me the impression he wears a mask for his audience to admire while keeping his personality under lock and key. I really considered giving him my number before my ride arrived. As cheesy as his pick up lines were, his magnetism was undeniable.

The rest of the band is just as entertaining and talented. Their drummer could have the makings of Jon Bohnam greatness.

They are a mish-mosh of talent that has found their genre, grunge music, but not their purpose. With a mix of cover songs and original songs, I sense they are still seeking the message they want to convey to the world.

That potential paired with an inside look to the early days of stardom could make for a great piece. An elevated addition to my portfolio, as well.

My phone dings five minutes later with a reply from the band's account. I have no idea which member is typing but I would guess it's not the lead singer. The tone is too cheerful to be the brooding, shaggy haired musician from the other night.

@BrokenCompassBand: Nice to make your acquaintance, @LaylaRose!! I'll share the idea with the band, but I'm certainly on board. Let me know what you'd need from us and we'll make it happen. Thanks for reaching out about the opportunity!

No man trying to make an image for himself as the strong silent type would use that many exclamation points.

I purposely avoided the part about being a journalist for a college newspaper, not some fancy blog or magazine. Hopefully they let that bit slide at the interview.

"Have you heard from Jack recently?" Just the mention of my ex's name makes me cringe.

"No. But don't put that kind of negative energy into the universe. If we don't speak of him, maybe he'll never show up again."

My emotionally abusive ex was supposed to be out of my life six months ago when I finally cut ties. But he continues to find opportunities to sneak through the cracks and back into my life. Much to his dismay, he hasn't snuck his way back into my heart. We were together for two years before I finally woke up and noticed all the patterns of emotional abuse and narcissism. McKenzie had to help me move my stuff out while he was in class and I moved in with her—perfect angel. Because I knew he'd do anything to get me to stay if he knew my plans to leave. I knew he'd try to pull some shit to manipulate me.

The only way to deal with people like that is to cut them off completely. No contact. No fodder for the flames. No ammunition. It was one of the scariest and most liberating things I've ever done.

"Let's hope it stays that way."

Ding.

Two days later I receive a reply from the band while shamelessly binging Audrey Hepburn movies and eating a pint of Tillamook Ice cream.

Eager to get the ball rolling, I reply in a flash.

@BrokenCompassBand: Good news!!! The band is on board. If you want to sit in on one of our rehearsals and interview us afterward, that would be great. We rehearse Mondays and Thursdays. So just let me know your availability!

@LaylaRose: Awesome! I'm free this Thursday. Just give me a place and time and I'll be there!

Three

Layla

L.A. WOMAN-THE DOORS

Maybe my usual flare jeans and white fitted shirt isn't the most professional attire for an interview, but we're talking about a grunge-rock band so I hope they appreciate my lack of formality.

Doing my due diligence ahead of time, I researched the address the faceless band member gave me via Instagram to make sure they weren't luring me to an abandoned house somewhere. Thankfully, the address turns out to be a music shop in Torrance. And that's exactly what I find when the Uber drops me off.

The sign above the store reading Wilson's Music looks a little worse for wear, but adds character to the storefront. Records and instruments sit in the window displays that look older than my mom.

As I step through, I'm transported into a world of music I've only dreamed of. The floor is layered in Persian rugs except for a corner of the store that holds all their vinyl records. A shag army green carpet sits beneath a rust toned sofa where patrons can listen to records and test them. The rest of the store has every instrument imaginable from guitars and drums to harps and mandolins. A couple people mill about looking at the merchandise for sale.

But the most niche artifact in the shop is a sign above the guitars that reads NO "STAIRWAY TO HEAVEN" and I can't help but laugh to myself.

A middle aged man with a grey ponytail stands behind the counter concealing all their most prized possessions such as first edition records and instruments that belonged to famous people—or were near famous people.

One of the guitars hanging on the wall behind the counter has a plaque that states it belongs to the shop owner who was at Woodstock and had a backstage pass sticker on his guitar.

Approaching the counter, I ask the man, "Are you Wilson?"

He peers over narrow reading glasses to examine me, ignoring the guitar he's restringing.

"Nah, I'm just the luthier. Wilson is closer in age to Willie Nelson than me. What can I help you with?"

"I'm a journalist," I say proudly, even though I don't have the official credentials to prove it. "I'm here to interview Broken Compass and observe a rehearsal."

Nodding his head, the luthier hums, "Mmm, gotcha. They're in the back. Practice room B." Gesturing with a pair of pliers, he points me toward an opening in the wall between two Les Pauls that I assume leads to the back rooms. I pass a room full of acoustic guitars before coming to the end of the hall where three doors make three sides of a square. The center door directly in front wears the letter B in chipped gold paint over the narrow window above the door knob.

Deep breath, Layla.

Then I enter.

Four men in various shades of black and gray turn their gaze on me, leaving their task of setting up equipment to view the intruder.

I feel like a doe surrounded by a pack of wild grizzlies. Four sets of eyes latch onto the weakest animal in the room.

No one speaks for a solid thirty seconds before one of the guys steps forward, the lead guitarist. He's also the tallest in the room. Lanky and towering, at least 6'2" with blond hair that resembles Jaime Campbell Bower. His smile instantly makes me feel at ease, genuine, and dimples for days.

"Hey, you must be Layla." He extends a hand for me to shake which feels keenly un-rock 'n' roll but is greatly accepted because it breaks some of the tension I'm feeling.

"Yeah. Nice to meet you. Are you the one I've been communicating with on Insta?"

"In the flesh," he runs his hands down his Black Flag shirt as if to check that he is indeed a living entity. "I'm Cameron. This is the rest of the band. That's Chris on drums," he points to the drummer with brown curls any girl would be envious of, and a thick beard to match. He's the shortest in the group but built like an ox. "Dallas on bass," average in height and build, he rocks the classic 80s hair metal hairstyle. "And this is our lead singer, Atlas."

My eyes swivel to the dark haired Adonis wrapped in black from head to toe. His jaw is clean shaven to amplify the chiseled form and full lips. Can a man be beautiful? Because I think this one is. It's hard to see his eyes beneath the shaggy hair hanging over his forehead but I feel their force. I feel the way he's weighing the scales of a second chance with me.

Intense doesn't even come close to describing his personality, at least on first impressions. He's gorgeous and he knows it which makes him lethal.

His whole aesthetic has *heart-breaker* written all over it. Woven bracelets, a couple burnished silver rings, and the sleeves on his shirt rolled up to the crook of his elbow to expose veiny, tattooed arms.

Lord help the woman who gives her heart to this man.

"Guys, this is Layla Rose," he introduces me by my Instagram handle which is also my first and middle name. "She's the journalist I told you guys about."

And that's the minute Atlas realizes his chances with me were just shot to hell. Even if it wasn't taboo to mix business and pleasure, musicians never want to date anyone that could use their pillow talk as material.

"Nice to meet you," Chris waves over his drum set without letting go of his sticks.

"Likewise. And it's just Layla, Layla Rose is just my social media handle." This is already giving me the impression it'll be a rocky start to the interview.

Get it together, Grayson, you have a masterpiece to write.

"I figured we'd start with the interview and then you could observe our practice. Sound good to you?"

"Sounds perfect." I give a thumbs up, *a thumbs up!* What the hell is wrong with me?

The guys take their positions beside their respective instruments while I plant myself on the barstool against the wall. Atlas is the only one that remains standing.

"Alright. Let's start with the basics. Tell me about yourselves. How long have you been a band?"

"You didn't look up anything about us before the interview?" The non-answer comes from Atlas, which fits his character.

Of course I looked up everything I could find about them. The only digital articles I found were from their high school days when a small local paper wrote about them performing at a county fair. Everything else I found came from their own social media accounts. For a band that's been playing a lot of gigs in esteemed bars, there isn't a lot of information about them on the internet.

"I'm not writing a research paper. I wanted the information directly from the source. I want to be the mouthpiece to tell your story."

Dallas nods and smiles, seemingly pleased that someone besides them is brave enough to face their fearless leader (unless they're a democracy). If Atlas appreciates my backbone, he doesn't let on. But he does answer my initial question.

"We've been a legitimate band for seven years."

While making notes in my notebook, I ask a follow-up question. "Was it a group decision? Or was it someone's idea?"

Cameron answers this time. "Atlas and I used to jam together. As our passion for music grew, so did our need for a full band. That's when we reached out to Dallas and Chris to be a part of it. Been together ever since."

"What made you want to work with Dallas and Chris?"

"Atlas was in the school band with them." I try to hold back the snort at the image of this pompous man in a band uniform by pressing my lips between my teeth. Turning my face downward to make a note helps as well.

"What instruments did you play?"

"I played snare drum," Chris replies with a quick tap of his own instrument. "Dallas played the clarinet."

My giggle has no hope of being restrained this time. "No way."

"Yes way. And Atlas played the—."

Atlas shouts "Don't you dare," at the same time Chris finishes his sentence with "tuba!"

I can't help myself. I burst into a fit of laughter that involves doubling over my notebook. Who would have thought big bad Atlas Woods was a band geek. I can't picture the brooding grunge rockstar before me in a band uniform complete with the feathered hat.

Between fits of laughter I ask, "Please tell me you have pictures."

"None that I know of," Dallas responds. "Except maybe the school year book."

Note to self: figure out where they went to high school.

The interview progresses at a smooth pace after that. The initial tension of an intruder in their midst subsides for the band's desire to share stories, artistic process, and their passion for the craft.

If there's one thing I've learned in my short time as a journalist, it's that people love to talk about themselves.

One thing is abundantly clear from the getgo: these four men love music. Their passion isn't just for performing and the allure of stardom. They love creating magic together, giving life to the music in their heads and the messages they want to share to the world.

And I wholeheartedly believe their stories need to be shared. They don't just write songs about love or breakups or good times with friends. Drawing inspiration from their heroes, they write songs about friendships falling apart. About growing up. About rough families and childhoods. Their music is soul deep. And I can't help but feel that each song is a little piece of their hearts carved out and displayed on a silver platter.

By the time we reach the end of the interview, I can already foresee the way their music will touch the lives of thousands. They have that kind of magnetism. Mark my words, Broken Compass will be a household name.

"Alright, final question," I fold my hands over my notebook. "I like to work personal details about people into my articles. It humanizes you so readers feel like they know you, not just your career. So tell me something about yourselves. It can be as simple as your favorite color."

I'm met with the usual uncomfortable silence that precedes people having to give a random fact. People love to talk about themselves but when you ask for something as simple as their favorite song, it feels too personal. People would rather tell you about their childhoods than their favorite movie and why it means so much to them.

And then Chris breaks the silence with an enthusiastic announcement. "I'm gay."

The rest of the band scoffs while I stare on in shock, hoping this isn't the first they've heard about his choice is partners.

"Anyone who hears your songs knows that." Cameron waves a hand as if this bit of information is not sufficient enough. But I jot it down regardless.

Dallas chimes in next, "I was named after Dallas Texas, where I was born and raised."

Cameron supplies, "My favorite movie is Titanic."

Not what I was expecting but I'll take it.

I turn my attention to Atlas. Before I can ask for a personal fact from him, he supplies, "I think there was room for Jack on the float."

"That doesn't count," Chris beats me to reprimanding him.

Atlas sets his heavy gaze on me and we exchange a wordless battle of wills. The gears in his head are turning over and over looking for something personal enough to appease me without being too personal at all.

"I play seven instruments." Impressive. "Guitar. Bass. Piano. Banjo. Harmonica. Tuba. And bagpipes."

After picking my jaw up off the floor and refitting it to my mouth, I ask, "Why? And how? What inspired you to learn such a vast array of instruments?" *Seven* instruments. And that's if you don't include his vocal chords.

"Sorry, Rosie, you only said one personal fact."

Touché...

Though, I'm not a fan of the nickname.

Finally, we reach the end of the interview and I sit on the edge of my seat waiting to hear what kind of magic they're going to make today. My eyes never stray from Atlas as I watch him close his eyes, step up to the microphone so his lips are two fingers length away, fill his lungs with air, and begin.

Four
Layla

BLACK HOLE SUN-SOUNDGARDEN

I've heard them live but something about this intimate setting takes my breath away. The way they play when no one is watching—no one but me. It's so personal and raw. Even if there were ten thousand people crammed into the tiny studio, I'd still feel like they were performing especially for me. That's how intentional their music is, how distinctive their ability to caress the soul is. Their music isn't for the masses, it's for the individual. They're playing for every lonely heart, every broken soul, every person who's ever felt overlooked. It's unlike anything I've ever heard.

When I saw them perform in a bar, they played a rowdy punk song and a couple covers. The song they're playing now is melodic with heavy tones of primal emotion. It's rough like callused hands from hard work, yet as graceful as a Degas painting.

The majority of artists, especially rock bands, make their way to the mainstream media with radio songs that are easily digested and easily forgotten.

But if I were a betting woman, I'd put all my money on this song being their hit single. The song that changes their lives forever.

As soon as they finish, I'm speechless. I just stare at them because they stole my ability to form coherent thoughts, let alone complete sentences.

"I hope that look on your face means you liked the song," Cameron teases.

His words snap me out of the trance they sprinkled over me and I find my power of speech.

"Yes. Yes. That was unbelievable. Oh my gosh. I don't even know what to say."

"Isn't that your job?" Atlas teases me with a dimpled half smile. "Who do you write for, anyway?"

"The Daily Trojan." I hope they weren't expecting the Rolling Stones.

But that's exactly what they thought, based on the shocked expression on Atlas's face. Or something just as prestigious. His pointed stare swivels from me to Cameron, saying enough with just that one look to tell me he and I are in big trouble.

"We took all this time and shared all this information about ourselves just to be published in some college newspaper?"

The urge to stand up for myself and my work overtakes my desire to be liked. So I rise from my stool and command his attention.

"Hey. We get at least ten thousand downloads every day for various articles we publish. A lot of our graduates have gone on to work for publications like the New York Times and Vogue. I myself have had an article published in the LA Times. Just because I work for a college newspaper doesn't mean this article won't get attention or be sold to someone else. All it takes is the right person to read the article to invest more time and money into you. Do you think the Seattle Times is the first news outlet to write a piece on Nirvana?" Feeling all fired up, I carry on with my momentum. "Everyone trying to make a name for themselves starts somewhere. You and I are no exception."

The lack of sound in the studio is deafening. It feels like a heavy miasma clouding the room.

"I can't wait to read your article," Cameron speaks up. Though it encourages conversation, it does little to break the tension.

I stuff my notebook and pen into my bag before slinging the strap over my shoulder.

"I'll send you the link once it's published," I say gruffly before grabbing the knob to fling the door open. Before departing I look over my shoulder to address the band as a whole. "Thank you for letting me sit in on your session and for being so vulnerable with me. I'll do your story justice."

That's a promise.

The bus ride home is quiet—thank goodness—but it gives me too much headspace to simmer on the interview. Despite my best efforts at self-sabotaging, I come to one finite conclusion: the only real attitude in the band is Atlas. I have no doubt the rest are thankful for any exposure, even if it is just in a college newspaper.

My stubborn side rears her ugly head in a determined mission to prove that the interview was not a waste of their time. I meant what I said about the power of the media, even if it's not a mainstream article. Every article has the power to make an impact. It just takes the right person to see it. So I'll write the best fucking article they've ever read and put Broken Compass on the map, even if it's the last thing I do.

As soon as I arrive at the shitty apartment McKenzie and I rent, I breeze past her, ignoring her salutations, and lock myself in my room with a bottle of water and my laptop. Tunnel vision consumes me as I put my thoughts to electronic paper, channeling my inner Hunter S. Thompson.

And I paint the picture of stardom yet to be discovered.

It's been a week since my article on Broken Compass was published in the Daily Trojan. Mira was so thrilled with the piece that it made the front page. In her words, I "really embodied the spirit of the band." While her approval gave me a small sense of satisfaction, the real delight came when I saw the band's social media growth, and announcements of more and more shows at various venues. They performed often enough before, but the correlation between their increased number of shows and my article being published is undeniable.

Cameron reached out via Instagram to compliment my writing and thank me for writing so favorably of the band. He didn't say it, but the undertone of his words leads me to believe that he was worried I'd slander their name after the rocky way we left things.

As annoying as Atlas's dismissal of my status was, I prefer a *kill them with kindness* approach. Ridiculing the band wouldn't have helped matters. But sending my article to club owners I've worked with in the past and seeing those same clubs on their roster gives me enough gratification to light a bonfire.

Come Monday morning, I open my email in the newsroom to see one with the subject line: MAGAZINE INQUIRY.

My hand moves faster than Sonic the Hedgehog to click on the email as I read through the opportunity I've been waiting for.

Dear Miss Grayson,

Your article in the Daily Trojan about Broken Compass caught my attention the other day and I was thoroughly impressed. I was wondering if you'd be interested in writing a few pieces for our online Magazine, CADENCE, covering a couple of other musical groups in the area.

Please reply at your convenience and we can discuss compensation.

Best wishes,

Travis Jarrin

Editor of *Cadence Magazine*

I've heard of *Cadence* before, I came across their online platform when I was researching Broken Compass. The magazine included the band in their list of top ten up-and-coming bands in Los Angeles. The fact that they saw my article and reached out about professional work is the ticket I need to further my career post-graduation.

A lot of my colleagues on the paper have jobs lined up as interns for papers across the country. Very little pay and long hours. And I know exactly where that would land them: getting a second job to compensate for the lack of funds after college while fetching coffee and sharpening pencils for people who don't care about their careers. That path leads to so many people leaving the journalism business in search of stability.

I don't want to be another statistic. I don't want to be another hopeful graduate who thrived on a college paper and then burnt out in the real world. I want to leave my own mark the same as Broken Compass. I suppose we are similar in our goals, even if our passions are different.

At the end of the day, we want to be household names, we want people to memorize the words we shared for their insight and magnitude.

As soon as there is a lull in the newsroom, I dial the number attached to the email for Travis Jarrin. After three agonizing rings, he answers with a gruff, "Yeah?"

"Travis Jarrin? This is Layla Grayson."

"Oh, good, thanks for getting back to me." I picture a middle aged man sitting at a cluttered desk pouring coffee directly into his bloodstream while signing off on various approvals needed for the magazine. "So, I have a couple bands I want to run spotlights on. Your article about Broken Compass is along the lines of what I'm looking for. I'll pay seventy cents a word. You in?"

Hindering the giddy jitters coursing through my veins, I reply, "Make it eighty cents and we have a deal."

"You drive a hard bargain, Miss Grayson, make it seventy-five and we have a deal. I'll email you the details. I need them in the next two weeks."

"Consider it done."

Just like that: possibility.

The click on the other end of the line signals my opportunity to almost literally jump for joy. I stifle a squeal and kick my feet under my desk in a way that must look childish but I don't care. My ego is too inflated to care what anyone else thinks at the moment.

And then my phone rings, knocking me off cloud nine with an alarming blast. The number isn't saved to my phone and I don't think it's Travis's number either.

But now that I'm a big fancy reporter, I'm sure I'll get plenty of calls from adoring fans.

"This is Grayson," I answer in my professional tone, despite it being a personal phone.

No adoring fans, no work related business, no one speaks on the other end.

But I hear the unsteady breathing of whoever it is that called me. If this were a horror film, the serial killer would definitely be on the other end of this call.

"Looks like I owe you an apology."

Most *definitely* not an adoring fan. Atlas Woods sounds positively morose about calling me.

"Is Cameron holding a gun to your head to say that?" I'm only half teasing. Cameron strikes me as more of a pacifist. But I wouldn't put using leverage over his friend past him.

"Not exactly." Not a no, either. "I'm sure you've seen we have a bunch of new shows lined up. I won't pretend your article didn't have something to do with that."

An apology and an admission of being wrong. Atlas must be quaking in his Doc Martin's.

"Did you read it?"

I've been dying to know. It wasn't like I could call him up and ask him. I'm not that desperate for his approval.

And I don't have his number.

Wait a minute, how did he get my number?

"I did." His thick voice answers

"And?"

"Annnnd. It was excellent. The way you wrote about us, it was transparent without giving too much away. You made us sound like we are already big rockstars."

"You are rockstars," I remind him.

"Yeah, we just haven't been discovered yet." A soft chortle tells me he's losing faith. Or at least he was before this upswing in attention. "But your article definitely has the people believing. Thank you again."

"It was my pleasure." That's the truth. I had as much fun writing the piece as I did sitting in on their practice.

"We have a show Saturday night at a pretty big club downtown. Any chance you'd want to come?"

Although his voice is lazy as if he couldn't be bothered to care, I detect the subtle trace of hesitation behind his words. Something tells me Atlas Woods has been seeking approval his whole life and can't shake the need to please. The compulsion to crave acceptance.

"Can I bring a plus one?" No way I'm going without McKenzie.

"Um, yeah. I guess. I'll put you and a guest on the list."

"Then I'll be there."

Another drawn out pause lingers in the electric current connecting our phones. I should probably put him out of his misery and say something, but I'm picturing an uncomfortable Atlas squirming on the other end.

"See you, Rosie." *Click.*

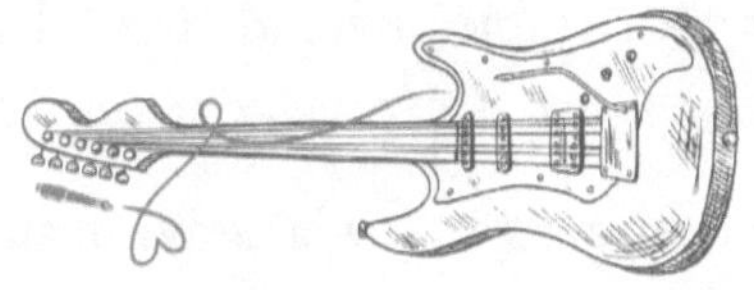

Five

Layla

SEVEN NATION ARMY-WHITE STRIPES

McKenzie was nearly impossible to drag away from her studies for a night of fun. She was quizzing herself with a flashcard app on her phone on the Uber ride to the downtown bar. But I let her drive herself crazy as long as she could before insisting she have a little fun tonight. There's a balance to supporting your friends and their crazy dreams while still encouraging them to live.

On any other Saturday night, I'd be at a dive bar listening to young bands or working on a piece in the comfort of my own home. I rarely attend clubs with obnoxious lines that wrap around the building. But since we get to skip the line tonight, I'll make an exception.

The breeze from the ocean is heavier tonight, leading me to wish I'd chosen something besides my suede mini dress and pumps. However, if this place is like all the rest, I know the combined body heat of party goers and revelers alike will suffocate me as soon as we step inside.

A burly guy who could pass for a Tank Abbott look-alike stands guard at the door with a tablet in hand, dressed in all black to look as imposing as possible. We step to the front of the line which earns us some scowls as I announce, "Layla Grayson and guest." The guy looks over his tablet, purposefully tilted so I can't sneak a peek at the other names on the list.

"There's no Layla Grayson on the list, ma'am."

What? Did Atlas forget? Or was he just trying to mess with m—.

"How about Rosie and guest?" If this works I'm going to strangle that arrogant, pompous—.

"Go ahead, ladies." The bouncer steps aside and sweeps his arm to gesture us inside. I hope Atlas is proud of himself.

As we enter through the neon illuminated corridor onto the main floor of the club, McKenzie leans into my side, looping her arm with mine, and asks, "Why would he put you under Rosie?"

"Long story short, I said I don't go by my middle name and Dumbass Woods latched onto that."

"Oh come on, that's not too bad. At least your middle name isn't Bertha." Poor McKenzie. She eliminated that name from her records the day she left for college.

The main floor of the club is a half circle of open space for an audience and dancers to congregate, bordered by a bar on the right and left that curve with the wall, and a stage big enough to fit a small orchestra in the back. VIP booths overlook the floor from the left and right. How one gets up there, I have no idea.

People have already filled the space to the brim, but that doesn't stop us from squeezing through the crowd to the front right of the stage to get a great view of the band. I brought my Sony a6400 to snap a few photos of the band live in action. It's a nice compact camera with good pixel quality for high resolution photos. At least good enough for a newspaper article.

"I want to be home by midnight," McKenzie informs me. Although she's shouting, I can barely hear her over the chatter and the rowdy music blasting through the speakers overhead.

"Sounds good to me," I shout back. That's when I feel a hand grip my elbow. I whip my head around so fast, ready to ram my elbow into whatever drunk douchebag thinks it's ok to grab a woman but stop short when I see it's Atlas getting my attention. A bend of his fingers signals for us to follow him through the door I didn't see in the wall, presumably leading to the backstage area where the band is gathered in preparation for the show.

"You made it," he observes as soon as the closed door drowns out the noise.

"Yeah. Thanks for making it so easy to get in," I chide. "I think it's only fair I know your middle name, now."

"Fuck no," he scoffs as if it's a ridiculous request.

"There she is," Cameron calls as soon as we're close enough. "The woman of the hour."

"Thank you, but tonight is about you guys."

Joining the circle of band mates, I introduce my plus one to everyone. "Guys, this is McKenzie. McKenzie, this is Atlas, Dallas, Chris, and Cameron. Meet Broken Compass." I don't miss the way Mckenzie's eyes linger on Cameron the longest, or the way he can't peel his gaze away from her after she finally breaks eye contact.

"We owe you big time," says Chris. "That article was stupendous. We gained eight thousand Instagram followers overnight. And several calls to book shows. We can't thank you enough."

"Yeah, you killed it, Grayson," Dallas adds.

"It was my pleasure. Thanks for agreeing to let me write about you. And it's really the luck of the draw if the algorithms push your article or not. We all got lucky."

"Don't sell yourself short." It's Atlas who pays me the compliment this time, or the closest thing to a compliment I'll ever get from him.

"What's the camera for?" Cameron points a long finger, perfect for playing guitar, toward the device in question hanging around my neck.

"She's a photographer," McKenzie answers for me with such enthusiasm.

I'm quick to clarify, "It's a hobby."

"Oh stop it." McKenzie gives my shoulder a playful tap. "You're talented. That's more than just a hobby. She takes amazing photos. She even did my headshots for grad school applications. Here, look." Extracting her phone from her knee-high boots, McKenzie proceeds to scroll through her Instagram to show Cameron and the rest the headshots I took of her for her resume. I'll give her this, she's sly. McKenzie makes sure Cameron has a good look at her profile and handle name so he can find her later. I just hope he's observant enough to pick up on it.

"Wow, these are great!" Chris praises. "Make sure to get plenty of my good side tonight, ok?" He says as he dramatically runs the back of his hand up his left cheek to let me know his best angle.

Five minutes to nine, the band takes their place on the stage before the curtain draws back exposing them to the monstrous crowd on the floor. The applause is deafening. I can feel the energy in the club prickle with anticipation, both from the audience and the band. This might be the largest crowd they've ever performed in front of, if I were to guess.

"Greetings, everyone," Atlas begins, earning another round of cheers. McKenzie clasps my hand with a giddy laugh. As many times as she's accompanied me to concerts and shows, she's never seemed as zealous as she is tonight.

"Thanks for being here tonight. We are Broken Compass. Now let's have a good time." Atlas's smooth voice lulls the audience into a state of euphoria before he's even begun to sing. But the second the instruments rise and his vocals carry over the crowd, the whole place is in an uproar cheering them on. The band opens with an original song called "Leave Me Be" about embracing your weird, embracing your crazy, and finding your people. I'll have to ask them later if it was written about their own found family experience.

It's the perfect song to begin, not just for the upbeat tempo that energizes the room, but for the uplifting nature of the lyrics. The crowd loves it. Any good set starts this way to set the tone for the night.

The band plays a mixture of covers and originals, varying in pace and mood to carry the souls in this club through an out of body experience. Some bands choke like Kershaw at the World Series, others let their nerves fuel their drive to give the performance of a lifetime. While tonight's show would be considered practically perfect by anyone else, I see more beneath the surface. I know the performance of a lifetime is still in their future.

After a chilling rendition of "Seven Nation Army," Broken Arrow finishes their set with an original called "Big City", reminiscent of Green Day before they went radio. The crowd eats every crumb left on stage as the band takes their final bow, bids them farewell, and bolts off stage as the curtains lower to the thunderous applause from the club.

The crackle of undiluted joy rushes backstage with the band members as they embrace each other in manly hugs before surprisingly enveloping McKenzie and I into their powwow. Their infectious excitement sends a thrill down my spine, coursing through the points where Atlas's hand rests on my lower back and McKenzie's arm drapes over my shoulder in the circle we've formed.

"That was..." Chris starts and trails off in search of the right word.

"Electrifying," Atlas supplies. For a guy who doesn't show a lot of emotion, he's radiating happiness like a golden aura outlining his silhouette.

"You guys killed it!" McKenzie says more to Cameron than the rest of the group. "Unbelievably good."

"Alright, Miss big time music critic, what did you think?" I meet Atlas's dark eyes before shifting my gaze over the others.

To quote my own article, "'Watching you perform is like standing on the precipice of something great.' You'll be unforgettable."

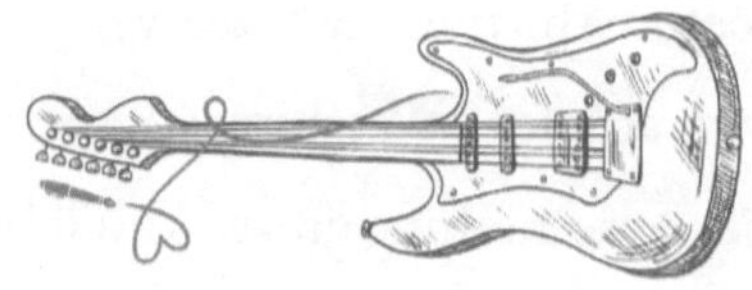

Six
Layla

DON'T STOP BELIEVING-JOURNEY

After some of the buzz from the evening has died down, the band starts to pack their equipment behind the privacy of the curtain. To celebrate a great show, they asked us to join them at a bar to which I was ready to deny for McKenzie's sake so she could get home to study. But she swiftly beat me to it and agreed, which is uncharacteristic for her but shouldn't be all that surprising considering the goo-goo eyes she and Cameron have been making at each other all night.

"Have you ever heard of the band NEEDTOBREATHE?" I ask from my perch on a speaker. I offered to help but the band insisted they have a system and I'd probably fuck it up. Which is true. I don't know anything about all the tech stuff.

"They're that Christian rock band, right?" Dallas says while hunched over a massive storage container of chords.

"Yeah." I'm kind of surprised one of them knows the band, considering the difference of styles. "Well one time they were talking about when they felt like they made it big. Ya know, selling out a 5,000 seat theater. Then a 10,000 seat arena. Et cetera. And the drummer said he felt like he'd made it big when he didn't have to lug his own gear in and out of every show."

Chris sighs dreamily thinking about such an accomplishment. "That'll be the day." Until then, the band is responsible for setting up and tearing down every last mic stand no matter how high on praise they feel.

But there's nothing that elevates that jittery excitement like a middle aged man in a sport coat staying after the show to approach the band.

"Broken Compass?" Every pair of eyes swivels to the salt and pepper haired man casually standing on the floor of the empty club with his hands loosely tucked in his pockets.

"That's us," Cameron walks toward the edge of the stage. "What can we help you with?"

"My name is Frank Ruben. I'm a talent agent for Marble Music." Consider my interest piqued. That label has a lot of big names on it. "I gotta say, I was pretty impressed with your performance tonight. If the crowd's reaction is anything to go by, you certainly made a name for yourself tonight."

Anxiety hangs in the air as every person on stage waits with bated breath for this Frank Ruben to continue.

"Thank you, sir," Atlas breaks the silence.

"How about we have a sit down at my office Monday morning and talk about our label representing you."

Playing it cool, the guys exchange looks as if to confirm their busy schedules would allow for such an inconvenience before Cameron replies.

"We should be able to make that work."

"Excellent." Mr. Ruben starts back toward the door. Before spinning around, he says, "I'll DM you the information. See you Monday, boys."

Then he's gone, leaving an injection of fresh adrenaline in the room. As soon as we're sure Ruben is out of earshot, we all release a collective symphony of shock. The guys come together in another group hug (a manly one, of course) before Cameron starts literally bouncing off the walls with excitement.

"A fucking label wants to represent us?"

"Sure sounds like it," McKenzie confirms.

The atmosphere carries the pure elation until the very last piece of equipment is loaded and we all load into the van bound for a bar they apparently frequent. Considering all the gear shoved into the back of the van, space is limited. They've truly mastered the starving artists vibe. Dallas drives since he doesn't partake in alcohol or weed. Chris takes the passenger seat, while Cameron is generous enough to offer his lap to McKenzie in the back considering the lack of actual seats. That leaves Atlas and I to squeeze next to each other behind the drivers side. With every twist and turn the van takes on its route, our shoulders bump, our thighs graze, and the tension of trying not to touch one another binds my limbs in a vice.

"How was my movement tonight?" Atlas's voice is just soft enough for me to hear and no one else. The brush of his breath against my ear gives him an unfair advantage.

Keeping my eyes on the road ahead so I don't catch the smoldering gaze I know he's wearing, I reply, "You certainly made an improvement." And that's the truth, his stage presence went from moody and mysterious to conveying "I can satisfy a woman" all while playing a guitar.

"Glad you approve."

Is this all the acknowledgement we're going to give this? I hope I don't have to tell him a fling between us isn't in the cards. I don't want to be another notch on his bedpost.

We pull up outside a hole-in-the wall place with just a simple neon blue sign reading *Blue Room* to mark its existence. It's one in the morning but we're all so buzzed from the night's events that no one is ready to retire yet.

The bar is both exactly what I pictured and not at all. I was expecting a larger crowd at midnight on a Saturday, but only ten to twelve patrons occupy the space aside from two bartenders.

However, the dive bar boasts the kind of cozy and relaxed atmosphere most bars spend thousands of dollars trying to achieve. This place achieved it by simply existing. No frills. No loud music. No trendy, unpalatable cocktail menu. Just basic well drinks, beer, and peanuts.

To top it all off, a couple of the customers are performing karaoke at a makeshift stage. An older gentleman who wears his age in the form of a bald patch atop his head is singing "Ghost Riders" into a microphone, while keeping a steady hand on his drink.

The lighting is low. The pool table is free. And the kind welcome of one of the bartenders tells me Broken Compass are welcome regulars.

"So you guys come here often?" McKenzie asks the group.

Cameron is happy to answer on behalf of the band. "It's kind of our post-gig ritual." The bartender sets out three beers and a soda for Dallas before taking our orders. "We like the ambiance. It's relaxing but they know how to have a good time, too."

"Does that mean we get a show tonight?" The weathered bartender eyes Cameron mischievously.

"Put me on the list, m'lady." Sure enough. Cameron's name is called on deck for karaoke. But before he leaves to serenade the bar, I raise my can of hard seltzer toward the center of the table.

"I'd like to propose a toast." All eyes on me, no one hesitates to lift their drinks in solidarity. "To Broken Compass: May you break hearts and piece them back together with your music for years to come."

"Here here."

"Huzzah."

Then someone shouts, "Cameron, get your ass over here," as the intro to "Ain't No Mountain High Enough" rises over the primitive sound system.

"Oh man, this is a duet. Guess you'll need to join me, McKenzie." Cameron extends a graceful hand toward my friend. Stars dance in her eyes as I swear I see the makings of a cute fairytale romance play out before me.

"If you insist."

The pair sing their hearts out without ever breaking eye contact while the rest of us watch, knowing we are privy to the start of something special. It's cute, really, McKenzie dated a few guys in college but her focus has always been her education and career. While I doubted a lover would make her stray from her straight and narrow path, maybe she finally met the man worthy of sharing in her success.

"They're cute together," Atlas leans ever so slightly toward me to strike the conversation. Though his eyes meet mine, he keeps his face directed at the duet on stage. "They really are."

"I saw you haven't published anything since the article about us. What are you working on now?"

"You've been looking for my articles?" My voice ranges somewhere between teasing and genuine appreciation. He's either very nosy or very considerate.

"The algorithms have been showing me lots of highlights from the paper." *Sure they have.*

"With graduation right around the corner I'm not working on anything big. Although an online magazine is paying me to do a couple pieces for them. Their editor contacted me and asked if I could go watch a couple bands and write a couple articles for their mag. Have you ever heard of *Cadence Magazine*?"

"Seriously?" Atlas jerks his stare from his band mate to give me his undivided attention. "They're a great fucking magazine. They asked you to write for them?"

"Just a couple freelance pieces." I downplay the offer. "But I hope it may turn into something more. I'm checking out one of the bands at a bar next weekend. Do you guys want to join?" I direct the question at the rest of the group so it doesn't sound like I'm asking Atlas out or anything. That would be more than his inflated ego could handle.

"What kind of music?" Chris asks.

"Well, it's a country dancing bar, so I'm assuming country or western."

"Ah, they got both kinds," Dallas references the Blues Brothers with perfect timing. "Hell yeah. I'm down. These guys don't like western but they can handle some Americana."

"I have no guarantees about the quality." Last thing I need is my reputation being questioned. "Just doing my job."

"Eh," Chris waves a hand, "it'll be worth it if we have a good time."

As our conversation wraps up, the love birds' duet comes to a close. Cameron rounds back to the table while McKenzie trots off toward the restroom.

"You're up next," Cameron looks at me from over his beer bottle. Then to Atlas, "And you."

I scoff, "And what, pray tell, did you choose for our song?"

That's when the tune of "Don't Stop Believing" by Journey begins. The intro is long enough for Atlas and I to share a resolved expression before taking the stage. He starts singing about a small town girl while I wait to sing my part about a city boy. Not that I've been keeping it a secret, but I don't broadcast that my parents made me take vocal lessons for six years because my choir director said it would help me improve my abilities.

It did.

The only problem was my passion wasn't singing, it was studying music history and sharing musicians I loved. They finally let me quit vocal lessons when I was sixteen and they realized what a waste of time it had been.

But at least my training comes in handy for occasions such as this. If it weren't for the vocal coach, I may have never learned to properly hone my alto sound. Not all of us can be Enya.

As soon as I start my verse, I feel Atlas's shocked expression swing my way. Maybe he was expecting something akin to a dying seagull. I'm not nearly at their level, but I can carry a tune well enough.

If he weren't such a professional, Atlas might've missed his cue to join me for the chorus in lieu of his astonishment.

I'll have to add *surprising Atlas Woods* to my resume.

We belt our hearts out, potentially having a little bit of fun by the end of the song, and take a bow when the karaoke version of the song fades out.

Dallas and Chris greet us with a round of whistles and whoops when we rejoin the table to find Cameron missing.

Interesting.

"Why the hell are you writing about music when you could be the one on stage?" Chris asks the question but the other two men are leaning over their drinks, eager for an answer.

"It's not where my heart is." And that's the truth. "My parents wanted me to do choir in school but I loved writing about music more than I did performing it."

"Well at least they got their money's worth," Atlas's voice is dry but his eyes dance with playfulness.

Planting my palms against the table top, I hoist myself back out of my chair and announce, "I'm going to find the little girls room. I expect you two to give us a show when I get back."

"There's no pole in here," Chris teases.

I meander to the back of the bar in search of a restroom and my best friend.

And I find her alright. With a blond guitarist's tongue shoved down her throat in the narrow hallway leading to the bathrooms.

Thankfully, they're too engrossed in their tongue tango to notice me so I slink away without disturbing the moment.

"That was fast," Atlas observes as I retake my seat.

"Well, the path to the bathrooms is blocked by a certain guitarist and law student having the time of their lives." I doubt McKenzie would mind me sharing what I saw considering they were putting on a show for anyone to see. Besides, Cameron will probably share it with the guys as soon as we leave.

Atlas just takes a sip of his beer to cover the tiniest hint of a smirk. He might try to wear a mask of indifference but the band is his life, members included. He's happy his friend found someone meaningful.

And with that, my icy wall keeping Atlas at a distance melts by one layer.

Seven
Layla

HONKY-TONK WOMEN-ROLLING STONES

Cameron and McKenzie are sickeningly cute.

After their night of reckless abandon at the Blue Room, McKenzie informed her new beau that she needed a week and a half of isolation to focus on her studies and then they could pursue something. Cameron–being the considerate gentleman that he is–stayed clear of McKenzie for the allotted time.

Meanwhile, I pursued my budding relationship with *Cadence Magazine* by attending a country western bar in my best 70s cowgirl aesthetic outfit on a Saturday night with a rock band. It sounds like the start to a bad joke: a rock band and a female journalist walk into a honky-tonk...

This country western bar did everything right in terms of setting the ambiance. European skull mount decor, rustic wood furnishings, and American flags everywhere. The center of the bar hosts a wide rectangular dance floor bordered by an orange glow so dancers can see their cowhide bound feet through every step. At least fifteen couples are already spinning around the floor to the time of the song playing over the speakers.

But the most impressive thing is how everyone moves as one cohesive unit although the pairs are dancing separately. Everything is so synchronized that no one trips over one another.

I am not that coordinated, so there is no way in hell I'll be cutting a rug this evening.

Winding our way through the sea of tall bar tables, we follow the hostess to a table marked RESERVED that the magazine claimed in my honor.

The floor is littered with peanut shells, crunching underfoot with each step so I feel the gritty texture beneath my boot.

I didn't want to say anything in front of the waitress but as soon as she's out of sight I comment, "Why don't they sweep the floor?"

"It's a country western bar," Dallas states as if that answer should be enough. After he climbs into his seat and catches the confused brow I've raised, he clarifies. "It's a thing with western bars. They give you a bucket of peanuts for the table and you throw the shells on the floor. They probably sweep it every day or two."

"You sound like a guy who's walked on a lot of peanut shells in his lifetime."

"My name's Dallas for a reason," he half smiles. "My parents are from Texas. I moved here with my Memaw in high school but I go back at least once a year. I've seen my fair share of western bars."

"Just add a trough for him to feed out of and it'll feel like home." Chris tosses a playful punch at Dallas's shoulder.

In the time between ordering our drinks and waiting for the band to take the stage, a comfortable silence ensues as we take in the dancers and the drinkers. Everyone is buzzed on life, high on comradery. The adrenaline the dancers exude must be infectious because the entire bar buzzes with manic energy like kids who've been seated behind a desk all day.

I never would have thought to find a bar like this in Southern California. Then again, I wouldn't expect to find Ethiopian food either but we have at least three Ethiopian restaurants in my neighborhood.

"So, how's McKenzie?" Cameron's voice draws my gaze back to my four handsome dates.

I'll be honest, he waited much longer than I anticipated to ask about my best friend.

"Please tell him something and put us out of our misery," sighs Chris. "He's been talking about her nonstop since last weekend."

Cameron responds appropriately by tossing a peanut at his friend.

Taking pity on the lovesick man, I offer, "She's good. When she takes her very rare breaks from studying, she asks if I've heard from 'the band' which really means she's wondering if you've called."

"How are her studies? Only a few more days until the LSATs, right?" *Not that he's counting.*

"Yeah, she takes the first round of testing on Wednesday."

"Shouldn't she have taken them last year?" Atlas speaks up. Upon receiving a quizzical look from everyone seated at the table he continues. "My cousin is a lawyer and she had to take hers the year before law school. Aren't you graduating this year?"

"I am, she's a year behind me."

"How'd you two meet?"

Swinging my attention back to Cameron, I reply, "I dated her brother in high school. Didn't last long. But I gained a lifetime friend out of it, so I'd consider it time well spent."

Before our conversation of friendship history and law school can continue any further, a voice over the speakers announces the band for the evening and the whole reason for being in a bar this far outside of my element.

"Ladies and cowboys, please put your hands together for tonight's entertainment. The Roundhouse Rebels."

The crowd welcomes the band of traditionally dressed cowboys onto the stage with hoots and hollers.

The band begins with an original song of theirs that revolves around a truck and a girl like most country songs. It's when they start getting into more of the western style music that the lyrics really find their depth. But I notice that the audience loves the cliche songs just as much as the more impactful songs.

To their credit, the Roundhouse Rebels really know their audience. They play mostly upbeat songs with happy messages that keep dancers on the dance floor. Even their slower love ballads have couples taking to the floor to sway in country western style to the melodic tune.

As eleven o'clock rolls around, the band announces their final song for the night will be "Save A Horse, Ride A Cowboy" which earns more enthusiasm than any other song of the night. I'm familiar with the song but I did not expect it would have a trance-like effect on the crowd, pulling them from their seats as they flock to the dance floor.

"Come on," Chris grabs my hand and tugs me off the barstool.

My eyes feel like the size of golf balls in their sockets. "What? No way."

"Please?" He pouts like a puppy. "None of these guys will dance with me in public."

"Or private," Atlas amends the statement.

The pleading, childlike look in Chris's eyes have such a strong effect I don't even realize I've agreed until we're practically to the dance floor. Thankfully, there is no line dancing involved in this song and all the people who watched the dancers through the night are jumping and bobbing in an uncoordinated rhythm which makes me feel a little less awkward.

Chris interlocks our fingers on one side while his other hand slips to a respectful position on my back and mine lands on his shoulder. Before I know it, we're prancing around the room like a couple of drunk idiots, mirroring all the other drunk idiots twirling and bouncing in a circle. The crowd moves around the dance floor as one mass of bodies without losing their step. Thank goodness for Chris or I would not have been able to keep up with them.

I have to admit, it was more fun than I thought it would be. My sense of self-preservation and fear of looking foolish evaporate with the humid air of sweaty bodies enjoying their lives without a care in the world. Although our music tastes may vary, the human psyche cannot survive without music and we all give into the transformative effect it melds into our souls. For the duration of a song, we forget about the outside world and just feel.

Everyone on this dance floor is feeling tipsy with joy.

No sooner does the song end than I pointedly take a step off the packed dance floor to cement the end of my dancing career.

Dallas and Chris leave for the evening while Cameron, Atlas and I stick around to finish our drinks. Considering their expertise in music and entertainment I pick their brains about the band for ideas to include in my article. Although country western music is not their scene, they are still musicians and talented performers.

We all agree that while the music was good and the band knew their audience well, their stage presence left something to be desired. Aside from a *hello* and *goodnight*, the band did not interact with the crowd. We live in a world where it's not enough to play an instrument well or sing like Chris Stapleton, you have to entice your audience from the stage.

"Does it bother you to critique a band?" Cameron asks from across the table. "I'd be too afraid to hurt someone's feelings."

"It used to," I admit. "I remember the first time I had to write a negative review. I was assigned to the school play in 11th grade and the lead actress was atrocious. I think the director was trying to give everyone opportunities over the years and she was a senior. She missed steps while dancing and forgot a line. Not to mention her acting was stiff. My editor encouraged me to be honest and guided me in writing an honest review without coming off as mean. But that didn't stop the actress's feelings from getting hurt. She wrote "BITTER BITCH" all over my car with one of those chalk markers after school."

Cameron's eyebrows shoot to his hairline. "Woah. Drama queens can be vicious."

"You can always tell the spoiled ones," Atlas says over the rim of his beer glass, oddly insightful. "They've never faced criticism."

"It's ok. My boyfriend at the time was Mckenzie's brother and they lived next door to the drama queen. So they egged her car in the middle of the night."

Swiveling my head, I observe the bar as it empties at a steady pace. Only a few people are left at their tables besides us and the dance floor is left vacant.

Across the dance floor I eye the stage and the dormant instruments belonging to the bar that wait patiently to be used. A mischievous gleam must have twinkled in my eye as an idea came to mind, because Atlas inquired, "What's that look for?"

Turning back to him, I narrow knowing eyes on him and ask, "Isn't the banjo one of the seven-million instruments you play?"

Atlas eyes the stage like a snake coiling in preparation to snap at him. "Yeeesss," he draws out the word.

"Can I hear?" I give him my best doe-eyes and cheesy smile in hopes it will work on him.

When all I get is an eye roll, I think he's about to reject my request. Until Atlas silently stands and walks over to the stage, removing the banjo from its stand. Cameron and I follow close behind with eager steps.

Atlas sits his pert ass down on the corner of the stage and removes a thumb pick from the strings of the banjo, fitting it onto his right thumb. He starts with the most basic banjo tune that will send shivers down any Arkansas hillbilly's spine, then moves into a cover of Slipknot's "Psychosocial" which I never would have picked for a banjo cover. But it works perfectly. The way the tempo emphasizes each note translates the song into some western-rock hybrid. It's incredible.

After he finishes the first verse and the chorus note for note, he removes the thumb pick to return it and the banjo back to their rightful places.

All the while, I stand flabbergasted beside Cameron who must be used to this kind of musical talent considering he doesn't look the least bit shocked.

"Ok, you have to start working some of these other instruments into your music," I declare—no—demand.

"We're a grunge band," Atlas reminds me, "banjos and tubas don't really work into our sound."

Time to break out my extensive knowledge of rock bands. "The Dropkick Murphys use bagpipes all the time. And Ozzy Osbourne includes the harmonica in multiple songs, especially in his Black Sabbath days. Those instruments set them apart from all other bands at the time."

Atlas is ready with his rebuttal. "There was nothing else like Black Sabbath when they came on the scene."

"And people have been trying to replicate them ever since."

Just like I knew Broken Compass would go far, I know in my gut this is their ticket, this is their secret weapon to get the attention they deserve.

"What if we change the intro to "Broken Man" from a guitar solo to a harmonica solo?" Cameron offers helpfully. "It's not our best song but it's still a crowd pleaser. We can give it a shot in the studio and see how it sounds."

The gears in Atlas's full head spin at rapid pace while he mulls the idea over. Finally, he rises with his eyes on Cameron before they lower to me and he answers. "Fine. We'll give it a shot."

"Yes," Cameron and I both hiss triumphantly at the same time before sharing a well timed high-five.

"You won't regret it. This is going to be epic. I just know it."

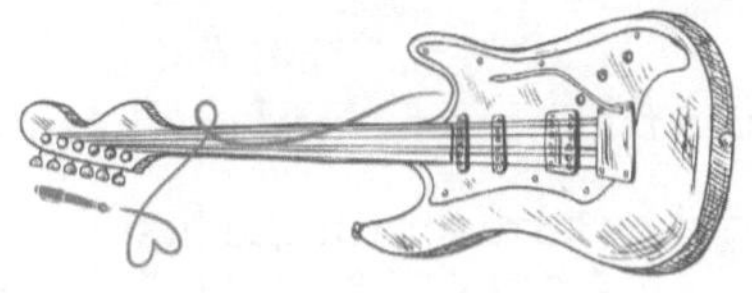

Eight

Layla

W**HAT I GOT-SUBLIME**

And it was. The band let me sit in on another rehearsal while they played with the inclusion of the harmonica in their song "Broken Man" the day after their meeting with Frank Ruben.

The label is interested in representing them but they need to get a full set together without cover songs.

Thankfully, Atlas has a little black book of songs he's written over the years ranging from barely an idea to completed pieces. Keeping it simple, they only include harmonica on one of the songs in case the label isn't a fan. But based on some of the other artists the label represents, I have a feeling this will be right up their alley.

Once McKenzie completes her LSATs, she and I spend the last couple weeks of the semester attending the band's various shows and hanging out at the studio in our free time. We've truly embraced the role of groupies for Broken Compass, only without the constant praising and only McKenzie is sleeping with one of the band members.

She and Cameron fall into a natural rhythm after their first date. I know the second they have sex for the first time, not just because we're girls who tell each other everything, but because Cameron starts spending more nights at our apartment than at his own.

After several years of denying herself the chance to grow close to someone for the sake of her career, it's endearing to see my best friend find someone who will give her the affection and happiness she deserves. And I couldn't be happier it's someone I actually like. Poor McKenzie has had to put up with way too many duds of mine over the years.

Not limited to but including Stalker Jack whom I dated for two years and then wouldn't leave me alone when I ended things. He was a narcissistic asshole who gaslit me on a daily basis until I cut ties.

The only problem was he knew my schedule and routine and couldn't handle the shame of rejection.

After I got the school involved, he left me alone. It's been three months since I've heard a peep out of him. Silence is bliss, but ominous.

At long last, after sixteen years of education and busting my ass, graduation day arrives. My final assignments have all been submitted and approved, I sent my articles to *Cadence Magazine,* and the last step before emerging into the adult world of work and freedom must be taken across the stage in the courtyard of the university. I don't pay attention to any of the speakers and I only recognize one quarter of the students being called, but when my name finally echoes over the sound system, the gravity of the moment collapses on me, sparking a rare emotional moment of reflection.

I hear a chorus of cheers from the audience between my parents and the rock band accompanying my best friend in the stands. I had no idea they'd be in attendance and a little sliver of sentimental affection creeps into my heart. We've all become closer over the past few weeks, going from antisocial college students to rockstar groupies and friends.

Once the pomp and circumstance of tossing my cap in the air is complete, I begin searching for it. Anticipating this little dilemma, I tied a friendship bracelet to my tassel so I could sort mine out from the other caps littering the lawn which proves to be useful as I spot it ten feet from my chair. Not sure how I managed to launch it that far considering I am about as athletic as a one armed crocodile.

As I stop to retrieve it, a masculine hand clutches the flat top before I can. Raking my eyes up the length of the arm, over the shoulder, and along a slender neck, my eyes land on the ghostly familiar face of my ex-boyfriend: Jack.

The same Jack I've been avoiding for months.

Though he wears a charming smile, I recognize the malicious gleam in his eyes, the spark of cruelty and wickedness the world overlooks because of the golden hair that flops over his forehead.

"I believe this is yours," Jack says by way of greeting as he extends the graduation cap to me. I hesitate before swiping it out of his hands, holding it in front of me like a shield.

"What are you doing here?" My voice carries a frigid tone I reserve for him.

"It's graduation," he says as though I'm an idiot. That was one of his favorite moves: talk down to me like I'm unintelligent. "I'm graduating. Just like you."

"And you happened to be near me, convenient." And likely calculated. "Thanks for finding my hat, I should be going."

His scaly hand clutches my wrist as I turn to leave. He crosses the space between us in the blink of an eye. Bending at the hips to lower himself to my level, another power move.

"Come on, Lay," his soft tone is doing its best to convey he's not a threat, much like a fox's smile. "I just wanted to say congratulations. You worked really hard for this." Lord knows he didn't. He used his charm and status on the baseball team to earn his grades.

I refuse to acknowledge anything he says as kind considering there's usually an underhanded motive behind it. So I reply, "Is that all?"

Puppy dog eyes stare back at me, the picture of innocence and sincerity. But it's all a mask.

"Lay," he draws out my name like I'm a petulant child. "I just wanted to see how you're doing. I'm not a bad guy."

My words taste acidic as I spit them toward the bastard holding my wrist a little too tightly to be friendly. "Violence isn't the only thing that can harm a person."

That grip on my wrist tightens. Like a true snake, Jack slithers in unnoticed and charming until he's cutting off your airway and sinking his fangs into you. You don't realize you're in danger until it's too late.

"I never hit you, Layla. But maybe I should have marked you so you knew you were mine." Something darkens in his eyes. It's almost imperceptible unless you know how to look past the bullshit and pretty-boy exterior to see the ugly soul trapped in smooth skin.

But before Jack has a chance to do or say anything else, a different voice that has lulled me into a trance through club speakers breaks the tension.

"Is there a problem here?"

Atlas's outwardly cool tone bears a hint of a threat, a threat Jack doesn't miss. He releases my wrist but stays planted less than a foot away from me without taking his eyes off Atlas.

"Who are you?" Jack's eyes narrow on Atlas before swinging in my direction. "What's this, Layla? Found someone new already?"

We broke up six months ago, even if I was dating Atlas, that's a perfectly appropriate amount of time.

Not to mention *none of his business!*

But Atlas steals my chance to correct Jack by answering, "Yeah, she did. You alright, Rosie?" With a curt nod of his chin, I know he's really asking me if Jack is going to be a problem.

I take a pointed step away from Jack toward Atlas who tucks me under his arm in a show of casual possession.

"Figures," Jack scoffs, "you always were a fame whore."

Atlas wraps a meaty hand around Jack's neck before Jack even has a chance to finish spewing the word whore. The slightest amount of pressure on his jugular and fear strikes Jack's expression in an all too satisfying light.

Atlas speaks in a hushed tone that does nothing to stifle the intolerance in his voice. "If you ever speak about a woman like that again—especially her—I won't hesitate to apply enough pressure to cut off all the air going to that thick head of yours."

I wouldn't have pegged Atlas as a violent man, but the promise of death in his voice sends shivers down even my spine. The fear in Jack's eyes is priceless.

"Problem here?" Cameron's voice announces everyone else's arrival over my shoulder. At the reminder of witnesses, Atlas drops his hand from Jack's throat. Thankfully, everyone around us is too wrapped in a blissful post-graduation bubble with their loved ones to notice.

"He was just leaving," I answer Cameron without looking away from Jack, telling him all he needs to know with just a glance.

Without another word, Jack turns on his heel and heads in the opposite direction. Hopefully that will be the last I'll ever see of him. Sucks that it takes the perceived protection of another man to make him get the message.

"Oh my god, are you ok?" McKenzie is on me in an instant, looking deep into my eyes like a traumatized kitten.

"I'm fine," I answer honestly. "I don't think he'll be making an appearance again."

Then, facing Atlas, I say, "Thanks for the help," trying to sound as appreciative and nonchalant as possible. I don't want to make this a bigger deal than it needs to be. But something tells me Atlas saw the tension between Jack and I, the power dynamic that he's been trying to hold over me since we met. The signs I didn't see soon enough.

"No problem." He returns my not-a-big-deal attitude.

Simple as that.

Nine

Layla

WITH **A** **L**ITTLE **H**ELP From My Friends-The Beatles

After a celebratory dinner with my family, I took an Uber to the address McKenzie sent me in Hawthorne; or as close as I could get to the address before walking the rest of the way.

With my cap and gown tucked into my bag, I follow the GPS to a small collection of single story duplexes compacted into a tight unit. According to the GPS, I need to follow the narrow driveway to the back of the property, to the last duplex where windows glow a rainbow of neon colors and music feeds a pulse through the foundation. No doubt in my mind this is the right place.

Thirty seconds after I sent a text to McKenzie that I'd arrived—because who knocks anymore—the door swings open breaking the barrier containing the music to reveal Dallas's shining face.

"Welcome, guest of honor." He greets me, beer in hand and a wide smile across his narrow face.

Stepping inside their home is like stepping into Superman's secret lair. The only light comes from neon strip lights that line the ceiling and windows, shifting through the colors of the rainbow. Speakers adorn all four corners of the living room which play the corresponding sound of the classic rock music videos playing on the television. A navy blue L-shaped couch is tucked into the corner where McKenzie keeps Cameron's lap extra warm and Chris sits at the opposite end, slouched against the backrest with an arm stretched out.

Opposite the couch is my dream come true, a floor-to-ceiling wall of shelves containing at least a thousand records and one section designated to not one but *two* vintage record players. And not the kind that look vintage but have modern electronics. These came straight out of the hippie age and my deepest fantasies.

Completely bypassing the people who showed up for me today, I skim my fingertips delicately over the record covers while I examine their collection. Names like ABBA, Billy Idol, and Tool stick out to me. Some of them are bands I've never even heard of before.

This collection must have been years in the making between all four guys.

"Impressive, huh?" Atlas's voice startles me out of my fixation. I hadn't heard him sneak up beside me over the volume of the music.

Unable to tear my gaze away from the beautiful collection, I reply, "It's amazing. How long have you guys been collecting these?"

"Not us," Dallas says from behind us. "Just Atlas. He had about half this many when we met him."

Turning to face him, he sees the question in my eyes but doesn't make me ask it.

"I got my first record when I was eight. The obsession kind of snowballed from there."

I'll say.

"Which was your first?"

Instead of simply telling me, Atlas stretches his corded arm to the top shelf on the left side to extract a record concealed beneath its cover and hands it to me.

The Lion King

Soundtrack

featuring music by Hans Zimmer

A tight smile tugs at the corners of my lips. Something about this is so innocent and pure of heart.

The edges of the record cover are worn and frayed, evidence of how often the record has been taken out and replaced to the case over the years.

"It was my favorite movie as a kid," Atlas shares with me. "My parents got it for me for my eighth birthday." It's not often you see a twinkle in someone's eye, but I swear I see the tiniest spark as Atlas drifts into the past, reminiscing about fond childhood memories.

"And that's not even all of them," Chris calls from across the room. "He has more in our room."

"You all share one room?" I can't keep the horror at how smelly that room must be out of my voice. The duplex looked small but I didn't realize it was that small.

"Ew, no," Chris corrects me. "Atlas and I have the room on the right. Dallas and Cam have the room in the back. Pitiful that four guys with decent jobs can only afford a shoebox two bedroom place."

As Chris delves into a rant about California politics and cost of living, Atlas jerks his head toward the hallway silently instructing me to follow him.

As promised, the door on the right past the tiny kitchen leads into a bedroom. One of the twin beds is neatly made with folded corners and a surface so flat you could bounce a quarter off it. The other is also tidied up but clearly not as pristine. That side of the room has yet another floor-to-ceiling bookshelf but only one. And this one is also bursting at the seams with records.

"Is there anything special about these records?" I ask as I help myself to them, flipping the covers over to view the song lists.

"Yeah, there wasn't room for them on the other shelves." A joke. Atlas Woods made a joke. And although my back is turned, I think I hear a faint chuckle as well.

"When did you start singing and playing instruments?"

"When I was seven." I'm glad to get an actual answer out of him. When I started asking more personal questions at the interview he shut me down immediately. Either he's more comfortable around me now, or the threat of his words being published was the reason for his behavior.

"School band?" I ask casually as I move on to the next shelf of records.

"Private lessons to help with my speech impediment." I jolt upright at that. Not just because the thought of Atlas with a speech impediment seems outlandish, but because his vulnerability with me feels purposeful, like an olive branch.

"I had a speech impediment most of my childhood. Doctors said it would go away and it didn't so a speech therapist suggested music to help me. My parents started taking me to private lessons and even when my speech improved, I asked to keep going. That's when I started picking up other instruments."

Forgetting I had the power of speech for a second, I stare at Atlas as he shares this heartwarming story of a rockstar who started out with humble beginnings.

"Still comes out sometimes when I drink too much, so I don't get tipsy very often."

I hadn't really noticed before. Being around the pop culture and music scene for so long, I was so used to people drinking at all different rates. Atlas almost always had a beer nearby, but I can't recall watching him drink much.

Then I remember how McKenzie's freshman year of college she was so nervous at parties she always had a drink in her hand. A tactile object for her to fidget with and act as some kind of security blanket.

My heart softens toward Atlas Woods just a little more.

"Thank you for sharing all of these with me." Although I don't say it, I believe he hears the rest. *And thank you for sharing your story.* "I have no idea when my obsession with vintage stuff started but I have a thing for anything retro. Record players, cameras, clothes, music. You have a time capsule of music here."

"Well, you're welcome to use them any time—carefully, of course. But music is meant to be heard, not collecting dust on my shelves."

Out of the kindness of his heart, Atlas let me peruse his music collection in peace for another two minutes before bringing up the elephant in the room.

"So the guy at graduation. Is he an ex-boyfriend?"

"Unfortunately."

"Has he been harassing you?" Wow, Atlas does not fuck around when it comes to getting to the point. He didn't even count to three before ripping off the bandaid.

"He was." I finally turn to face him. "I broke up with him six months ago. Stopped hearing from him three months ago. Until today. The narcissistic bastard doesn't like being the fool. Getting dumped is like a smear on his reputation in his eyes. But I don't think he'll be a problem anymore."

Atlas's thoughts are so loud but I can't make out a word he's thinking. The only clues that I have are the pinched skin between his brows and the frown his mouth has formed. Not to mention the bulging vein in his temple. The only response he grants me is a small nod and an "Ok" before he heads for the door of his room. I take that as my sign to leave his inner sanctum.

Back in the small living room, the music has lowered to a decibel I can actually hear conversations over. McKenzie leaps out of Cameron's lap when I reenter and dashes to the television stand, removing a wrapped box topped with a gold bow before thrusting it towards me with a little bounce.

"What's this?" I ask, eyeing each of the people in the room.

McKenzie groans. "Ugh, people always say that when they get a gift but they'd know if they just opened it."

"It's from all of us," Cameron semi-answers my question. "Congrats on making it out of the education system."

Every pair of eyes ping-pongs between me and the box in my hands. Kneeling on the builder-grade carpet, I start unwrapping the gift. I'm one of those people who doesn't just rip into it but undoes the tape holding the paper secure to reveal a brown gift box. My heart stutters when I slip the lid off. I must be hallucinating or something. Because there's no way I'm holding a 1970s Leica M4 camera. Aside from the Canon AE-1, the Leica M4 was the quintessential 70s camera. When you think of what a vintage camera looks like, this is always what comes to people's minds.

And they aren't cheap.

I turn wide eyes to the group of friends surrounding me, letting my stare speak volumes since they rendered me speechless with this act of generosity.

"Happy graduation, Rosie."

"You guys…" I don't even know what to say. "Thank you. Where on earth did you find this?"

"There's a guy in Venice Beach who restores old cameras," says Chris. "It works and everything. He adapted it to work with modern film or something like that. Either way, he said it's usable."

"I can't believe you guys did this." I'm not much of a crier, but I am feeling especially emotional right now, more so than I did receiving my diploma.

Stuffing those squishy emotions back in their hole, I waddle on my knees toward the couch and say, "Everyone gather close. Let's christen this thing together."

"Actually..." Dallas hisses through his teeth as he scoots closer to Chris and Atlas, "We kinda already did."

"Had to make sure it works," Chris says as if he was doing me a favor. "There's a surprise on there for you to develop later." They all chuckle, clearly all in on the secret image to be revealed in development. But I laugh with them and hold the camera out, lens centered at the core of our little group, and snap the camera making the click of the lens and the flash go off in synchronized harmony. Music to my ears.

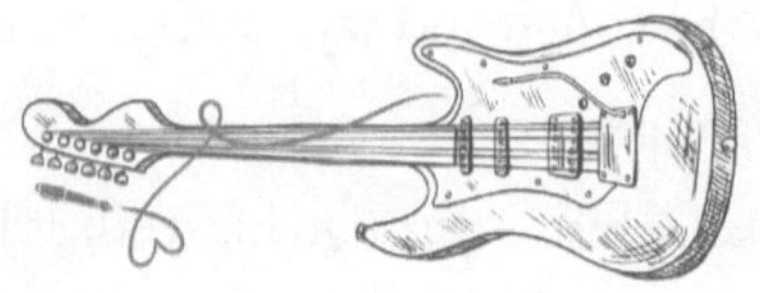

Ten
Layla

HEAT ABOVE-GRETA VAN FLEET

The surprise was in fact a photo of Dallas and Chris making demonic faces leaning over the camera while Cameron and McKenzie sport cheesy smiles. And Atlas crossing his arms with a look of indifference on his face, nothing new.

Both the surprise photo and the one from graduation night made my collage of photos taking up half my bedroom wall. The black and white moments frozen in time. Cherished memories that bring a jolt of serotonin to my brain every time I catch a glimpse of them.

With a copy of the group photo in hand, I stride down the narrow driveway toward the band's living quarters and let myself in to share the news I just got over the phone.

"Miss Grayson." Travis says in his formal way of greeting.

"Yes, sir."

"I'm calling to offer you a full time position writing for Cadence Magazine. *I was very impressed with your articles. It doesn't pay*

much, you're welcome to do freelance work on the side, but we'd like you to join the team."

Mr. Jarrin's voice is so nonchalant, as if he didn't just offer me a dream job.

My immediate answer should be yes! As much as I hoped Mr. Jarrin would like my work so much he'd hire me, I thought it was a fool's dream.

Trying not to stumble over my words, I say, "Wow. Thank you so much, sir. I'd be honored."

"Perfect. As I said, it doesn't pay much but as the magazine grows, so will your paycheck. I'll send the job application to the email we have on file. Have the application and your resume to me by Friday. Sound good?"

"I'll have it to you by Thursday." I reply trying to sound as professional as possible. I pray he doesn't hear the childish excitement in my voice.

"I'd expect nothing less from you. I'll be in touch."

The second I hit the red button to end the call, I leap out of my bed that I've been rotting in all day and perform a little happy dance for the Raiders bobblehead my parents brought me from their trip to Las Vegas. Thank goodness no one was around to see that embarrassing moment.

In a matter of sixty seconds, Travis Jarrin just changed my life and made all my dreams come true. I'll be paid to write about music. As in adult money and an adult job doing what I love. Not shoved in the corner of a newsroom taking notes and making coffee. Though it's probably for the same pay.

With excitement fizzling beneath my skin I need to tell someone. Maybe the first person I see on the bus will do it.

When I step into the guys' abode, I don't register anything else beside the sight of McKenzie squatting on the floor surrounded by hundreds of records she has taken off the shelves which lay bare against the wall. She looks like a madwoman. But I am clearly the only one who thinks so considering no one else seems the least bit entertained by the crazy lady tits deep in vinyl records.

"Hey, Layla," Cameron greets me. It's only then that McKenzie lifts her head long enough to set eyes on me and says hello before she spins toward the shelves to set the records in her hands back into place.

"Uhhh hi." I glance from my naratic roommate to the guys who are lounging on the couch as if manic, organized McKenzie is a usual sight for them. "What's going on?"

"The records had no structure," McKenzie calls over her shoulder. "So I'm putting them in alphabetical-chronological order. First organized by band name, then oldest to newest album."

"Isn't it cute," Cameron says without taking his eyes off his girlfriend. They are truly perfect for each other if he thinks her overly organized quirks are cute.

"Girl, never let that man go."

Setting my sights on Atlas I ask, "And you're ok with her rearranging all your stuff?"

Atlas pauses writing in his notebook to look up at me and shrug. Then he takes a sip of water and continues jotting down...whatever it was he was writing. Probably lyrics.

"How long has she been doing this?" I ask, taking a seat on the floor so my back can lean against the arm of the couch.

"About two hours," Dallas supplies. "She was looking for a Blondie record and couldn't find it so she decided this storage system needed a revamp."

Sounds about right. One time, McKenzie couldn't find the cinnamon in our spice cabinet so she threw out all the mismatched bottles of spices and started over buying every spice provided by McCormmick, as well as a spice rack so she could see if one was missing. Lord knows I never put a spice jar anywhere except its rightful, alphabetically assigned spot.

McKenzie brakes her stride to shoot Atlas an incredulous look. "How can you not have Led Zeppelin IV?" Her astonishment is warranted, that is a true crime for a music lover.

"It hasn't come to me yet?" Atlas answers like that is a normal statement.

The look on Mackenzie's face is priceless. "What? Like it hasn't waltzed through the front door yet?"

"Here we go," Chris laughs.

Atlas sets his pencil on his lap and his water on the floor before setting his sights on McKenzie as if he is about to drop a profoundly insightful bit of knowledge on her.

"I didn't go looking for any of these albums," he declares. "They've all been given to me or I found them looking through record stores or something. My philosophy is that they don't mean as much if I just order an album on Amazon. I let the albums choose me."

McKenzie raises one blonde eyebrow before returning to her work, refusing to acknowledge his statement.

I, on the other hand, tilt my face up so I can see Atlas and say, "That's kind of beautiful. Like all these albums were meant for you. No matter what kind of journey they've had."

Atlas just nods.

"Did that start with the one your parents gave you?"

"In a way. They gave me that one for my birthday. Then three more for Christmas. I was too young to buy my own so my first few albums were all gifts. After that, I felt like that's how it was supposed to be. Every album has a story. Like my first edition Star Wars soundtrack I found at a yard sale. Or the complete set of Simon & Garfunkel albums my old neighbor gave me cause she knew I collected records."

"There's memories linked to every record." I surmise with a warm smile.

The nearly imperceptible quirk at the corner of Atlas's mouth tells me all I need to know. In a way, the records are more than just great music and pieces of history, they also represent friendships that have come and gone, moments in time, anyone who's ever looked at a record and thought of him.

With the lull in the conversation, I prepare to take my moment for the big announcement, except Cameron beats me to it.

"You guys want to hear something cool?" With a couple nods and affirmations, Cameron continues. "I got an email from the editor of *Cadence Magazine* who was asking if one of their journalists could shadow us as we record our first album and detail the 'road to stardom,' as he put it."

"Seriously?" Dallas's slack jawed expression locks on Cameron beside him. "That's awesome. I know they aren't huge but still, that's gotta be great for our careers."

"He said it might even lead to a cover issue." Then Cameron tilts his head downward so he's looking at me beneath bushy brown-blond eyebrows. "He also said they'd have a new journalist coming on board soon he'd assign to our band once she's officially hired." I pinch my lips between my teeth to contain the word vomit on the verge of leaving my mouth. "Any idea who that could be, Miss Grayson?"

At once, Atlas lifts his gaze from the notepad to me, McKenzie whips her head around so fast her hair fans in a perfect circle, and the remaining band members drop their jaws to the floor.

Unable to contain it any longer, I throw my whole body into making my announcement in one long stream of words, "*Cadencemagazine*offeredmeajob."

No sooner do I speak the words into existence before McKenzie has tackled me to the ground in a boa constrictor hug and the guys shout their enthusiasm into the air. I don't know what kind of reaction I expected but Chris, Cameron, and Dallas dog piling on top of us was not on my bingo card for the day. Nonetheless, their outpouring of support warms a frigid part of my heart I didn't realize needed to be thawed until now. This group of friends has filled a void I didn't know existed. McKenzie has been more than enough for me, but all of us together feels like family.

It feels like home.

And now, I'll be paid to write about my friends' success.

Once the band has unleashed me from the snuggle struggle on the floor, Atlas extends a hand to help. I take his outstretched palm and he lifts me to my feet, landing us toe to toe.

"Congratulations, Rosie. You earned it."

"Hell yeah you did," Chris agrees from the kitchen where he's preparing a pitcher of margaritas. "Just make sure you write about me like a musical god, ok. I'm talking Apollo and his magic drum set who grants orgasms with the power of his music."

"That's a tall order," I tease.

"If he's Apollo can I be Zeus?" Says Cameron.

To which McKenzie chimes in, "Does that make me Hera."

Seeing a pattern form I insert my two cents, "You know the Greek gods are notorious for having open relationships and sleeping with everyone and their mother, right?"

Cameron and McKenzie's eyes snap together in a silent exchange I can only assume means they are both too possessive to let that happen. Chris reenters the living room distributing plastic cups filled with a pungent margarita that smells mostly like tequila. Once everyone has a drink in hand, he lifts his to the center of our circle of friends and says, "Cheers."

"To Rosie," Atlas raises his cup.

"And to our mutual success," I add. We all raise and clink our cups before taking a sip of the so-called drink before scrunching our faces in unison.

"Chris," Dallas says through clenched teeth. "Is there any lime juice in this at all?"

Chris shrugs his shoulders. "We ran out."

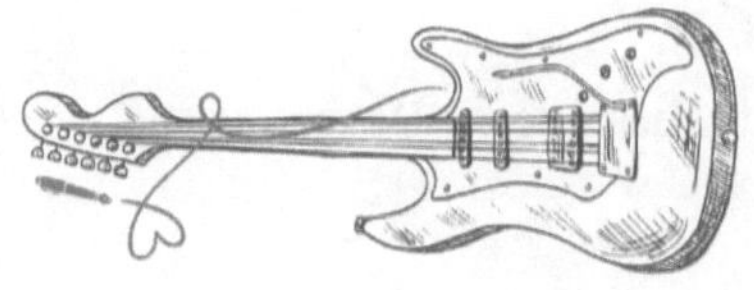

Eleven
Layla

SHE **W**ORKS **H**ARD **F**OR the Money-Donna Summers

"This is our humble beginnings," Mr. Jarrin says to accompany the wave of his hand toward the open office space. I guess an office is a generous word for what *Cadence Magazine* calls home. It's really an open concept warehouse style room with four desks, a copy machine, and a mini fridge topped with a mini microwave beside the mini coffee machine.

It's my first official day on the job and I stressed all morning about what to wear. With McKenzie's input, I decided on burgundy parachute pants and a crocheted top. Professional but still sporting hints of my personal style.

Then I stressed on the entire drive to the office that I wouldn't make it on time, that I just dropped major cash on a used car thinking I'd have consistent pay only to get fired day one.

Not only did I land a spot right outside the building, but I was also ten minutes early. Mr. Jarrin was not the least bit surprised by my punctuality. And judging by the denim and t-shirts, I'm a little overdressed. But it's better to be overdressed than underdressed, in my book.

"This is Paul," Mr. Jarrin gestures to the front desk on the right side where a middle aged man with wild salt and pepper hair briefly looks up to acknowledge my existence. "And that's Smitty." The desk behind Paul is home to a guy I'd guess is in his thirties, who's exhaustion is evident by the designer purple bags beneath his eyes.

"Did your parents really name you Smitty or is it a frat name?"

Smitty sets the coffee he was drinking onto the cluttered desk in the little open spot between a collage of sticky notes and splayed magazines.

"My parents named me John Smith because they are unoriginal assholes and my frat brothers called me Smitty. Between the two, I feel like Smitty is less cliche."

"You make a good point."

Mr. Jarrin leads me to the empty desk on the left side behind what I can only assume is his desk. His desk has two monitors and five used coffee mugs. The disorganized spread of paper looks even more exaggerated with the pristine desk behind it that only holds a monitor and keyboard atop the wood veneer.

In a way, my new boss matches his desk. His pants look fresh but his white t-shirt beneath the gray button down could use some laundering. Like most balding men, he compensates with a beard but that also needs a little attention. He looks like a man who devotes all his time to his business and rarely takes care of himself. The price of being a business owner.

"This will be your home away from home on the days you're in the office." Mr. Jarrin steps aside so I can get acquainted with my desk. "I know you live a ways away so we only need you in-office a couple days a week and you can work from home the rest of the time. Unfortunately this job requires a lot of working late which is why you're on salary."

"Not a problem, sir."

"Don't call me sir."

"Yes, sir," I give him a little salute which earns me a dramatic eye roll.

"You're going to be a handful, aren't you Grayson."

"Yes, but I'm also going to be wildly successful and I'm affordable."

"You make a good argument."

Mr. Jarrin takes a seat in his rolling office chair which looks far more comfortable than the rest in the office. Perks of being the boss. Picking up a notepad and pen, he instructs, "Pull your chair over here."

I half expected him to add *kid* to the end of that sentence but he doesn't. It sounds like something the boss would say to the new girl in the office. But the amount of respect he shows his employees while maintaining his position as the authority earns my own respect.

I roll my $20 office chair to the other side of the empty desk so Mr. Jarrin and I occupy the same space. I feel like I need something to take notes on as well but he rolls right into the discussion.

"So let's talk about this assignment," he begins while reading through a couple of his notes that resemble a child's handwriting more than an adult's. "Obviously I'll need you to write a couple articles outside of this assignment on occasion, but I want this to be your main focus. I want to give readers an indepth look behind the curtain at the music industry."

"The humble beginnings of rock stars," I quip.

"Precisely. Your article gave Broken Compass the boost they needed and now they are one of the hottest undiscovered bands. As soon as they release their album and go on tour, they'll be even bigger. I want the inside scoop. I want the notoriety of being the first to recognize their talent. You're friends with them, right?"

"I'd say so." Warmth returns to my chest when I think about the quick nature of how we all formed our little family. "My roommate is dating the lead guitarist."

"Even better." That earns me a meaty thumbs up. "The reason your article did so well and turned a lot of heads is how personal it was. Not just the personal facts about them but how you made readers feel like they were in that rehearsal with you, a part of the experience, like they are everyone's best friends. Keep that rolling."

"Got it."

Something between a smack and a bang interrupts our flow of conversation. Out of the corner of my eye I catch Paul smack the side of his monitor as if it's one of those prehistoric monitors from the 90s shaped like a giant cube. The monitor jiggles at the force of his impact, then Paul goes back to typing so whatever he did must have worked.

"Got any ideas for what to name this series?" Mr. Jarrin's voice pulls me back to our meeting.

"Uhhh, off the top of my head, how about *Road to Stardom*?"

"Too cheesy."

"*The Rock Star Experience*."

"Sounds like you're offering a gigolo."

"*Due North*?"

"What, are we a GPS?"

I let my brain run over words rapid fire in my head for a second before coming up with. "The Rise of Legends."

Mr. Jarrin brings his thumb and pointer finger to his bearded chin as he considers it for a moment. Eyes downturned he gives a little "hmm" then replies. "That could work. Sounds promising. Not just for us but for the readers. Confident in the band's ability to make it big."

"They'll be playing the superbowl someday," I remark. "Mark my words."

I spend the rest of the day getting organized and drafting my first article about the band, sort of an intro to what the series will cover and a brief introduction to Broken Compass. The magazine releases new issues twice a month virtually and physical copies sold online.

From what I've gathered, Smitty, Paul, and I are the writers that fill the magazine. Mr. Jarrin is the brains and organization behind it doing everything from editing to formatting to the legal parts of running a business.

Mr. Jarrin wasn't lying when he said the job involved long hours. Because it's my first day and I don't have a lot of material yet, I helped him virtually format everything for the next issue to release and brainstormed ideas with the team until 7:00 in the evening. It's nearly 8:30 by the time I get back to the apartment. Considering the giggles I hear from behind McKenzies closed door, I'm guessing her other half is in there with her. So I choose to leave them alone in favor of taking a well deserved hot shower after sitting in traffic with terrible air conditioning in the California summer heat.

It's one of those showers that feels restorative, healing, like it washes every inch of worry, stress, and tension from your body so you walk away a new woman. Feeling refreshed, I pop some chicken tenders from the freezer into the microwave and pour myself some water from the filter in the fridge.

As I'm scrolling on my phone waiting for the microwave to deliver my classic college kid dinner, a new message banner drops from the top of my screen reading the name of the sender: ATLAS WOODS. I click on the message out of sheer curiosity that quiet, antisocial Atlas Woods would text me at 9:24pm on a Monday evening.

> **ATLAS: How'd the first day go?**

He's texting me to see how my first day at the magazine went? What does that even mean?

> **LAYLA: Our master plan to take over the music literature world is coming along nicely.**

ATLAS: I'd expect nothing less.

ATLAS: Was everyone nice to you?

LAYLA: A little overwhelmed and in desperate need of my magic, but otherwise very professional.

ATLAS: They're lucky to have you.

LAYLA: Hey, how does the headline *The Rock Star Experience* sound to you?

ATLAS: Makes it sound like our bodies are for hire.

LAYLA: My boss said something to that effect too.

Feeling like it's only the polite thing to do, I make myself comfortable on my bed and text back:

LAYLA: How about you? How did your day go?

Since there is no reply for a solid sixty seconds I worry that I overstepped an imaginary boundary. Then the little typing bubble pops onto the screen and I release a tense breath I didn't realize I was holding.

ATLAS: Oh, ya know, just counting down the days until music can pay my bills instead of making coffee for rich people.

Atlas and Cameron both work at a trendy coffee shop in Manhattan Beach. The kind with neon signs that say BUT FIRST COFFEE and themed backdrops for social media posts. I've heard them both complain about wannabe fashion and lifestyle influencers setting up tripods during the morning rush and causing a back up. And naturally, those people never tip.

LAYLA: Watch out! Your PR team will probably start making you guys pose for dorky pictures to post on social media. You may even have to do trending dances.

ATLAS: If that day ever comes, you have permission to slap me.

LAYLA: You certainly know how to tell a woman what she wants to hear.

Silence.

And then:

ATLAS: When's the next time your boss wants you to shadow the band?

LAYLA: Your first recording session. Thursday, right?

ATLAS: Right. Fingers crossed it goes well. The boss's boss will be there to see what she's investing in.

LAYLA: Bring your A-game, Woods, this is only the beginning.

More silence.

ATLAS: I can't believe how fast this all is. We haven't even recorded the album yet and it already feels like so much has happened in such a short amount of time.

ATLAS: Feels like our future is within reach and we're just climbing the ladder until we can grab it.

LAYLA: You guys worked really hard to get here. Enjoy the ride. And don't forget why you started making music in the first place. It's easy to let the work and boring details cloud the reason you love what you do.

ATLAS: Is that how you feel about your job?

LAYLA: Yes and no. I love what I do. But I also need to make a living. I know I'll have to write articles that don't interest me as much so I make them interesting. But if I let my passion for writing get bogged down by work, then I'm just another cog universities spit out into the workforce. Gotta stay realistic while keeping the dream alive.

ATLAS: Sounds like quite the juggling act.

LAYLA: *gif of a circus clown juggling bowling pins*

ATLAS: *gif of a man eating popcorn*

Well call me a monkey's uncle, I never would have pegged Atlas Woods as the gif sending type.

> ATLAS: You can do anything you set your mind to, Rosie. No doubt about it.

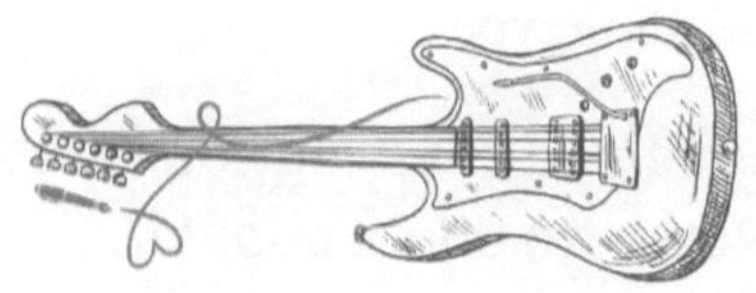

Twelve

Layla

W HOLE LOTTA LOVE-LED ZEPPELIN

I've seen the magic behind how a song comes to life in Atlas's mind. I've seen how the notes coalesce with the words to form a perfect symphony while he acts as the vessel for the song to arrive into the world. Bit by bit, little by little, it all comes together through a marriage of natural talent and focused work.

Now, I get to witness how those songs are recorded for the world to hear. McKenzie and I are sitting in the control room watching the band set up their gear–the things they were allowed to bring, anyway. The recording studio provides all the sound equipment but the band was allowed to bring their own instruments.

The producers made an exception for me to observe the session but not for McKenzie, he said it would be too many people. So naturally, I claimed she was my lovely assistant and essential to the process. The producer didn't buy that one bit, but played along with it anyway and allowed her to sit in for this *one* session, which he made clear by holding a single finger up.

As the band warms up, Mr. Ruben walks into the control room with a sophisticated looking blonde on his heels. If her tight french twist and Louis Vuitton's didn't establish the power dynamic in the room, her upturned nose would. She doesn't utter a word, just stands behind the guy at the control panel, crosses her arms, and observes the guys as they finish their warm-ups.

"Nice to see you again, ladies," Frank Ruben greets McKenzie and I.

"Pleasure to see you again as well," I reply. That's when CEO Barbie turns around to scan us where we're perched on the sofa.

"Who are you?" Her voice sounds like she should be an absolute doll but her tone suggests power and authority. I imagine she's honed this approach over years of working her way up the ladder in a male dominated industry. Something I'm all too familiar with.

"Layla Grayson." I project confidence even though her withering stare makes me feel like a lowly peasant. "Journalist for *Cadence Magazine*. And this is my assistant McKenzie. We have a continuous series following the band's rise through the music industry."

I only get a "hmm" in response to that claim. "And you need an assistant?"

Mr. Ruben leans closer and says in a hushed tone that we can still hear, "She's also the lead guitarist's girlfriend."

"I see." She gives McKenzie a once over. "This will be the only exception. We limit the amount of people in here for a reason. Too many cooks in the kitchen can get messy."

"Understood, ma'am." As soon as the woman turns her back on us, McKenzie offers her a half-hearted salute.

Once the band is set up, Mr. Ruben leans over the little microphone and presses the call button to speak to the band. "Alright
guys. Let's make some music. We also have the record company's
CEO Dana Boem sitting in on this one." No pressure or anything.
"Go ahead, guys."

I've heard them perform this song countless times. Big clubs, the
practice room at Wilson's, even practicing the harmonies in their
living room. And all of those times surpassed what I'm seeing now
for one simple reason: they aren't performing with heart. Something about the recording studio and I'm guessing the pressure
weighing heavy on their shoulders is messing with the band's mojo.
They aren't bad. They just don't have the same spark as usual.

And I'm not the only one that notices. Mr. Ruben and Ms.
Boem's spine's stiffen, their posture expressing exactly how they
feel about this take without having to utter a word.

Frank leans over the microphone and calls for the guys to stop
and start again. His exact instructions are "Give it the heart I know
you have."

So the band begins again. And it's still not enough. No matter
how many takes they do it's just not *right*.

Ms. Boem departs through the door and enters the recording
studio with a poised strut that looks well rehearsed.

"Boys," she greets them while folding her hand in front of her
abdomen. "This isn't the band I've heard so much about. This
isn't the band I've seen countless videos of online. Take five and
then bring those guys in here because the boys before me right now
are not it."

Talk about putting the fear of God in someone.

Ms. Boem leaves the recording studio to reenter the control room just as I slip into the hallway.

I don't want to place the blame on Atlas but he's the front man, the lead singer. His energy carries the band. So when he steps into the hallway as well I notice the tension right away. It's evident in the way he runs his hands through his dark locks. The bulging veins in his arms. The way he paces a six foot stretch of the hallway, back and forth.

"Hey," I grab his attention. "What's going on?" I try to use a soothing voice that doesn't imply I think this is his fault.

"I don't know," Atlas responds without looking up from the carpeted floor. "I don't know. Maybe it's the pressure of it. Maybe it's because this isn't our normal space. I don't know but it feels *off*, somehow."

"You've played in countless venues, to any number of people. Why is this any different than playing at Wilson's?"

Atlas takes a long breath to pause and consider the situation, taking stock of his surroundings and his emotions. With every blink I see the gears in his head turning over and over.

"Yesterday, Ruben said our album doesn't have enough sex appeal," he announces. I've got to admit, that's not what I thought would be bugging him. "He said the powers that be want more sex appeal from the band. They want a radio errotic song and they need to be able to market more than just our music."

Ok. Now we're getting somewhere.

"Alright. Well, that's not ideal but do you think it's doable?"

"I don't want to be some sex symbol, Rosie." Atlas finally stops to stare at me, face to face, heart to heart. "I want to be a musician. I want to be known for my music and the work we put into our craft, not just radio songs and bare chests."

"Ok, I'm gonna be honest with you." Inhale. Exhale. "That's Hollywood, Atlas. That's the way this industry works. We've seen it for decades. From Elvis thrusting his pelvis to hot chicks on cars. Every band that has made it big has done their fair share of vulgar music for whatever time period they thrived in. People want something they can relate to. Something to get their heart pounding. Something that makes them feel alive when their miserable, mundane lives just won't do it.

"Don't give the people some silly sex song about banging girls and getting high like those who came before you. Reach out to their souls and give them something that makes them feel the rush of sex they so desperately crave."

Inhale. Exhale.

I have no idea how Atlas will react to this but I can only hope he understands where I'm coming from. We don't always see eye to eye but when it comes to the big stuff, I feel like we match.

Atlas takes a deep breath of his own then nods. No response, no words, just a nod. But that's better than yelling in my face so I'll take it.

Pointing one painted nail toward the door to the recording studio I say, "Now march your ass back in there and find something to hold on to so you feel inspired. I know your compass is broken but try to find your way, ok?"

I was hoping my little pun would break the tension but he doesn't even crack a smile. However, Atlas does in fact march back into the studio and throws his guitar strap over one shoulder. I can see by the look in his dark eyes that he's digging deep to find whatever will inspire him so he can do his job.

Atlas lifts his eyes to me, stares for a long second in a way that feels like he's trying to communicate telepathically, then monitors his hands as he positions them for the first chord of the song.

We all hold our breath as we wait for the band to begin.

And when they do, it's magic.

Pure magic.

Whatever Atlas found within himself was enough to not only reclaim his passion and his fire, but lead the band into a beautiful harmony of instruments and words to create something truly magnificent.

As soon as the band finishes, I see the back of Ms. Boem's head bob and nod, not to the beat of the music but in confirmation that she got what she came for.

This is the small assurance that she's pleased. They still have a label to represent them.

She leans over the microphone to address the band. "Good work, guys. Come back tomorrow to record another song. And I believe you have some homework as well."

She must mean the "sex" song. Figures she'd be the one behind that.

Before exiting the room, Ms. Boem turns to me and says, "Miss Grayson. While I'm pleased about the coverage the band will be receiving I want to make one thing clear. We will cooperate with you as much as you cooperate with us. Don't make this label look bad or our cooperation will start to fade. Understood?"

I confirm. "Understood."

I hope this lady makes the guys rich and famous, otherwise it's all pointless.

Cameron bursts into the control room to lift his girlfriend off her feet and plant an excited kiss on her. At least someone is having a good time. Chris and Dallas seem to be in good spirits too, but I see the hesitation in Atlas, the fear that he won't be able to deliver. Fear for his future and their image. And I just hope he can find a way to appease the label without selling his soul in the process.

"Let's go to the beach to celebrate a great first session," Dallas suggests. "Bonfire."

McKenzie perks up at the suggestion. "Ooo, I'll swing by the store and get marshmallows."

"And beer," Cameron adds.

As we file out of the room, I give Atlas's elbow a little pinch so he brings his gaze to me.

"Hey. Whatever you found to lead them through that, it worked. You guys did great."

I offer him a sympathetic smile and he offers me the slightest curve of his mouth back.

Better than nothing.

Thirteen
Atlas

Dangerous Woman-Ariana Grande

Maybe Layla had a point.

The Beatles are known for so many classic songs that have become household staples. Yet their raunchier songs still earned them attention.

Not to mention all the artists discovered on social media platforms because one risqué song was picked up by the right person and went viral. Those songs can be used to hook an audience so they listen to more of your music and find a piece that speaks to them. These days, it just takes one viral song to make a career.

But I don't want us to be a one hit wonder band. We're so much more than that. So I latch onto another piece of the puzzle Layla laid out for me.

People want to feel something profound, they want the intensity and adrenaline of sex, not just the provocative nature behind it. Society is desperately craving artists to make them feel alive. So that's what I'll give them.

Now I just need inspiration.

It's been a while since I've been with anyone. I used to look forward to the mind-numbing fucking after a show with someone I didn't have to keep up appearances with. But I've felt uninspired as of late. A routine orgasm just doesn't do it for me anymore. I don't know what I need but girls throwing themselves at me isn't it. I like the chase, the back and forth flirtation, the build up to the moment of combustion.

Maybe that's what I should write about. It's not about the finish line, it's about the electrifying, heart-pounding, patient desperation to get there.

With that thought in mind, words start taking form, notes. They're just out of reach but growing closer to form a tangible melody that ignites a song. Phrases that need to be aligned in just the right order to create a sequence bold enough and meaningful enough to be memorable.

I start to hear all the other instruments in my head. As soon as one piece clicks into place the rest follow. I hear the sultry seduction of the bass, the vibration of the drums, the lyrical tune of the guitars to accompany the words. It needs fine tuning but there's something there.

There's a hit song waiting to be crafted.

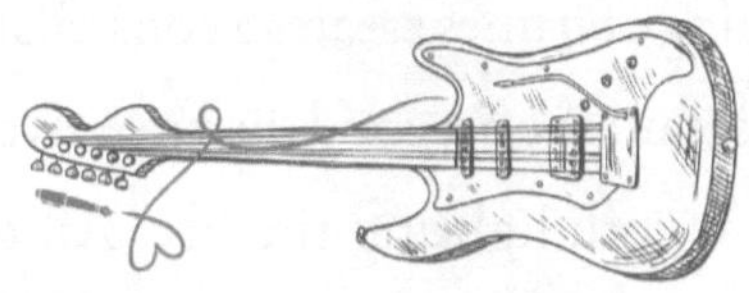

Fourteen

Layla

EAT YOUR YOUNG-HOZIER

"Marshmallows secured," McKenzie announces as she slides into the back of the van with a grocery bag of much more than just marshmallows.

"Is that deodorant?" Chris squints to see through the cheap plastic.

McKenzie shrugs her shoulders innocently. "I was out."

"Ya know I'm almost out of toothpaste," Dallas starts but Chris silences him.

"Then go to the store tomorrow. This was not a shopping trip. It was simply recon for bonfire supplies. Just because McKenzie broke the rules doesn't mean you get to."

"Who made the rules?" Cameron's voice is far from serious.

"The bonfire gods, obviously." I feel the eye roll from Chris even though I can't see it. "Now let's get this show on the road."

Dockweiler beach is the only one in the area that you can have an open fire on. So we are not the only crowd on a Thursday night to form a fire pit and bring out the s'mores supplies. The red-orange twinkling of flames creates a constellation up and down the coastline. We set up shop a good distance away from the crowd as the boys get to work lighting the fire. All of them. Because obviously fire draws all the male specimens in the vicinity and the task takes more than just one person.

But it's no time at all before we're all gathered around the fire in a small huddle roasting marshmallows on sticks while ever-organized McKenzie sets up a conveyor belt of s'mores ingredients to expedite the process. Dallas is playing music off his phone but it's just background noise to the chatter and banter between friends after a successful first day.

Atlas is seated beside me and I realize that's on purpose when he angles his torso in my direction, leaning his head toward me to speak in a hushed tone.

"I started working on a song," he tells me.

I peer up at him through my lashes, rearing back just a little so his entire face is within my field of vision.

"Really?" I make no effort at all to hide the shock in my voice. "That was fast."

"I was thinking about what you said and, sometimes, the music just comes to me. It's out of my control. I started writing music in the first place because these songs would play on repeat in my head and I had to get them out somehow."

"Alright," I wave a hand to welcome this new song into the universe. "Let's hear it."

Pulling his phone from his back pocket, Atlas hands me the device after opening it to a notes page where the words to the song are written.

If she'd let me love her
I'd do it on my knees
If she'd let me love her
I'd love to hear her say please
I'd beg for just one taste
I'd beg for a tease
If she gave me her heart
I'd show her my expertise
Teeth, Tongue and Oxygen
She's everything to me
And if she'd just let me in
I'd show her what lovin' means

I read them a couple of times because...damn! I have no idea what the melody sounds like but I can already tell this will be a song for women to swoon over.

Still scanning the words, I say, "Wow. Sexy. Intimate. Mature but also playful. I think you're on to something, Woods. What does the song sound like?"

Before Atlas can show me, Chris interrupts, "Are you two going to share with the class whatever Atlas has on his phone? Please tell me it's embarrassing childhood pictures."

"Sorry to disappoint." I hand the phone back to Atlas. "It's actually a steamy song."

"Ooo even better," McKenzie huddles closer to the fire as if that will encourage Atlas to perform. "Sing it for us."

Atlas averts his gaze to the phone. For a guy who has played on stage to hundreds of people, he certainly lets his timidness shine through when it's a more intimate group. "I only have the first couple verses done. But maybe you guys can help with the rest."

Nodding his head in consideration, Chris says. "Ya know, I've always felt my true calling is in writing erotic songs."

And that is Cameron's cue to shove half a chocolate bar into Chris's mouth to prevent him from saying anything else on the matter.

With Chris's forced silence, Atlas clears his throat before letting the music pour from his mouth. A sultry collection of notes accompany the subtly arousing words he wrote to form a song that makes everyone's panties wet. We're all hooked, listening with bated breath as he performs the first two verses for us around the bonfire.

I can already hear a steady bass to accompany the tune, the way the band will use their instruments to amplify the vibe. It would honestly be the perfect slow and erotic strip tease song. And I'm not the only one who thinks so.

As soon as Atlas finishes, Cameron leans over to his girlfriend and says loud enough for the group to hear, "Hey babe. Do you want to take a little walk with me? To the van?"

McKenzie swats his chest looking half tempted. "Don't be crude."

"Damn, dude," Dallas adds. "That's good. Even has me in the mood. Do you think it's the kind of thing the label would want?" It takes me a second to realize Dallas directed the last part to me.

Once I come down from the little high Atlas's smooth-as-sin voice gave me, I'm thinking clearly enough to reply. "Absolutely." I say with pure confidence. "I'm sure it's better than they were hoping for. With so many bands trying to make it big, I feel like they throw in a half-heated sex song for the same reason the label wants you to include one. But fans overlook it for the better songs they put their whole heart into. There's promise, here. It's good." I swing my gaze to Atlas beside me. "It'll blow them away."

I'm starting to think Atlas isn't capable of writing half-hearted songs. He throws all his passion into every song, every note is crafted with reason.

He doesn't do anything without purpose.

Some moments in my life leave a mark on my soul. My first CD player blasting "Why Not" by Hilary Duff when I was a kid. The first time I drove by myself after getting my license. Sitting on the floor of the guys' living room after they gave me my graduation gift. And I want to capture those significantly insignificant moments forever.

Sitting with my friends around a fire on the beach, laughing without a care in the world because it feels like everything is going right for once. This is one of those moments. So I take my Polaroid camera out of my oversized bag and snap a quick photo. I know I'll barely be able to make out everyone's faces through the shadowed glow of the fire, but I'll still know. I'll still be able to look back on this photo and remember the pure happiness I felt for a fraction of time.

> ATLAS: You really think the song is good enough?

I was plugging my phone into the charger before bed when Atlas's message popped up on my screen. Now I'm lying here thinking about how to respond.

> LAYLA: Are you doubting yourself, Woods?

> ATLAS: It's just not my usual thing. I try to write about things that matter. Things that will inspire.

> LAYLA: Well, hopefully you inspire a lot of sex with this song.

> ATLAS: -_-

> LAYLA: And I think you'll also inspire people to love their partners. What may seem silly and inconsequential to you may touch someone else who's in a rough place. You never know how the things you put out into the world are going to affect someone. Maybe it'll be the mood booster someone needs to take their shot.

Silence. Then:

> ATLAS: Thanks, Rosie.

ATLAS: And thanks for today. I appreciate it.

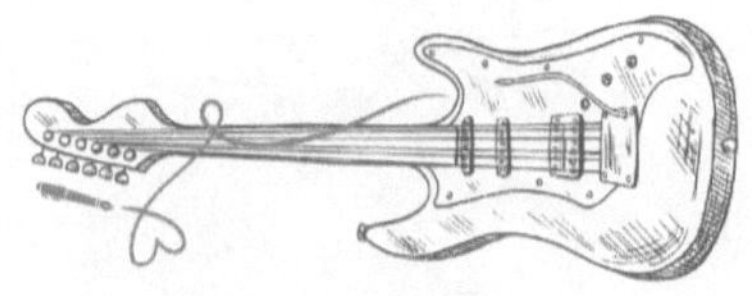

Fifteen

Layla

I THINK I'M IN LOVE-Eddie Money

"Come on, it's just one dance move."

McKenzie looks way too thrilled to be directing the boys in trending dances for social media. And Atlas looks like he'd rather slide down a banister of razor blades than give in to social media fads for the sake of marketing.

It's been two months since the first day of recording for the band. Atlas finished the song the band dubbed the "lovin' song" but the label renamed it to "Blood and Oxygen" once they heard it. Cameron said he could see the dollar signs in Ms. Boem's eyes when they performed it for the first time. She expedited the recording and producing process so they could push out the band's first single and generate hype for their upcoming album.

And thanks to the power of the internet, that hype turned into a global social media sensation when a famous influencer created a strip tease type dance with a belt to the song. It wasn't long before the entire internet started removing their belts in a series of choreographed moves and everyone was melting over the thirst traps. And once the book girls got a hold of this song, they amplified the streaming numbers by the thousands.

Naturally, the label wants the band to jump on board with their own music for publicity's sake and perform their own version of the dance. And as expected, Chris was more than willing to perform an errotic dance for social media, Dallas and Cameron were reluctant but willing to do it, and Atlas was Atlas, putting up a fight every step of the way.

He's still the grumpy stick in the mud he's been from day one. But now I understand that his hesitation isn't about being a contrarian or an asshole, he just doesn't want to be a sex symbol.

Too bad for him, he's also the lead singer and everyone and their mother is begging to have his babies.

It's weird seeing your friends go from humble musicians who play in bars and clubs to famous rockstars overnight. While the world see's hot guys who can sing and play instruments, McKenzie and I still see the goofy bandmates who formed a brotherhood with a common passion. The guys who sing Karaoke at the *Blue Room* when they have a bit of free time to just be themselves.

Standing in a straight line, the guys each hold one hand on their belt buckles while McKenzie points the phone camera at them in the practice studio. The dance is simple, a bunch of sideways hip thrusts to the beat of the song and then slipping their belts from the loops in time with one another before wrapping the belt around their necks. All while lip syncing to the verse.

Although, I'm not sure it can be considered lip syncing if they are the artists who perform the song.

"Alright guys, show me your moves in three, two, one." Momager McKenzie points to the guys to direct their start and they perform it as if they've been practicing in the bathroom mirror all this time. As soon as Chris removes his belt, his overly loose pants drop to his ankles revealing red and white heart boxers. The guys are paying too much attention to their own coordination to notice.

Not wanting to ruin the moment, McKenzie and I hold in our laughter until she hits the red button to stop the recording before we burst into a fit of laughter. That's when the rest look to their left to see what has us doubling over. All three fully clothed band members toss their belts at Chris. I should have seen that coming. What I didn't see coming was Dallas saying, "Man, we see enough of your naked ass at home. Pull your pants up."

That only causes McKenzie and I to laugh harder. "Wait, this is normal behavior?"

Chris holds his hands above his head in the shape of a halo while the guys go back to their instruments to continue rehearsals. They still have two more songs to record before the album can be finalized and released to the public. The label already has shows lined up for them to promote the release.

Including a huge festival in Palm Springs. Big names from all over the country come to this festival. One of the headliners for the two day event is rumored to be Taliah Summers, the biggest pop singer in the last five years who's steadily collecting more Grammys than any pop artist before her.

Thanks to the band's notoriety, my articles in *Cadence* have been getting record views and I've been cited in several other journals. It's a mutually beneficial relationship that continues to elevate everyone's careers.

Except McKenzie who starts her final year of college in a few days. So we planned a campout at the festival to send her back to school with great memories to carry her through the year as she morphs back into overworked-law student Mckenzie.

It seems like it's been ages since my roommate and I occupied the apartment at the same time. So when I walk in to see her sitting on the couch with trash TV on, I pounce at the opportunity to catch up. Drinks and snacks in hand, McKenzie and I lounge on the couch in the most unflattering positions angled toward the TV. Two women with duck lips are arguing on the screen but their chatter is just background noise to our own gossip.

I've been catching McKenzie up about work and what it's like when I go into the office. Things are always chaotic but I thrive in that environment.

I know I shouldn't be surprised but I'm still taken a smidge off-guard when she asks, "Are any of your coworkers hot? Potential suitors?" Her eyebrows dance on her forehead to emphasize her excitement about my dating prospects.

"Uh, no," I crush her hopes instantaneously. "Paul is happily married and Smitty is a scatterbrain. I can't handle *that* kind of chaos."

"Shame," McKenzie tilts her head back toward the TV as I shovel more gummy worms into my mouth. "Cam and I could use another couple to go on double dates with. I love spending so much time with him but sometimes it's fun to hang out with other couples, ya know?"

Not even a little bit.

"Sorry to disappoint you. These are my hard work and making a name for myself years. There will be plenty of time for romance in the future."

"What if the love of your life fell into your lap?"

"Let's be real, Henry Cavil isn't falling into my lap any time soon."

"What if it was the right place, right time and there was something worth pursuing?"

Straightening my spine, I position myself so McKenzie can feel the full weight of my squint as pieces start falling into place.

"Kenzie," I draw her name out slowly. "What are you up to?"

"Nothing." Likely story. "It just seems like there might be some chemistry between you and Atlas." There it is.

"Ha." The half-hearted noise leaves me before I can think twice. "Unlikely. He's cool and I think we've become friends but let's not forget how that relationship started."

"Oh come on. Danika hated Julio at first but now she's obsessed with him." Mckenzie flings an arm toward the screen, referencing the poorly acted reality TV show we've been binging.

"I hardly think the actors from *Love Uncharted* are a worthy example to help your case."

Falling back into her slouch McKenzie mutters, "It was worth a shot."

Heaving a sigh I respond, "I don't know Kenzie. He and I have come a long way in terms of friendship but I just don't think romance is in the cards for us. I don't see him that way. But," McKenzie lifts her head like a prairie dog when she hears the conjunction, "I will admit he and I have grown closer. Sometimes it feels like we really get each other. Like we understand one another without having to explain too much."

Leaping off the back of the couch McKenzie twists her torso to point a finger right in my face. "A-ha! I knew there was something there."

"Kenzie. That doesn't mean it's romantic. I feel like you and I get each other too. I feel the same way about the guys that I do about you."

"But you two would be perfect for one another," she whines, slumping down again. "You said you had some chemistry when you first met before the interview."

As the queen of changing subjects, I ask, "How about you and Cameron? It's been a few months now. Has anyone uttered the infamous L-word yet?"

A soft, feminine blush creeps across her cheeks which tells me more than her words might.

"Not yet," she says, biting her bottom lip. "But I think he will soon. There have been a lot of almosts. Like the other day we were having some alone time in the back of the van—"

"Sterilize the van. Got it." I hold a thumbs up.

"–And he looked at me for a long moment, tucking some hair behind my ear. He looked like he wanted to say it but kissed me instead."

"Aww," I stretch my bottom lip to make the pouty *that's adorable* face. "Maybe he's just waiting for the right moment."

"Maybe he wants *me* to say it first." The shock in McKenzie's eyes tells me this is the first that notion has come to mind. "But I don't want to say it first. It's embarrassing for the girl to say it first."

"No it's not." I try to calm her. "Do you love him?"

My best friend stares at the TV for a long, tenuous moment but I doubt she's really watching it. She's probably picturing her boyfriend's curly blond hair and soft eyes that show how many smiles he's worn in his lifetime. A dreamy expression smooths her features and I know the answer before she even replies.

"I think I do."

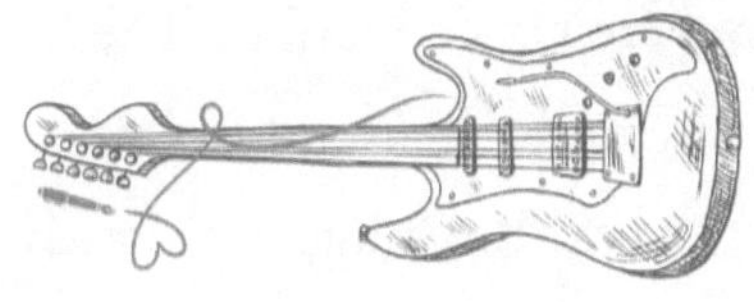

Sixteen

Layla

Free-Zac Brown Band

I always dreamed I'd get to attend one of these festivals and flash my snazzy PRESS badge at every gate. But I never imagined I'd get to do that *and* be a groupie for one of the most anticipated bands of the weekend.

This will be Broken Compass's first major performance since their song went viral online. And they will be presenting a few of the songs from their album for this crowd, unheard by anyone except the label and us. Unleashing new music at a festival as large as this one is risky but if the crowd loves the songs, the reward will be worth it. The success will generate even more buzz in anticipation of the album release.

But if they don't like the songs...

Let's just pray they do.

I have full confidence in the band and their music, as I have from the start. There isn't a shadow of a doubt in my mind that the audience will fall head over heels in love with the new music.

While *Cadence* couldn't afford to pay for all of my expenses, any costs for the festival are tax-deductible. The band got McKenzie and I all-access passes for the weekend and we set up a couple tents in the camping area so the big things are already covered.

There is no actual PRESS badge for reporters so I made myself one to seem more official. Hopefully no one notices that the other journalists are going badge free.

As much as Dallas teased me about the badge with my little headshot from the magazine's website, it's been helpful to convince artists that I'm a legitimate journalist and not just a groupie. Though, my celestial sheer dress over the burgundy bodysuit probably isn't helping me look professional.

I've already gotten a few brief interviews on top of shadowing the band to record their experience. Not to mention the countless photos I've already snapped. I specifically brought the Leica M4 to capture the festival so the photos have a true nostalgic feel to them, not just a filter. The difference is always obvious and I'm going for authentic, not curated.

I'm angling the camera toward the in-ground pool of the retro bungalow where several of the VIP guests are swimming when I feel a tap on my shoulder.

Imagine my utter shock to find Donovan Gentry standing behind me with a boyish grin that's been plastered all over the press for this festival. This will be his first solo performance since splitting up with the boy band that made him famous in the first place.

I always hate it when musicians do that. It's one thing for a band to fall apart, it's another for a member to get too inflated an ego and think they can succeed on their own.

"Hi," his smooth voice itches under my skin. "Can I buy you a drink?"

Donovan looks over his shoulder to the outdoor bar where several other big names are ordering drinks.

Looking from the bar back to him I answer by holding up my camera. "I'm actually a journalist." In my experience, most musicians don't want to get mixed up with reporters for fear their dirty laundry will be hung out to dry on the front page of every reputable magazine.

Donovan tilts his head so he has to peer through a dense set of lashes to make eye contact. It's a calculated movement, giving the impression of vulnerability. "In that case, can I offer you an interview?"

He's got balls, I'll give him that.

"You're willing to sit down with a journalist you've never met, you don't know what magazine I work for, and you want to give me an interview with no strings attached?"

"Just one string, actually." Let me take a wild guess. "You also let me buy you a drink." It's an open bar but I understand his meaning.

With a nod I agree to his terms and follow him to the bar. Donovan Gentry is by far the biggest name that's agreed to speak with me this weekend so I can't pass on an opportunity like this.

Pulling out all the stops, Donovan moves the barstool back for me to take a seat before mirroring me in the stool opposite. When the bartender asks for our drink orders he replies, "I'll take a gin on the rocks. And for the lady..."

He turns to me so I can place my own order. Thank goodness he's not one of those guys that tries to order for a girl.

"I'll have a club soda with lime, please." Meeting Donovan's inquisitive expression I supply, "I'm not drinking until I'm done working." Although it wouldn't really matter since we live in a time when sobriety is as normal as marijuana use.

But Donovan accepts that with a head nod, no further questions on the matter, and changes the subject. "So, how long have you been a journalist?"

"You don't even want to know my name first?" I quip. But when Donovan points at my chest I realize he knew my name the second I turned around. As well as the magazine I work for considering they are both printed in bold letters beside my photo on the nifty little badge I made.

"Oh. I'll make sure to note how observant you are. 'Rumors Are True: Donovan Gentry Can Read.'"

"I hope I earn a better headline than that." I'll admit. He is pretty charming. From the way he gives me a half smile every time he talks to the slight tilt of his head so his chestnut curls sweep over his brow. I can see why girls and guys alike swoon in his presence.

Before asking any of my own questions I answer his. "I just graduated in the spring with a degree in journalism. I've been working for *Cadence Magazine* for only a few months."

"You write with the voice of someone with a lot of experience, not someone who's only worked for them for a few months."

Color me shocked. "You've read my work?"

The bartender sets our drinks on little paper napkins embossed with the drink sponsor logo. Donovan takes a sip of his clear liquor while I forget about my drink altogether.

"I have. I heard there's this band called Broken Compass that's making a rise in the music industry. Can't go online without hearing their song. So naturally I looked into them and found your series about them."

Grabbing hold of my senses again, I take my club soda in hand to swallow the awestruck lump in my throat.

"Well, if you still agreed to an interview then it must not have been half bad."

"Good enough that I kept reading." Am I blushing? My cheeks feel tingly. "Consider me an open book. What would you like to know, Layla Grayson?" Donovan opens his arms as if bracing for a hug, which tugs the top of his button up white linen shirt open far enough to see a sprinkling of dark hair on his chest.

This could either go very well for my career or very poorly, but it's worth a shot.

"Alright, Donovan Gentry. You've answered every question about your split from the band with vague answers. 'I was headed in a different direction.' 'Creative differences.' All that jazz. So what's the realest answer you can give me about why you went solo?"

"Ouch, right for the jugular," he mimics a knife slashing his throat with his index finger. Taking his drink in hand he continues, "But I appreciate how direct you are without being insulting. Most reporters who ask usually phrase it in a way that either makes me out to be the bad guy. Or it sounds like they've already made up their mind about me."

"I believe everyone deserves a chance to tell their side of the story. Afterall, there's your story, there's their story, and the truth lies somewhere in the middle."

Donovan appraises me for a moment, never breaking eye contact as he considers how to answer me without breaking any legal restrictions I'm sure have been locked on the topic.

"Alright," he leans forward to brace one elbow on the bar. "What I can tell you is that the 'creative differences' was absolutely true, just a simplified version. As we grew older, the band wanted to continue to cater to a younger demographic whereas I felt that we should grow with our original audience." Out of the corner of my eye I notice Donovan trailing drops of condensation on his glass with his pinky finger. "I didn't want to stay a teen boy band heart-throb forever. I didn't want to be pigeonholed into a demographic I would eventually get too old for. A forty year old man singing to teenagers is downright creepy. And I predict the band will eventually wither away for that very reason."

My head bobs in understanding. He makes a valid point. When you don't progress, the world moves on without you. It's the same reason why older artists are revamping their music or using social media to promote themselves, now.

Leaning back in the stool to get a good look at the man before me I ask, "So what do you want readers and your fan base to know going forward?"

Donovan looks away for a second and then back at me, multan eyes locked on my face.

"I guess I want them to know I am still me. I still have nothing but love and respect for my former bandmates. And I plan to continue making music that we can all grow with."

I guess maybe he isn't just an egocentric asshole who thinks he's more talented than his bandmates afterall.

"And what do you mean by you're still you? Who is Donovan Gentry without the band?"

I know that sounds harsh but I hope he understands what I'm trying to do.

"I'm a musician first and always will be. The most important thing in my career will always be the fans. I'm still the same guy they've listened to when they cried or the guy they listened to at parties. I'm still the same guy who prefers tea over coffee." He's referencing an old interview from when his original band first found stardom. "And I still love making music."

"Alright, one last question, Donovan: how are you feeling going into your first solo performance since leaving the band?"

A hissing noise breaks out as Donovan sucks air through his teeth, leaning back in his stool to mirror my position.

"Nervous." It says alot about him that he took the honest approach. "The fans could hate my new direction or my own artistic style."

"Or they could love it." I reminded him.

"And that's all I can hope for. I can only hope I meet their expectations and then some."

"Well I'm looking forward to your show," I confess. "If your enthusiasm and dedication is any indication of your skills as a solo artist, I think you'll knock 'em dead."

I get a full smile from Donovan for that vote of confidence. I'm not spiteful. I want to see people succeed. And I hope whatever he has in store is exactly what his fans want.

He's performing tonight before the main event while Broken Compass is in tomorrow's lineup. So tonight will be a night of fun before the band makes their biggest debut ever tomorrow.

"I appreciate your vote of confidence, Layla." A mischievous grin spreads across his face as I see an idea forming in his eyes. "Alright, Layla. I've answered your questions. Now it's time for you to answer mine."

I could remind him that wasn't part of the deal but I have to admit I'm intrigued. And maybe...partially...just a little under his spell.

"Go ahead, as long as you don't print any of it." If he doesn't like my journalism joke then this is already over. But to my relief he laughs a little bit.

"What's your favorite band?"

"Fleetwood Mac."

"Favorite color?"

"Red."

"Favorite place you've ever been?"

"Here." That answer takes him off guard. Realizing he might think I'm referring to this moment in time with him I clarify. "This festival is by far the most fun I've ever had. I love the atmosphere. Everyone is so laid back but everyone just exudes excitement. We're all here for the love of music. I love people watching. I feed off everyone else's energy and all I'm getting here is a beautiful amalgamation of friendship and joy. Everyone is living for the moment instead of worrying about the future."

A sweet, genuine smile graces Donovan's face making him look even more handsome.

"I like that." *I like that.* That's all he says but it feels like so much more. It feels like *I like you.*

But before he can ask any more questions McKenzie inserts herself into the picture.

"There you are!" She huffs her exclamation. "I've been looking for you everywhere. We're going to find spots in the grass for the next show." It takes my best friend a second to realize who is seated across from me but she hides her momentary shock rather well.

"Sounds good," I say to her as I rise from my seat. To Donovan I say, "thanks for the interview. Keep a lookout for the article."

"Oh, I plan to," Donovan beams.

But before I go I say, "Hey, Donovan. One last thing?"

"What's that?"

"Smile." He chuckles a little as I raise my camera and take his picture before he can think about it too much. Then McKenzie and I are walking toward the concert stage where the guys must be waiting.

The very second we are out of range, McKenzie bounces on her toes and asks a question she already knows the answer to. "Was that *Donovan Gentry*?"

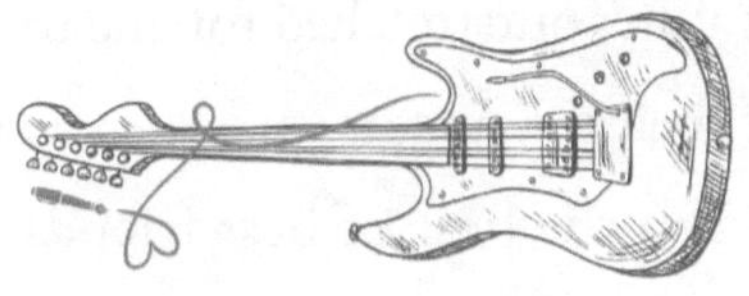

Seventeen
Layla

Bro Hymn-Pennywise

I've never attended a festival before but I'm fairly certain it's normal to pass joints around with complete strangers. Not that we should trust what's in them. But when Chris doesn't keel over and die after taking a hit, I'm fairly certain it's safe. I haven't used weed since my last frat party but I take two puffs off the joint and pass it along, offering my thanks to the owner of said joint.

It's not long before I start to feel the mild tingling effects of the drug numb my skin and my senses, but I didn't smoke enough to lose all my inhibitions. So I'm absolutely certain I don't want any of the drink the same guy tries to offer Mckenzie and I. Noticing this, Cameron loops his arms around McKenzie and angles his body between us and the stranger, effectively forming a blockade. I'm not usually one for having a guy mark his territory over a woman, but it has its uses in moments such as this.

Cameron and McKenzie sway to the music while Cameron rests his cheek beside her temple. It's sickeningly adorable.

"My god, you guys are cute," I say over the music right before pointing a finger at my outstretched tongue to demonstrate how sickeningly sweet their romance is.

But, seeing as I'm the best of best friends and all, I lift my camera to my eye and click a photo of the two of them looking so perfectly happy from a profile angle. The flash alerts them to my not-so-sneaky move causing both their heads to whip in my direction. Taking one hand off of Cameron's arm clasped at her sternum, McKenzie angles her index finger in my direction and declares, "I want a copy of that."

"As you wish."

As the penultimate band packs up their gear on the dimly lit stage, Donovan Gentry's face is broadcast all over the screens bordering the stage to remind the audience who the final act of the night will be. The second his promotional poster illuminates the night, McKenzie sing-songs, "Ooo, it's Layla's new boyfriend."

I feel four pairs of eyes shoot to me in a flash. One set feels particularly hot against my raw skin.

"Your what?" Atlas's voice carries a hint of disdain.

"No, he's not." I correct them. And to McKenzie I say, "Thanks for that. He gave me an interview earlier. That's all."

"He seemed pretty smitten to me, when I walked up."

I hold my breath for a second to let all the air in my lungs sustain my sanity before releasing it in a heavy exhale. "We were just talking. He gave me a more straightforward answer about why he went solo than he's given any other journalist. He wants people to know he wasn't being vindictive."

"So why did he leave the band?" Dallas askes.

I raise my eyebrows and inform him, "Guess you'll have to read the article and find out."

"He also bought her a drink." Considering I was just a very helpful best friend getting a cute picture of McKenzie with her boyfriend, she is not returning the favor by inciting discourse on this matter.

"It was an open bar and I had club soda. Calm down, guys."

Ironic that the same man we are speaking about is the same man to save me from having to talk about this topic any longer.

An overly enthusiastic voice is projected across the crowd through the speaker system to announce the final act of the night, "In his first solo performance *ever*. Ladies and gentleman, give it up for Donovan Gentry!"

Donovan walks on stage in a pair of black trousers and a modernized paisley shirt, short sleeve considering the high temperature of Palm Springs in the summer.

As soon as he reaches the center microphone and adjusts it to his height he addresses the crowd. "Hello Palm Springs." The crowd goes nuts with cheers. "Before we start, tonight, I want to thank all of you for being here and for giving me the chance to show you what I'm made of. Now let's have a good time."

The band on stage starts an upbeat tempo with basic chords and progressions before Donovan starts singing what sounds like the perfect radio song. His album isn't releasing until a month after Broken Compass's, which I'm thankful for. No need for a new band to compete with a fan favorite.

We dance and bounce and enjoy his set. I have to admit his solo music is pretty good. I have no idea how much of it he wrote himself but the delivery is just as important and his performance had the audience screaming his name. If the crowd at the festival is any indication, Donovan's solo career will do just fine.

After the last song has been sung, the stage lights dim, and the booze has sufficiently worked its way through everyone, our little group heads back to the campgrounds for the after party. AKA drinking around a fire and eating munchy food.

"Alright, does everyone have a drink?" Chris asks before he plops down beside me around the campfire. He's satisfied when we all nod and raise our cups to confirm. "Perfect. It's time for a game of Truth or Drink."

"Don't you mean Truth or Dare?" McKenzie asks.

"No. Dares are either lame or too over the top. Besides, I'm a nosy nelly and I want to ask personal questions."

"You already do that," Dallas teases.

"But now it's socially acceptable. Ask someone a question. They can answer or drink. And then that person gets to ask someone else a question. Easy enough. So, who wants to go first?"

"Why don't you do the honors?" Atlas gestures to Chris across the fire.

"Well if you insist." Chris scoots closer to the fire as the evening temperature starts to drop. "MmmMcKenzie." Chris's head whips in her direction. "Is Cameron's dick closer to the size of a Truly can, or a long neck bottle?"

"Dude." Cameron shakes his head emphatically at his friend. But when he sees McKenzie raise her hand to measure over the length of her own Truly can, Cameron's voice cracks as he chastises her. "*Babe.*"

"What?" She shrugs her shoulders innocently. "You should be proud of your dick. And I don't want to drink on the first question." Turning toward the campfire to address the group she announces, "Longneck." And Cameron buries his face in her shoulder, clearly not too upset about his longneck size being exposed.

"Dallas," McKenzie changes direction. "What's the most embarrassing thing you've ever done in front of the guys? And keep in mind that they can confirm or deny if it's really the most embarrassing thing you've done."

Dallas rubs a hand over his scrunched face before confessing.

"One time, on a drive back from a gig in some other town, I couldn't hold my...bowels any longer. So I made the guys pull over on the side of the highway."

"That's not very embarrassing, it happens to everyone." I say.

To which Cameron replies. "Oh, there's more."

So Dallas continues. "As I'm doing my...business...with the van blocking my view of the highway, a car pulls up behind us and a couple of really hot girls get out to see if we need help. But instead they walk up to see me dropping a deuce in the dark. Full squat."

Everyone aside from Dallas bursts into a fit of laughter.

"They ran screaming for the hills." Chris can barely breathe through his heaving laughs.

"Alright Chris, your turn. Top or bottom."

"Pft. Easy. I'm a lover at heart, so top. But I've dabbled in the art of being a catcher a few times and I gotta tell you–"

"Whoa. I didn't ask for details."

"Fine. Fine. Atlas." Everyone's gaze shifts to him. "I can't help but notice you haven't been hooking up with groupies after shows, in a while."

"I thought we were your groupies?" I put on my deeply offended face.

"You're official groupies, not casual groupies. Anyway, Atlas, when was the last time you got laid?"

Atlas looks around the group, considers his options, then lifts the plastic cup in his hand to his mouth to take a strong pull from it. A chorus of disappointed ahhs resonates around the campfire. But rules are rules. And We really shouldn't have expected anything less from him.

"Rosie," Atlas looks at me over the tops of his knees. "If Donovan Gentry calls you and asks you out, would you accept?"

"Ooo, good question." McKenzie adds her support.

"Uhh, how would he call me? I didn't give him my number. So I feel like this question is baseless."

"He could call the magazine," Dallas oh so helpfully supplies.

"Yeah." McKenzie is really on board with this idea. "And he's famous, so I'm sure he has people for that."

Atlas levels me with a look to ask, "So, would you?"

I meet his stare, considering the question. What would I do? Of course I noticed how handsome he is. And I had a good time talking to him today. But I was also doing my job. And my job is the most important thing in my life, right now. I have to focus most of my time to my work.

But, I've also been feeling the familiar ache of a dry spell. It's been a while.

The honest answer is I don't know what I would do. So I do the only thing I can and take a drink which earns me a lot of boo's.

"Lame." Chris bumps his elbow into me. "I'd ride that man like a wild mustang."

The game continues for a little while longer as the campfire turns into embers and we peel off one by one. Since McKenzie and Cameron commandeered the smaller of the two tents, I decide to share the bigger tent with the guys. There's an odd sense of peace in sharing a sleeping space with men you feel completely safe with. No risk of waking up to one of them trying to take advantage of a sleeping girl. I knew my relationship with the guys was special long before this, but my comfort around them really solidifies that.

"Scoot over," I direct Atlas since he decided to take the queen size air mattress all to himself.

"You're sleeping in here?" He asks like I've offended him.

"Obviously," I answer as I climb in and flop down on the air mattress beside him. "Cameron is showing McKenzie his longneck and there's no way I want to share a tent with them."

"Yay, slumber party." Chris jokes in the dark.

To which Dallas opposes while flopping onto his stomach. "No. Just sleeping. I'm exhausted."

One by one, we all fall asleep to the gentle thrum of chatter across the campground, like the steady heartbeat of the world.

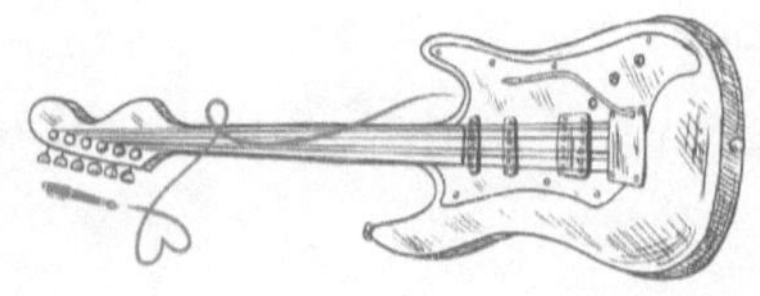

Eighteen

Layla

I CAN'T GO ON Without You-KALEO

Whoever's arms I'm wrapped in feel like home. The embrace is so heartwarming I feel a deep sense of peace. I can't say I've felt that too often. I could lay here forever and—

Wait. Who is holding me?

Memories from last night filter back into my mind as I recall sharing a tent with the guys so McKenzie and Cameron could have the other tent to themselves. Crawling onto the air mattress with Atlas and...presumably falling asleep. Which means it's Atlas's warm chest I'm nuzzled into right now. His steady embrace I'm savoring.

And that is crossing way too many lines.

Steady breathing. The rise and fall of our chests is in perfect synchronization so they press together with each breath. Do I dare move and break this moment of blissful peace?

I do. And it's worth the risk because when my head tilts to see if he's awake, a sleepy-eyed Atlas is blinking bleary eyes down at me.

This close, his face consumes my entire line of sight. It's not fair that his dark hair is perfectly tousled with sleep, not a rats nest like mine probably is.

"Morning," he says as if he's trying to hold his breath while speaking.

"Morning," I reply, afraid to break the spell. Then we say nothing as we just stare at the other, soaking in the warmth and serenity.

Unable to control my eyes, my gaze flicks to his mouth. His lips have that perfect masculine fullness. Looking back to his eyes I catch the way he examines my mouth too. It's almost like he wants to—

"Why didn't anyone tell the sun I'm hungover?" Just like that, Chris breaks the spell cocooning us in the tender moment. I roll away from Atlas before anyone notices we were cuddling.

Oh shit, I was *cuddling* with Atlas.

It's surprisingly cool for a summer morning. But I guess we're getting closer to the colder months every day. Not that it gets that cold in California. But the early hours of the morning can get a little chilly for us hot-blooded SoCal babies.

I choose not to acknowledge the cuddling or sharing a bed or fluttering butterflies in my stomach as I collect my overnight bag and head to the restroom to clean up for the day.

That was so weird. Considering Atlas and I began as two people who tolerated one another, it's weird to think I just shared a bed with him and we cuddled in our sleep. I haven't shared a bed with anyone in months. Not since breaking out of Jack's hold. I keep telling myself I like being single. I like the freedom. I don't need someone in my life.

But...this morning's cuddle session scratched an itch I've been ignoring. I miss intimacy. I miss the oxytocin that comes from hugging someone and sharing body heat.

I miss sex.

Which is exactly what I'm thinking when Donovan Gentry crosses paths with me and I can't help but notice his adorable bedhead.

He flashes me a sheepish but endearing smile as we grow closer to one another. Once I'm within ear shot he says, "Morning, you."

It's amazing how he makes that greeting sound like we are old friends reuniting.

"Morning," I reply. "Did you stay here last night?"

Donovan points to the RV and camper section of the campgrounds. "Stayed in a camper last night. I'm too high maintenance to sleep in a tent. You?"

"Shared a tent with my friend." He doesn't need to know I shared a tent with three other men. Even if it was platonic. "I saw your set yesterday. You did great. And the crowd loved you. I have a feeling your solo career will rival that of Harry Styles."

With a little cock of his head he says, "Woah, high praise and high expectations."

"Seriously, Donovan, I think your music was fantastic and you gave one hell of a performance."

"Can't wait to read your article about it." He gives me a lopsided smile before sauntering toward the restrooms. I have to refrain from peering over my shoulder to see if he is doing the same. But I swear I feel the weight of his stare on my back.

Today's look that I would never wear anywhere but a music festival is a rhinestone bustier bodysuit beneath a fringe skirt paired with comfortable combat boots considering how much standing and walking takes place at festivals.

Once McKenzie is up and dressed we start making the rounds, killing time before the band goes on this afternoon.

Day two of a festival is a whole different ball game. Once the frivolity of night one wears off, people are left slightly more sluggish and in desperate need of hydration. But as the day goes on and people drink their hair-of-the-dog to prepare for night two, the energy returns.

Around three o'clock the guys bound over to us with an extra skip in their step. Tired of the heat, McKenzie and I have been lounging in the shade trying to hydrate as much as possible.

"Guess what Guess what Guess what?" Chris runs his words together. "Our show time was moved!"

"What? To when?" McKenzie beats me to it.

Cameron asnwers, "The opening act for Taliah Summers got so fucked up yesterday they had to go to the hospital. So they moved our show time to seven. We are the opening act for Taliah freaking Summers."

Now I get why the guys can barely contain their excitement, even Atlas is smiling and that almost never happens. And it's a real smile, too, not his half smile trying to play it cool. It's genuine and pure and handsome and—*stop it, Grayson.*

"You guys, this is huge." McKenzie and I leap into the air. "This is going to be great for your career. You're going to kill it."

"We gotta give them a good show," Dallas interjects. "They were expecting M@nny–" Yes, that is actually how the punk singer spells his name "–we can't leave them disappointed when they thought they were getting someone big."

Chris makes a *pft* noise and says, "What are you talking about, they're going to forget about Lanny after they hear us perform. We are motherfucking Broken Compass."

"And don't you forget it," I add with a smile.

McKenzie and I are hanging out backstage with the guys before they go on but we plan to head to the VIP section of the audience for the actual show. Rarely do we ever watch them perform from the crowd but we don't want to miss the full experience of this moment in history.

Chris is playing a rhythm with his drumstick on a crate, Dallas is pacing, and Cameron has McKenzie nestled between his legs and his arms encircling her. They're all a ball of nervous energy.

But Atlas is just sitting on the ground in front of some of the equipment containers, legs bent in front of him and one arm draped over a raised knee. The picture of cool and collected.

But if there's one thing I've come to realize, it's that Atlas has his nervous ticks just like the rest of us. One of his hands is braced against the floor and his thumb is tapping away to the same pace of a hummingbird heartbeat.

Before he can see what I'm doing, I lift my camera to quickly snap a photo of him in this position. He looks like the perfectly controlled rockstar he always portrays to the rest of the world. Sometimes I wonder what it's like inside his head, where no one can hear his thoughts. No one knows if he's stressed or excited or feels the weight of the world on his shoulders.

When he hears the click of the camera, he turns his attention to me and narrows his eyes as if I just slighted him. I send back a cheesy grin to tell him *I'm an innocent angel. Don't be mad at me.*

He just shakes his head but I detect a faint smile adorning his lips.

That's when Ms. Boem and Frank Ruben grace us with their presence backstage.

"Boys," she greets them in a belittling fashion to remind everyone who's in charge.

"Ms. Boem," Dallas replies first. "We didn't know you'd be here tonight."

Her tapping heels come to a halt just far enough away from everyone that she can survey us in total. "Well I wanted to check in on the label's largest investment, currently. And I wanted to hear your plans for your performance. Especially now that you've been moved to a prime slot. I pulled some favors to get you boys here."

"Well," Cameron begins, "You've already seen the set list, we plan to start with–"

"That's not what I mean. I mean how are you going to make this show more memorable than the rest? How are you going to woo the audience?"

The guys exchange glances that transition from confused to worried and back again.

Atlas is the first to speak in their defense. "We didn't really expect to be the opening act for Taliah Summers."

"How about crowd surfing?" Dallas offers helpfully.

"Too cliche," says Ms. Boem.

"What if Atlas goes into the crowd to sing during a song?" Cameron suggests next.

"Not enough spark."

Chris is next to pipe in, "What if Cameron smashes his guitar?"

"What if I kick in your drums?" It's said in jest but it's obvious Cameron feels almost as protective of his guitar as he does his girl.

"How about kissing a girl in the audience?" Ms. Boem makes it sound like a suggestion but we all know it's not.

"How do you know he doesn't want to kiss a man?" Chris adds not so helpfully.

"Because I'm not an idiot." Ms. Boem's head swivels on her slender neck to face Atlas. "Sex sells, Mr. Woods, as you know. In the age of social media people will definitely capture it and you'll go viral again. Take one for the team and kiss some random girl in the audience. But make sure she's pretty. We need the crowd to go wild."

I imagine this is the moment Atlas wishes he could actually shoot lasers from his eyes to incinerate Ms. Boem. I mean, what kind of insane request is that? She's practically whoring him out. He's been adamant that he doesn't want to become a sex symbol for the sake of his career but that's exactly what Ms. Boem is trying to do.

And I feel guilty for encouraging it, in a way. I told him to write a sexy song and add it to the album thinking it would be overlooked for their better songs. But Atlas is too good a song writer and that plan backfired.

Now his label is trying to capitalize on that success and they need him to sell his soul in the process.

Something in Atlas's jaw ticks before he opens his mouth to say, "Fine." And that's the end of it. He has no other choice.

Part of me wonders if Ms. Boem had this planned from the start, as soon as she got the guys the gig. And knowing he wouldn't be a fan she waited until the last second to force the notion on him. It's not really a choice. It's a command.

Clicking her heels on the hard floor as she struts away, Ms. Boem calls over her shoulder, "Knock 'em dead, boys." And Ruben follows with only a thumbs up for encouragement. He didn't stand up for the guys.

Rising to his feet, Atlas paces a small circle then slams a fist on the container he was sitting by, keeping his eyes turned to the ground.

"Fuck," he hisses between his teeth.

"You could always ignore her," McKenzie suggests. "Beg forgiveness instead of ask permission, and all that."

"The label could drop us," Dallas reminds the group. "We can't walk away for five years without paying out the ass. But they can drop us for a number of reasons and I'm sure Dana could find one."

Well that answers that. Looks like Atlas's hands are tied.

The band starts to prepare for their set but I take a moment to approach Atlas.

"I'm sorry," I say with as much honest sympathy as I feel. "I know this isn't what you want."

"It is what it is." He doesn't bother to look at me as he pulls his guitar from its case and swings the strap over one shoulder.

"I'm sorry I pushed you to do the song, too." I have to get it off my chest. He's the one in this predicament and while it's the labels fault, I still feel an ounce of responsibility.

Atlas swings his eyes to me and says, "It's not your fault, Rosie. We wanted success, and now we have to deal with the consequences. I just hope we don't lose sight of why we love making music."

I hope so too.

That's what I want to say but instead I offer encouragement. "Then go out there and show these people that Broken Compass is the real deal. Not just pretty faces who sound good with autotune. You're true artists."

I get one of Atlas's half smiles that I'm so used to and give him a big thumbs up as McKenzie and I head to the VIP section.

It's different down here amongst the non-groupies. But we're blessed to have the VIP passes to get such a good view.

I anxiously scan the crowd to assess all the girls in the audience, wondering which of them Atlas might go for. There's a beautiful blonde in the front row wearing one of those sparkly chainmail bras. And then a fiery redhead a couple rows behind her with lucious injected lips. Then a stunning girl here in the VIP section with lilac hair and legs for days.

But it occurs to me that I don't know Atlas's type. I've never seen him with a girl before. This act Ms. Boem wants him to play that he's some sex-god-ladies-man is ridiculous considering none of the guys fit the narrative. I've seen Dallas make out with a girl here and there. But never bring any home. I've seen Chris disappear with a guy after a show. But even he keeps his private life relatively tame. And despite Cameron and McKenzie not being able to go two minutes without physical contact, they keep it PG in public.

The boisterous voice of the MC draws me out of my wandering curiosity as the announcement of the band incites an uproar of cheers. The guys step on stage one by one and I can't help but notice that the screaming intensifies when Atlas appears last. He walks to the mic front and center, already adjusted to his height, and puts on the mask they want from him. The heartthrob, the bad boy, the rockstar who only cares about music and getting laid, even though I know that's not who he is.

Most of the shows at the festival introduce themselves with the energy and exuberance that will get the crowd pumped. Atlas, however, takes a different approach.

He leans into the microphone until his lips are a hair's breadth away from it and speaks in a low sultry tone. "Good evening, Palm Springs." He slipped the mask on so easily. His voice may say he's in his element working the crowd into a frenzy, but his eyes scanning the faces of everyone is his tell.

"I'm Atlas. This is Cameron on guitar, Dallas on bass, and Chris on drums. And we are *Broken Compass*." He says the band's name as one would speak to a lover. Just their name alone causes an uproar.

Ruben helped the band design the set list and he was insistent that they start with "Blood and Oxygen" since it's the song that went viral. I can't argue with him there. Remind the audience why they like the band then introduce them to more music from the album.

As soon as the bass intro trickles through the speakers the cheers reach an all-time high nearly blasting my eardrums.

The crowd is eating up every second of sexual tension Atlas is projecting into the air. His intentionally raspy voice sends vibrations through the earth that shake even me.

As soon as he starts walking toward the end of the stage I know he's scouting for the perfect girl to make out with. This is the perfect song for it, and the only opportunity considering it's the only love song on the album.

Atlas squats to balance on the balls of his feet, microphone still in hand, as he makes direct eye contact with a number of women who would sell their left foot and give up reality television forever if it meant they could steal a kiss from Atlas Woods.

Unsatisfied with what he sees, Atlas starts making his way toward the VIP section in search of the perfect prey. That's when he locks eyes on me. He finishes the last verse of the song just as he arrives at the edge of the stage, standing five feet above the rest of us.

I'm fallin' apart just waiting for you
Your lips are drawin' me in
If you'd let me love you
I'd be your blood and oxygen

As Cam carries out the rest of the song on guitar solo, Atlas swiftly drops off the stage into the VIP section with such grace and ease you'd think this was a well rehearsed dance.

And the bastard starts prowling toward me like a wild animal stalking its next meal, taking his sweet time playing with his food. The crowd parts for their idol with every step he takes. At first I think he's just messing with me. Then I think there must be a girl behind me he's after. But There's no mistaking where that dark gaze has settled. My heart rate rivals that of a shrew the closer he gets.

There's no way he's actually following through on this. What is he thinking?

Atlas doesn't pause for dramatic effect when he's within reach of me. He just cups the back of my head and brings his mouth to mine for a searing kiss that rocks the foundation of the earth. Standing a good eight inches taller than me, he leans down to meet my upturned head and for a moment I forget I'm kissing Atlas: the quiet asshole. In this moment, I'm kissing Atlas: the confident rockstar. Atlas: the sentimental softy. Atlas: the man whose devotion runs so deep he would do anything for the sake of his friends.

Atlas: the man who cradled me in his arms this morning.

His kiss is deep and inviting, his hand on the back of my head soothes me into a false sense of security. And then the enthusiastic mayhem of the crowd yanks me out of the moment to remind me what just happened.

Atlas gives me a devilish wink then returns to the stage. Bracing his palms against the edge of the base to lift himself back up in one fluid motion, microphone still in hand.

One of the band's best qualities is the ability to seamlessly transition between songs. The tempo picks up just a bit and the key changes as they drive straight through one song into the next. Atlas doesn't miss a step as he takes his place back at center stage, replacing the microphone onto the stand.

Meanwhile, my mind starts to frantically reel over the last sixty seconds as I begin to question everything I know about Atlas Woods and myself.

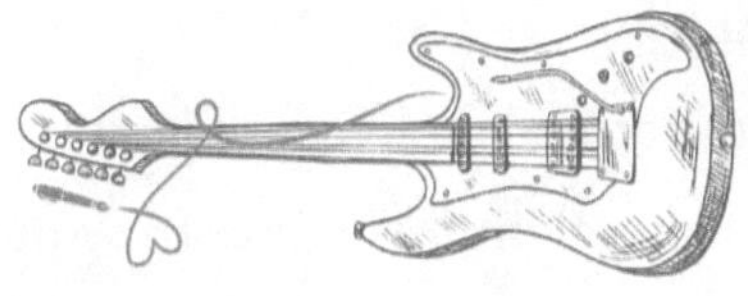

Nineteen
Layla

HAVING A BLAST-GREEN DAY

"You arrogant flesh-monger," I seethe as the band walks toward us after their set.

"Flesh-monger?" Cam questions.

"It's Shakespeare," Dallas informs him.

"You asshole," I punch Atlas's chest but I think it did more damage to my knuckles than to him. "What were you thinking?"

Atlas rubs his left pectoral where I punched him, which helps my ego just a little. "I was thinking that I didn't want to kiss some random stranger. At least I know you don't have any crazy diseases from making out with everyone at this festival."

I smack the same spot on his chest with the back of my hand. "You could have warned me."

"I didn't get the idea until about thirty seconds before."

I swallow my retort that's waiting on the tip of my tongue when Ms. Boem and Ruben approach us. Ruben looks thrilled, probably because the audience loved all the new songs the band showcased tonight.

Ms. Boem, on the other hand, looks like she's containing a fiery rage, clenching it in her tight fists. Once the pair close the circle of bodies, Ms. Boem uses her I'm-trying-to-sound-calm-but-I'm-furious voice to let everyone know exactly what she thinks of Atlas's actions.

"Mr. Woods," she locks her beady eyes on him, "When I suggested you kiss a girl in the audience I did not mean this one." Ms. Boem drives the point home by pointing an accusatory finger at me. "I didn't even realize the two of you were an item."

"We're not," I hastily correct her.

A heavy sigh leaves Atlas before he says, "I saw an opportunity and I took it. I didn't want to make out with some stranger who's been fucking god knows what all weekend. At least I don't have to worry about catching any diseases from Rosie."

Ruben leans toward me and not-so subtly asks, "I thought your name is Layla?"

"It's an annoying pet name," I whisper back.

"Regardless of your intentions," Ms. Boem continues, "I cannot prevent you all from seeing Miss Grayson or prevent her from attending shows, but the label's cooperation with *Cadence Magazine* will not continue."

"*What?*" Atlas and I ask at the same time.

"It wasn't her idea, she didn't do anything wrong." Atlas comes to my defense.

"It doesn't matter. Her constant presence has proven to be a problem for the band and incited behavioral outbursts. I am limiting the temptation."

"It won't happen again," Atlas pleads.

"I know it won't." The smugness in her voice grates my skin. Ms. Boem's true colors are showing as she smiles to say, "Don't forget that the entire band's success is at stake if you act out again. You wanted to be famous, this is the price of fame."

Always needing the last word, Ms. Boem turns on a heel and struts away for the second time today; her loyal pet Ruben close on her heels.

"Rosie, I'm so sorry. I didn't mean for this to happen." Atlas is standing directly in front of me now, both hands grasping my slumped shoulders.

When I turn my gaze to his I see the utter despondency burning there. The worry lines creasing his brow and around his frown.

"It's fine." I can't keep the remorse out of my voice. "You couldn't have known this would happen."

"We'll still give you interviews and bring you to all the concerts you want on the tour." Dallas tries to soothe me. "Whatever we gotta do."

"I know." I force the corners of my mouth up. "Thank you. It's ok, though. Maybe this is a good thing. I don't want to be known only as Broken Compass's biggest fan. I need to flex my writing muscles to other artists."

"Rosie." So many unspoken words hang in the air with his nickname for me. So many unspoken things linger in his eyes.

But I can't dwell on this. I won't get anywhere by wallowing. So I mentally pick myself up, dust myself off, and get back on the horse.

"I need to go call my boss and give him a game plan," I tell the band. But first I need to come up with a game plan.

"Layla, wait." I don't slow down for McKenzie but she catches up anyway, my best friend and constant support. She loops her arm with mine and asks, "Are you ok?"

"Yeah."

"One word answers aren't normally a good sign."

I stop dead in my tracks to face my best friend and let a little honesty shine through. "I just need to figure out how I'm going to spin this for my boss. I know the guys can still get me into the concerts and all. But the behind the scenes is really what makes this series."

McKenzie gives me a sympathetic lift of her brows, rubbing my arm with her hand to console me. She's the touchy-feely one in this friendship.

"You're smart and quick, you'll think of something. And I've always got your back.

"Plus," she says excitedly as an afterthought, "you still have that exclusive interview with Donovan Gentry you can surprise him with."

She's right. That interview is huge considering how close-lipped he's been. It could really help the magazine and my career.

"Hey Layla?" McKenzie's voice tells me I'm not going to like whatever she has to say. "How was the kiss?"

All I give her is an eye roll. But in my head I think *earth-shatteringly magical*.

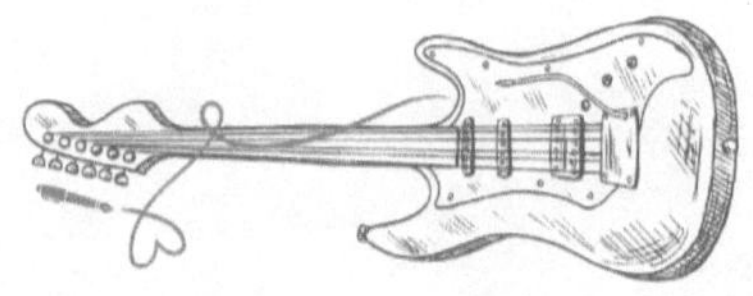

Twenty

Layla

YOU CAN'T ALWAYS GET What You Want-Rolling Stones

Only those who have lived paycheck-to-paycheck, never calling in sick, and taking any extra overtime they can to pay bills fully understand how exciting it is to see their hard work result in financial security. The day the guys got their first royalty checks was a day for celebration. As those checks continued, the breath they'd all unanimously been holding was finally released. Not only did they move out of their shoebox apartment into a rental house on the beach, they also scaled back their hours at their respective jobs. In hindsight, they didn't really need those jobs anymore, but putting all your faith in a pipe dream is too daunting to let go of the stability. They have a five year contract with the label, but in case the music career is a bust, they still have their old jobs to fall back on.

I can appreciate that hesitation. There are too many cautionary tales of people putting all their eggs in one loosely woven basket of dreams that falls apart.

But what if it works out? What if putting all your faith and hard work in one dream is what it takes to succeed?

Either way, the band will be going on tour soon which means saying goodbye to the mundane jobs that have kept the dream afloat for so many years.

The debut album releases in two weeks and then they set off on a nationwide tour playing in twenty-five different cities over the course of fourteen weeks. The tour starts and ends in California with the first show already sold out. One leg of their tour will be opening for the band Stevenson which is a huge honor in the modern music world, considering the other acts that have opened for them have gone on to win Grammys.

It'll be strange not having them around while McKenzie and I go about our everyday lives. But seeing people you love lake history feels just as euphoric as being a part of it.

Although McKenzie and I are more supervisor material than manual labor, we pitch in to help the guys move their stuff into the new house. But since I'm the only other one with a car, my contribution is transportation of smaller objects. It took two extra trips to move Atlas's record collection alone.

No one is more excited than Dallas that everyone will have their own room considering he has been sex-iled from his and Cameron's room off and on for weeks. But with only two bathrooms and one shower, ground rules have been set in place for no showers longer than twenty minutes, no two person shower parties, and aerosol spray in every bathroom. I'm counting my lucky stars that I've never had to live with this many men.

With one last load of moving boxes crammed into my little sedan, Atlas and I make the final drive from the Hawthorne apartment to their new house. Even if it is a rental, reaching the adult level "lives in a house" is one we all hope to achieve.

The Rolling Stones "You Can't Always Get What You Want" is playing on the radio as we drive without conversation. I think after a day and a half of moving, all the guys are too exhausted to think let alone talk. At least I thought so until Atlas asks, "Did you ever call that Gentry guy?"

My head swivels in his direction for a second before turning back to the road. In that brief second glance, I try to gauge why Atlas might be asking that. His expression is neutral but...I don't know, there's something in the way he purposely avoids my gaze that makes me think there might be more to it.

"No, I didn't."

Did his body just sink into the passenger seat a bit?

"Why do you ask?"

Atlas shrugs one shoulder and says, "Just curious. I don't get a good vibe from that guy."

A snort leaves me in response. "You're a *vibes* guy, now? I thought I was the one who lived their life by intuition."

"Fine. A gut feeling, then."

"That's the same thing!"

"Semantics." Classic Atlas, even when he's being nosy he carries himself with such laidback confidence as if he has every right to dig into my personal life.

"He's on the guest list for the release party." He announces. It doesn't take a genius to figure out that he's trying to calculate my reaction.

"Good," I say. "He can tell me what he thought about the article I wrote on him."

The article was well received and got a fair amount of attention. Travis was over the moon about the traffic the online magazine was getting in response. Surprise surprise, Atlas had nothing to say on the matter. Though by the way his jaw ticks, I assume he read it.

"This release party is shaping up to be a big affair, huh? Inviting people like Donovan Gentry. Any other big names on the list?"

"A few," he admits.

"Are you bringing anyone?" Although Atlas has been known to flit from groupie to groupie, I haven't seen him with anyone in the short time I've known him.

Atlas sighs, it's a heavy sigh that signifies I touched a nerve. Then he replies, "The label wants me to. They even had a list of options for me. But that feels disingenuous."

"They had a spreadsheet of women for you to escort?" The nerve of these people. "Are they asking Dallas and Chris to bring a date too?"

He shakes his head. "I was told that as the lead singer, my image is the one they want to *refine* the most. But it seems like they just want to create an image for the tabloids to latch onto."

I shouldn't be surprised after the stunt Dana pulled.

"I can't believe them. This kind of behavior is unacceptable. It should be brought to people's attention."

"Don't!" Atlas is quick to thwart the idea brewing. "Please, Rosie. Don't draw eyes to this. The band needs all the positive attention it can get before the release. If I have to take an up-and-coming pop star to a party for the sake of the band, that's a price I'm willing to pay."

"I thought you didn't want to be this guy," I remind him. The bitter sting of those words seeps under my skin. I feel like a bitch for calling him out on it, but Atlas can't forget who he was before fame sunk its claws in.

Atlas's silence hangs between us for a moment before he responds. "This industry promotes originality, but only the images they approve of." *Ain't that the truth.* "We see it all the time with female artists. The weirder and bolder their style on stage, the more successful they become. Since our band isn't exactly playing colorful, upbeat music, we have to lean into the mysterious side. That's just how it is."

I've been watching their dreams come to life before my very eyes. But I never stopped to consider what their dreams might cost them.

I only hope their dreams don't require them to pass the point of no return. The point when they lose the heart of the band.

"I guess that's show business, baby."

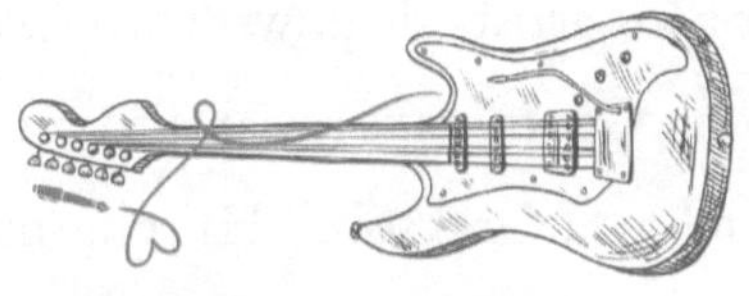

Twenty-One
Layla

Hey Look Ma, I Made It-Panic! At The Disco

Magicians turned a rooftop bar in the heart of Hollywood into a gilded cornucopia of glamour. Faces I've only seen online pass me by as I take in the extravagance of the event. From twinkling lights to flaming centerpieces to a signature champagne cocktail ignited by edible glitter, the label really leaned into the fire theme from the album cover to incinerate this party.

Also on theme is the hibachi grill to serve guests, but I'm not criticizing that choice since it happens to be a favorite.

The guys are "fashionably late" just like the label requested. Since Cameron and McKenzie are an item, it made sense for her to arrive with them. While Dana is not fond of my presence at this party, she couldn't prevent me from attending as one of the band's invited guests. While I am technically here for personal and not professional business, it doesn't hurt to get the lay of the land and rub elbows before the real party starts.

I've just finished speaking with a producer who's interested in having a couple of his artists sit down with *Cadence* when none other than Donovan Gentry taps my arm to get my attention.

"Well if it isn't Layla Grayson." His charming boyish smile glitters under the glow of the flaming torch above our heads. "I thought you must have been a hallucination at the festival until I read your article about me."

"Donovan Gentry," I greet him, since apparently we are on a full name basis. "Nice to see you again. I hope you approve of the light I painted you in."

"Oh come on," he nudges me playfully. "We both know journalists don't need their subject's approval."

"Not in the slightest. But it is nice to hear, sometimes."

After inserting a flirtatious chuckle, Donovan answers, "Well, I appreciate what you wrote. It was nice to read something positive for a change. And if I'm not mistaken, I think your article was the catalyst for a wave of praise that came shortly after. So thank you."

"I should be thanking you. Your exclusive interview gave *Cadence* the boost it needed."

Leaning in ever so slightly so his head dips closer to mine, Donovan lowers his voice to say, "Let's just call it a mutually beneficial relationship."

I blink. Then I blink again. I knew he was flirting with me at the festival but I thought it was a one time thing, an in-the-moment sort of choice driven by the atmosphere. Apparently, I was wrong.

"What are the chances I can share another drink with you tonight? No article attached."

Do I want that? Do I want a casual night with one of music's hottest stars? Do I want to see where it could go? It's not like I'm looking for anything serious but...I doubt he's looking for serious either. Maybe it wouldn't be so bad to have a bit of fun. He's nice, good looking, enjoyable company. Maybe it would be a good story for the grandkids one day.

Actually, I'm more the fun aunt with wild stories from her glory days kind of girl.

And this would be one enticing story to make.

"Your chances are looking good," I bat my lashes subtly.

Our flirtation is interrupted by the DJ for the evening broadcasting his voice over the speakers to get the crowd riled up.

"Ladies and gentlemen and everything in between. I hope you're having a good night." The party-goers erupt with applause. "It is my deepest pleasure to introduce to you the men of the hour, the maestros behind the music, the reason we all came out tonight: BROKEN COMPASS."

Applause, cheers, squeals from the girls bouncing up and down by the entrance. All the noise welcomes five of my closest friends to the celebration in their honor.

I join the whooping and shouting to cheer on four guys who have worked exceptionally hard to get to this moment.

The four of them strut into the party in well styled outfits they never would have picked for themselves but look effortlessly good on them. Knowing the guys, they would have been happiest in jeans and t-shirts. But the well trimmed clothing and unique styles fit them so well.

Then I notice the bimbo draped over Atlas's arm and my appreciation for them goes out the window.

He gave me fair warning. I know he didn't want to bring a date but he felt pressured. Yet I still feel a ping of jealousy when I see them walk in together looking like Rock 'n' Roll Ken and Barbie. She's blonde, petite, her lips look like they've been injected just enough to entice men. And now her very existence is making me abandon my women-supporting-women mentality because she's where I want to be.

Why couldn't I have figured this out before now? The night of their release party—the same night I agree to go on a date with Donovan Gentry—I finally realize I wish Atlas and I were together. I finally accept how good we would be together.

And it might be too late.

Is it because he's like a toy someone else is playing with so now I want a turn? AM I being possessive?

No, this feels too surreal to be that trivial.

As the crowd settles down while the band makes the rounds, I head to the bathroom. I wish I could step outside for some fresh air but we're already outside so what's the fucking point?

Should I tell McKenzie? She's been pushing this for months.

Have I missed my chance? Just because Atlas told me he didn't want to bring this assigned girl to the party doesn't mean he won't be tempted by a willing sacrifice. He's a red blooded male, how could he resist someone as beautiful as her?

I don't want to ruin my makeup so instead of throwing cold water on my face, I wet a paper towel and dab it to my chest and neck to ease some of the heat bubbling inside me.

When I step back into the party, I spot the band being ushered around by Dana as she shows off her prized breeding stud to all the music industry big-wigs. Atlas looks less than thrilled which means they're probably talking to someone from the business side of things, not the creative side. Atlas couldn't give two shits about how music makes money and the best way to market the band. He cares about the people who make music come to life.

McKenzie, on the other hand, looks deeply fascinated by whatever the man is saying. With the mind of a shark, she's always invested in information about the logistics of the music industry.

The blonde woman is nowhere to be found.

When McKenzie spots me across the floor she waves, turns to Cameron to tell him something I can't make out, then leaves the guys to greet me.

She's a vision in silver, tonight. The stylist must have had a hand in dressing the rockstar's girlfriend because the metallic silk sheath dress compliments her figure beautifully, but the shade of silver doesn't wash her out. To add a bit of a classy edge to the look, her eyes are painted with darker shadows and studded jewelry adorns her features. She looks hot and badass all in one bundle.

"Look at you!" I exclaim as she bounds over. "You look so hot."

"Awww. Don't stop," she beams in the midst of a twirl to show off every glorious angle. "Cam could barely keep his hands off me."

"Speaking of can't keep their hands off," I intentionally lean around McKenzie to bruise myself further with an eyeful of the girl practically humping Atlas in front of everyone.

"That's Michelle Michelle," McKenzie informs me. "She's on the same label and they want to cross promote."

"What kind of a name is Michelle Michelle? They couldn't come up with anything better?"

"Apparently that was her TikTok handle and she had a cover song go viral for half a second. Another producer who works with Frank brought her on."

Unable to watch the show any longer, I turn away from her and Atlas. "At the risk of sounding petty, does she seem kind of desperate to you?"

"Well, I think it should be you over there with Atlas, but no, you don't sound petty. She's really laying it on thick. You should have heard her when she climbed into the limo. She was all *'OMG. It's Atlas Woods. Oh my god, I can't believe it's you.'* It was so annoying. She wouldn't stop touching him. Rubbing his arm, putting her hand on his thigh, touching his—"

"Alright I get it, Kenz." If McKenzie is offended by the slight snap in my voice she doesn't show it. "I have nothing to be jealous of," I say aloud like I'm trying to convince myself. "Donovan Gentry asked me out."

"What? You said yes, right?"

"Of course I did. He's nice and hot. Why not see where it goes."

"That's my girl." McKenzie slaps my ass for emphasis.

Cameron interrupts our little moment by asking, "What are we congratulating Layla on?" In typical Cam fashion, he slings an arm over McKenzie's shoulders, pulling her close.

"Donovan Gentry asked her out."

Cam's eyebrows shoot to his hairline, "Woah, nice work, Grayson."

"What's nice work?" Chris asks as the rest of the guys join us.

Cam relays the information for everyone else, "Donovan Gentry asked Layla out."

If it wouldn't look weird, I'd bury my face in my hands. I don't have any brothers but this must be what it feels like, for all of them to be privy to my love life even when I want to keep it private.

Except for one, he does not feel like a brother. So I'm intentionally trying to avoid looking at him so I can't read his expression.

Dallas does one of those descending whistles guys do when they see something unbelievable happen. "Impressive. Where is he taking you?"

"Look, we haven't talked about the details yet. Let's not make this a big deal."

"OMG, Donovan Gentry is so hot." I thought McKenzie was exaggerating when she quoted Michelle Michelle by using text lingo in real life, but apparently not. She's even more beautiful up close with glass skin and rosy cheeks. "He's such a good singer, too. Don't you think so babe?"

Babe?

Atlas and I finally make eye contact. Even though he's trying to play it cool, I can see the flicker of annoyance in his throat where a vein pulses rapidly.

"Can't say I've paid much attention to him," Atlas answers his date.

Even though Michelle Michelle is draped on the arm of one of the hottest rockstars to emerge in the last five years, she's still gushing about Donovan and runs on a tangent about his boy band career turned solo.

But I don't catch any of it as I'm locked in a trance by Atlas's hypnotic stare. Realizing it might be too obvious, I shift my gaze to his date as she rambles on but I still don't catch a word as my mind reels over the notion that I want Atlas. It shouldn't surprise me since McKenzie (and probably everyone else) have noticed the gravitational pull between us. But it does. And now that he's here with someone the label approves of, I don't know what to do about these feelings.

These kinds of parties last into the early hours of the morning, but around 1am I decide to get an Uber home, pricey, but probably just as expensive as parking in this part of LA.

The band performed a couple songs from the album and killed it, as usual. But as someone who has heard them play countless times, I noticed some of the magic was gone without a crowd of fans. Playing for people who have a financial investment in your success or just want more exposure probably doesn't carry the same endorphin high as people who genuinely love your music.

"Heading home?" Atlas's steady voice breaks the dull silence of the city at night. I'm waiting on the sidewalk beneath the party. My Uber app says my driver should arrive in less than ten minutes.

"Yeah," I reply without much elaboration.

"You weren't even going to say goodbye?" He comes to stand beside me, shoulder to shoulder, as we both stare into the darkened building across the street.

"You guys seemed kind of busy. I let McKenzie know I was leaving. I have some work to do in the morning." My voice comes out almost monotone, like I'm dictating my to-do list.

"Mm." That's all he says. Not even a full word, just a sound, and I'm not sure if it's one of disbelief or understanding.

More silence. Always silence. He never has anything to say even when there's so much I can tell he's not saying.

"So did the label get lucky and form a love match between you and *Michelle Michelle*?" Trying not to gag on that name is a challenge of its own.

"I think we both know she's not my type."

Trying my hardest to keep the vitriol out of my voice, I respond, "I think anyone besides her can see she's not your type."

A heavy inhale precedes Atlas asking, "So, you're going out with Gentry, huh?"

Considering this is the second time that he's brought up my flirtationship with Donovan, I turn to face him with a little extra sass in my movements.

"Yeah. Is that ok?"

Atlas mirrors my position to fire back, "He just doesn't seem like your type."

"A hot musician who's nice and interested in me? That doesn't seem like my type?" I'm lonely, and he's willing. What more could a girl ask for, right?

"He just seems more two-dimensional, ya know? A basic melody without a harmony to back him up."

"I'm sure this observation was made after countless hours spent together determining his character. Have you even spoken more than five words to each other?"

"I wasn't keeping count." The finite tone in Atlas's voice makes my blood boil.

I turn back to the road when I see headlights round the corner. A silver Honda Civic with a glowing Uber sign on the dash rolls to a stop in front of us. Atlas opens the door before I can reach for the handle and waits for me to climb in. For a second I wonder if maybe he'll leave the party with me.

My eyes plead *come with me. Don't go back to her. Don't conform to the image Dana wants. Come with* me. But that's a fool's dream, just wishful daydreaming.

So I drive the nail in the coffin of this unproductive conversation by wishing him farewell. "Congrats on the album, Atlas. I hope it does well."

He says nothing, just shuts the door on me before the car pulls away from the curb. Even though I know I shouldn't, I peek over my shoulder to watch Atlas walk back inside. But he stays on the curb watching the car drive away until I can't see his form anymore.

Twenty-Two

Layla

C IGARETTE-Shaya Zamora

I stare at my phone for a beat, uncertain how to respond or if I should respond at all. I haven't spoken to Atlas since the launch party a day ago.

The album releases at midnight tonight, so I assume he's trying to hide the ball of jittery nerves he is right now. Atlas would never want anyone to see a side of him that isn't cool and collected.

Then again, if he's reaching out, maybe he really needs something.

Thirty minutes later I meet Atlas at the Hermosa Pier on The Strand. Palm trees and street lights alternate down the sidewalk as people mill about between bars and restaurants. Every business is playing music but none are playing the same playlists creating an amalgamation of gentle noise as background for the moment I spot Atlas leaning against a palm tree. A steady hand raises a joint to his lips, pulls so the cherry glows, then drops back to his side as he expels a puff of white smoke through parted lips.

"I didn't take you for a smoker," I alert him to my presence.

Atlas doesn't seem the least bit startled as his head swivels smoothly on his neck in my direction.

"Only when I'm stressed," he admits.

"You know it's illegal to smoke a joint in a public space."

"Yeah, but everyone does it." He's not wrong. Any heavy party holiday this beach is filled with all kinds of substances no one is supposed to have but everyone partakes in anyway.

Using his shoulder to push off the trunk of the palm tree, he cocks his head toward the pier and asks, "Want to take a walk?"

"Sure."

We walk in silence until we pass all the people loitering on The Strand. If I'd known we were going to walk out over the ocean, I would have brought a jacket since the breeze is stronger on the pier. Atlas dressed appropriately with a lightweight leather jacket, as opposed to my short sleeve top which does nothing to deflect the gust. At least I had the wherewithal to pair it with flared jeans.

When Atlas offers me a puff of the joint, he notes how tightly I've banded my arms to my chest. "Cold?"

Obviously. "A little."

I want to cling to my bitterness but Atlas makes that pretty damn hard when he slips his jacket off his frame and swings it over my shoulders. How can I be mad when he does something like that?

These rare moments of gentlemanly kindness are probably what earned my affection in the first place. So simple, so inconsequential and easy to overlook, but they make such an impact on my heart.

"Thank you." I pull the collar tighter at my neck. I almost feel bad for taking his protection from the wind but at least he has a long sleeve on.

As soon as we reach the end of pier where the light is dim and the waves crash against the pylons, Atlas drops the roach to the weathered wood, extinguishes the heat with his boot, then sets the cold butt of the joint on the railing so he doesn't forget to dispose of it when we're done.

If he'd flicked that thing into the ocean I probably would have walked away.

The anticipation has me on the edge of my seat. I just want to tell him to spit it out, whatever it is he wants to say.

"I'm sorry, Rosie." He stares across the darkened waters as he speaks. "I shouldn't have started shit with you—especially not you."

"So why did you?"

His shoulders rise and fall with a heavy breath as he leans his elbows on the railing. "That launch party should have been a fun night. But it was just more pressure added to my plate. More people to impress, more people to please. Another layer added to the mask they want me to wear. I felt the pressure of it all and took it out on you. But you didn't deserve that. So I'm sorry."

I'll hand it to Atlas, he could have just ignored the problem, acted like nothing ever happened. But he didn't. He owned up to it and apologized *promptly.* There's a lot of men in this world who aren't capable of that.

"Apology accepted. And I should probably apologize for–"

"No," he angles his body so he can stop me with a hand on my wrist. "You have nothing to be sorry for. I'm just glad you forgive me."

"Of course I do. You're one of my best friends, Atlas." I don't know if something just happened between us, or if using the word friend shut a cracked door. It's hard to dissect whatever this is and how he feels about it.

Peering over his shoulder, Atlas examines the street and asks, "I saw a bar with live music back there. Do you want to go listen?"

"Always," I smile. We head back the way we came and he doesn't forget to throw the roach away.

Be still my beating heart.

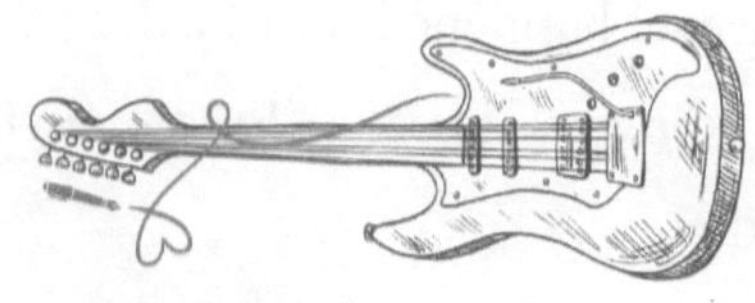

Twenty-Three
Atlas

IT'S A LONG WAY TO THE TOP (IF YOU WANT TO ROCK 'N' ROLL)-AC/DC

The launch went better than expected. It was wise of the label to follow the release with immediate tour dates. We have two shows in LA, a break for a couple days, then off to see the country.

I've never been a nervous performer but something about this first show has my blood racing faster than usual. This is hands down the biggest show we've ever done. Even from backstage I can hear the rumble of the crowd. Their excitement is manifesting in my veins with nervous tension.

This night is the start of the rest of our lives, this is the beginning of the career we've worked so hard to achieve. Working for next to nothing, slumming it in a tiny apartment while working dead end jobs, banking on our dreams paying off debt. And it's finally here. We've made it to the pivotal moment in our lives that felt out of reach for so long. Yet it doesn't feel real, and it doesn't feel satisfying.

All because when I see Cam and McKenzie embrace, when I see her wish him luck with hearts in her eyes, I wish Rosie was looking at me the same way.

I don't wish ill on anyone, but since the buzz around Michelle died down after a couple weeks, they aren't investing as much in her anymore. So there's no need for us to pretend to be more than acquaintances. The release party was the last time I had to interact with her. But that one night might have changed the course of what could have been with Rosie. I wanted to hop in the car with her when she drove off and tell her we should be together. She should be the one with me. We've shared so many big moments over the last few months together and I want to share everything to come with her as well.

But I didn't.

With Dana breathing down my neck, I can't bring Rosie into the mix.

I had a responsibility to the band to save face and make the label happy. So I let her drive away angry and went back upstairs to play my role. Seeing the joy on the guys' faces almost makes it all worth it. I want this as much for them as for me. I just wish I didn't have to let her go to make it happen.

I'm grateful she forgave me, but I wish I could tell her why I can't act on this chemistry between us.

"Almost time, guys," the tour manager alerts us.

The six of us gather in a circle, arms over shoulders, heads bowed inward. This is my family. These people matter more to me than anyone else in the entire world. Whatever happens after tonight, *this* is more important than any fame or fortune.

"Alright guys," Cam speaks up when I don't say anything, "Tonight's the night. Let's give 'em hell."

The guys must be able to feel the undercurrent of tension because they each give me withering looks of concern.

I will not choke. As soon as I'm behind the mic and the lights are bathing us, I'll drift into my own little world. I know it.

We break apart but Rosie wraps her delicate fingers around my bicep, holding me back.

"Hey," she says with a sympathetic smile. "You got this."

Three little words, but they fill me with courage. I don't know if all is forgiven, but I'm sure that she is doing what she can to make this night a success.

Before I walk off stage I lock eyes with her and ask, "Are we ok?" I just have to be sure.

That sweet Rosie smile that melts me graces her face as she assures me, "We're good, Atlas."

A heavy weight that's been pressing on my shoulders finally lifts as I walk on stage with the confidence of Goliath. Maybe—just maybe—everything will be ok.

The show was our best one yet. The label was happy, the crowd was ecstatic, everything went better than we could have asked for. Sometimes, a magical presence weaves through the stage connecting us in a way only music can and we feed off one another's energy, hypnotised together so every shift is felt before it happens. We were perfect, for lack of a better word.

For the encore we still like to play a cover song to honor the greats that came before us. Tonight we played "It's A Long Way To The Top (If You Want To Rock 'n' Roll)" by AC/DC. I even brought out the bagpipes which had the crowd in a frenzy as I showcased my weird talent. Thank you to Bon Scott for making it cool.

The song set the tone for the rest of our lives. We've dreamed big for so long. Tonight was the result of believing in a dream that felt impossible.

One step at a time, we're crafting the life we want.

We had some business stuff to talk over with the tour manager so the girls took off about an hour before us. It's 2am and we are all beat. The high of performing died down sometime around discussing lodging for the first leg of the tour. Since this was a local show, we drove ourselves.

"Alright, who's driving," Chris asks with a yawn.

"Picks, man," Dallas suggests. Whenever none of us want to do something like unclog a toilet, we throw four different colored guitar picks into a bag or a hat and draw. Whoever draws the red pick (mine) has to do it.

Cam, Dallas and I each throw our pick into a Crown Royal bag, I grab my spare from my back pocket and toss it in. Chris holds the bag out as everyone takes a turn drawing without looking. All at once, we hold our fists in the center and open them palm up at the same time.

Too bad for Dallas, he got the red pick.

"Ugh," he groans. "Alright. But we're taking my way home. It's faster."

Normally I'd argue with him, but as long as I don't have to drive, I don't care.

Since we're playing here again tomorrow night, we leave our instruments behind and load into the van. Chris and Cam take the back seat so I take the passenger seat to keep Dallas awake.

About ten minutes from home, Dallas speaks up over the music on the radio in a tone I've never heard from him before. It sounds like he's at peace, I don't know how else to describe it. "Tonight was the best night of my life, man."

An all-encompassing warmth seeps out of my chest, coursing through my extremities until I feel it in my finger tips. Tonight was amazing. Tonight was everything we ever wanted. And it can only go uphill from—

"Dallas. WATCH OUT."

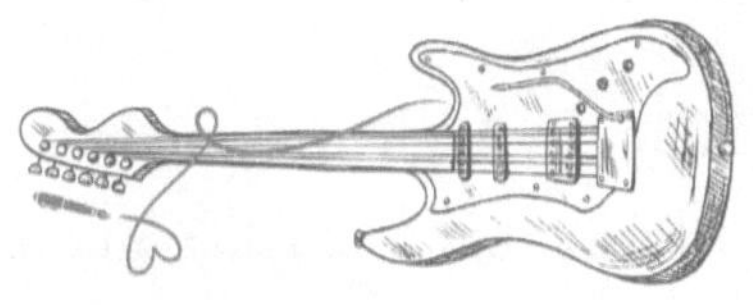

Twenty-Four

Layla

How To Save A Life-The Fray

Why is there ringing in my dream?

I'm lost in the kind of sleep that only comes from pure exhaustion when it sounds like my alarm is blaring beside me. But when I open my eyes, it's still pitch black in my room.

Cranking my neck to look at the glowing phone beside my bed I see Cameron's name illuminated on the screen.

What the?

"Cam?" I ask groggily after picking up the phone.

His heavy breathing is the first warning bell, the second is the anguish in his voice.

"Layla." I jolt upright. I've never heard him sound so distraught. "McKenzie didn't answer."

"What's wrong?" I rush the words out faster than my brain can really process them. But something in his voice makes my nerves shake.

He sniffs. Is he crying? "You guys need to get to Torrance Memorial. Now."

McKenzie and I burst through the doors to the emergency room in whatever the hell we could find lying on our bedroom floors. For me that's the dress I wore tonight and slippers. For McKenzie that's one of Cameron's shirts she sleeps in and a pair of baggy sweatpants.

The nurse directed us to room 213 and that's exactly where we find two out of the four guys. McKenzie immediately encircles Cameron's neck with her arms while I go to Chris and give him a shoulder to cry on. We are all sharing the same pain, we're all sharing the same grief and disbelief. How is it possible that we saw someone just a couple hours ago and now he's gone? How can he be gone?

Silent sobs bounce off the tile walls of the hospital room. The overhead fluorescent lights are off but a lamp in the corner sheds an orange glow from the corner, seeping into the dreary room to cast shadows where obstructions prevent the light from trickling any further. The blessed silence holds space for us to process as much as we can, to collect our thoughts, to lean on one another for support.

The collective atmosphere is *this can't be happening*.

"None of us saw the car coming until it was too late," Chris says through heaving breaths. "One minute everything was fine and then we were blinded by the headlights and then..." I don't think any of us have the heart to speak it aloud.

Chris looks worse than Cameron, he has a bandage on the side of his head. Cam has a few scratches but nothing major. They were far enough back in the van that they didn't take the brunt of the damage.

I have to ask, because he's not here and that worries me given the circumstance. "Where's Atlas?"

Considering he was beside Dallas in the passenger seat when it happened, I can't imagine what he's going through—or what kind of injuries he sustained.

"He stepped out to smoke a joint," Cameron utters into McKenzie's shoulder. I'm sure that isn't advised by the medical staff.

"Are you going to be ok for a minute?" I ask Chris with a calming hand on his shoulder. I don't want to abandon him if he still needs me. But he nods and encourages me to find our friend.

The garden the hospital sectioned off for smoking is just a short walk from their room. I used to think smoking areas were a little outdated considering how bad it is for your health. But right now, I'm grateful Atlas has a quiet place to go and deal with the tidal wave of emotions consuming him.

That's where I find Atlas, standing beneath a cherry blossom tree that is just starting to lose its leaves in preparation for regrowth in the spring. He has a joint balanced between two fingers but based on the little pile of ash at his feet, I'd say he hasn't smoked much of it, it's just been burning time beside him.

I stand directly in front of him, looking into empty eyes that don't stare back at me. I don't see the same man who lived in this body a few hours ago. He's been broken beyond recognition. I'm someone who believes we can be remade, healed. But I'm not naive enough to think it will happen overnight.

We don't need words, so I wrap my arms around his neck and pull him into me. I don't give him an inch of room to pull away or reject the comfort I know he needs. Because strong, stoic Atlas Woods would never admit he needs a hug.

At first I don't think he'll hug me back, he's stiff as a corpse. But then his hand drops the joint and I feel him ease into the hug, letting his body take the comfort he craves. Slowly, his arms rise one at a time until he's holding me back, crushing me into him. We don't speak, we don't need to. It might make things worse. We just grieve together in the same space and rely on the other for support.

Although I'm shaking with restrained tears, Atlas is the sturdy one, the constant rock of this group who shoulders every storm that passes.

How he's managing to handle this storm, I don't know, though. This is too much for one person to bear.

After what feels like forever, I pull away far enough to really take a look at Atlas. He has stitches over his left eyebrow and a purple bruise forming a crescent moon around his eye.

Running my thumb over his cheekbone I ask, "Is anything else injured?" Besides his heart.

Atlas lifts his right hand to brush jittery fingers against his left shoulder. "My shoulder is a little bruised. So are my ribs. But nothing...permanent."

It's amazing how in times of grief silence speaks so much louder than words. There's nothing I could say that will help as much as my silent presence. But it's moments like these that prove you can feel someone's heart without placing a hand over it, you can feel love and connection through shared experiences.

"Do you need more time or do you want to go back inside?"

Atlas takes one more hit of the almost extinguished joint before smothering it under his boot and tossing it in the trash. Then he laces our fingers together and leads me back into the hospital. Before we enter room 213, he drops my hand to pull the door open for me. That moment was just for us. It was what we both needed.

The five of us stay in the hospital until the guys are discharged. McKenzie, Cameron, and Atlas all squish into the back of my car while Chris takes the passenger seat. I imagine it's hard for all of them to be in a vehicle right now.

"Someone needs to call his family," Chris breaks the deathly silence. It's a task no one wants to do, but someone has to.

"I'll do it," I speak up. That responsibility shouldn't fall on any of their shoulders. I know it won't be easy, but I would do anything for these guys. Including informing their best friend's family that their son is dead.

Twenty-Five

Layla

WELCOME TO THE BLACK Parade-My Chemical Romance

The show scheduled for the following evening was canceled in the same press release announcing Dallas's death. But the tour is still scheduled to take off after the funeral. There's too much money on the line to cancel now. The label brought in a session bassist to fill in until a more permanent replacement can be found.

Apparently, a few days is all the bereavement a band needs before getting back to work.

McKenzie and I have spent every day at the guys' house. I called Travis immediately to inform him of the situation and he gave me the leave to take as much time as I needed. There were a couple of articles I had to finalize for him, and he offered to let me write the piece about Dallas but I declined. It's too soon for me.

The piece shouldn't be written at all, but the universe had other plans.

Besides, after being the one to deliver the tragic news to Dallas's parents, I don't want to be responsible for writing his obituary as well.

The Friday following the accident, with the help of the PR team at the label, a beautiful service was held for Dallas. It was closed to the public but a few familiar faces from the music world were in attendance.

I don't think the guys realized just how beloved they were in such a short time until the outpouring of condolences and love for Dallas was broadcast across the internet. We all had to stop looking at social media because it was impossible to scroll posts without seeing something about Dallas and the band. Even though the majority of fan girls focused their attention on Atlas, Dallas had his own groupies. And despite the date and time of the funeral not being publicized, there were still people at the gates of the cemetery trying to pay their respects.

Following the funeral, a luncheon was held at a local event space with photos of Dallas around the room. I helped comb through the guys' stuff for pictures to use. Pictures of his family, pictures with the band, a few of my own that I've snapped over the last several months.

The organizer even asked if they could display Dallas's bass beside the enlarged picture of him. It feels right that his bass is a part of this. Aside from his family and the band, music was his one true love. It seems like something he would have wanted.

Even though Frank and Dana and other people tried to get the guys to speak on the band's behalf, no one was willing—or ready—to talk about Dallas publicly. We've all made comments and shared our love for him in the privacy of the house. But speaking to other people—people who just want the exclusive story from one of his closest friends—feels too daunting a task to take on.

"I think I'm going to go home, guys," Atlas announces as he stands from our table at the luncheon. He's been so reserved since the accident, but I can't blame him. I wish words were enough to make the pain lessen. I wish I could carry some of the burden for him. But I know that no amount of condolences and reassuring words will ease his suffering.

"No worries, man, we'll see you at home," Cameron assures him.

"Here, I'll drive you." I stand from my seat as well.

There's no half-hearted insistence that I stay. Atlas just nods and offers me a, "Thank you."

The house is lifeless when we get back. No sounds beyond the gentle waves in the breeze. No movement or air. It feels suffocating.

I throw my keys in the bowl by the door while Atlas fetches a couple bottles of water from the fridge. I've noticed that no one has drank alcohol since the accident. The driver was drunk when he crashed into the van. He came out alive but with a broken leg and a sentence for second degree manslaughter as well as driving under the influence. The case was closed the moment he got behind the wheel and ran the red light.

We both take a sip of our water, then we just stare at one another. None of us have had the proper words to say anything besides "does anyone want pizza?" Because we had to eat at some point. Just going about daily tasks like brushing our teeth and cleaning out the dishwasher feel overwhelming.

Someone has to be the first to bring it up, *really* bring it up. So I lay a gentle hand on Atlas's good shoulder and ask, "How are you doing? Really?"

He averts his gaze from mine as though the way I'm looking at him physically pains him.

"I'm fine, Rosie." His irritation breaks through. "I don't need codling. I'm the one who's still here."

Atlas steps past me and heads for the stairs leading to his bedroom on the second floor. I know the smart decision would be to let him leave and cool off. Emotions are running high today. But stubborn, take-no-shit Layla doesn't let him walk away like that because sooner or later we'll have to deal with this. If I have to be the bad guy turned punching bag so he'll actually process what he's going through, fine.

So I follow him up the stairs as fast as my heels will let me. I stomp into his bedroom uninvited feeling a bit of my anger at the situation direct itself toward him.

"I was only asking because I care," I state firmly. "You don't have to be a dick about it."

"How do you expect me to answer?" Atlas shrugs his shoulders after removing his jacket. "I'm not going to ask for your pity because I don't deserve it. The only person we should be thinking about right now is Dallas."

I take a steadying breath before continuing. I can't begin to imagine what Atlas is feeling, but he can't ignore his own emotions and bottle them up. They'll just ferment and sour and explode.

"You can't neglect yourself just because he's not here." I keep my voice as steady as someone who's trying to keep a rabid beast from attacking.

"My best friend died!" He reminds me vehemently, shoving his hand into his chest with brutal force. I hear the emotion start to crack his voice. "I don't want to think about myself when he deserves all my attention. He deserves more than he got. He deserves to be here!"

"It wasn't your fault." My own voice is hindered by fervor.

Feeling my own tears emerge, I sense the moment of weakness in Atlas and rush him before he can run away. I wrap him in an embrace and bury my face in his chest, mourning the way we need to: together.

Too engrossed in his own feelings, Atlas finally allows himself to cry for a moment and nuzzles his nose into my neck, letting the tears soak my skin. We stand in each other's arms and just cry. I've done plenty of crying in the last few days, but always in private. And I'm not certain if Atlas has done the same. But he lets the tears flow and lets his emotions get the better of him. He needs this. He has to put on a brave front and be the face of the band for the tour. He has to be the guy the label wants and woo thousands of screaming fans. He won't be able to do that if he keeps all of this in.

But he doesn't have to be that for me.

I'm a firm believer that crying can be healing, that it can do wonders for the soul if you just give yourself over to it completely. I think that's what we all need.

I have no idea how long we've been hugging but at some point the tears slow down and the air around us shifts. People do weird things in times of grief. Some people break things. Others go on a cleaning spree. I once heard that crows will fornicate with each other on top of another crow's corpse as a form of grieving.

Some people do wild things to remind themselves they're alive.

Maybe that's what lingers unspoken between us when we both lift our heads to lock eyes. Maybe that's what Atlas sees in my gaze, because I see a need in his. It's uncertain and hesitant, but I see the silent query.

Neither of us speaks as we mutually agree to this and slowly dip our heads toward the others lips. We're a breath apart, almost there. When we meet, it's tentative, tender, testing. This is uncharted territory that feels just as right as it does wrong, given the circumstance. So we ease into the sensation of the kiss and the closeness until we're sure this is what we're doing.

But after that initial contact and realizing this has been a long time coming, Atlas and I attack each other like animals. Pawing at one another to remove clothes, or at least enough to grant easy access, frenzied touching and pulling and maneuvering.

Before I know it, Atlas's hand is beneath my skirt and his pants are undone so I can stroke him. We both moan into the kiss as we touch each other. He's hard. I'm wet. There's no point in waiting when what we both need is a couple strides away.

Removing his hand from my skirt, Atlas leverages his hand beneath my ass and lifts me until I'm seated on his desk. Spreading my knees farther apart, he centers himself between my legs while I slide his dick out of his pants and line him up with me.

One more second and then he's inside me. No gentle push and pull to ease into it. He's primal in his desire and thrusts at a pace that sends electrifying friction through my core. Hands on my neck and jaw, he angles me so he can kiss down my throat along the tendon. All the while rutting inside me.

One of his hands slips to my breast to knead the flesh over my dress, eliciting more groans of pleasure from me.

I can't say I'm that close yet because my clit has been unattended to. But I can tell this is just what he needs right now, his therapy. This is how he's processing his grief. We can talk about the rest later. Right now, he needs me. So let him use me to cope. Hopefully after he releases some of this pent-up tension he can face his loss head-on.

The telltale increase in speed and the heaviness of his breathing signals his release before it happens. His entire body tenses with one last low growl before he spills inside of me, resting his forehead on my shoulder. I feel his shortness of breath on my collarbone as he composes himself and the aftershocks ripple through him.

Atlas lifts his eyes to mine but I don't see the affection I was expecting, or relief or sadness, I see fear.

With quick strides, Atlas slips out of me and crosses the room grabbing a tissue from his bedside table to wipe himself off. If I didn't know any better, I'd think he was eager to get away from me, as if my touch burned to the core.

With his back to me, Atlas breaks my heart in a way I didn't know he was even capable of.

"That was a mistake," his voice comes out even toned. "You should go." He doesn't even turn around to say it to my face.

Normal Layla would have thrown a fit, she would have demanded more respect, she would have slapped him across the face.

But with the torrent of hormones and emotions flooding my brain, I don't have the words to express how hurt I am. I don't know what to say to such a cowardly act from one of my best friends. And after I just let him fuck the grief away with my body?

So I say nothing as I pluck my underwear off the ground and flee the room, the whole fucking house, and drive off in a puddle of his semen.

Shit. We were reckless not to use a condom.

What the fuck was that? *What the FUCK was that?* After everything that's happened, how could he use me like that and then discard me? I know he's hurting but that doesn't give him the right to treat me so disrespectfully. He didn't even have the guts to look me in the eye.

I'm crying for so many reasons as I drive away. But mainly because I know nothing will be the same after today. The family we built just crumbled to pieces before my very eyes.

Two days later, I dig through my phone to find the number that's been on my mind.

Or more appropriately, the person that's been on my mind. Perhaps the person who can help me forget about all of this for a little while.

The line rings three times before he answers with a casual, "Hello?"

Taking the fingernail I was chewing on out of my mouth, I say, "Hey Donovan. It's Layla. Layla Grayson."

His instant delight at hearing my voice soothes the worry I had before making this call. "Hey, Layla. Nice to hear from you."

"I'm glad you answered. Listen..." *just do it, Grayson.* "Are you free to get together sometime? Soon?"

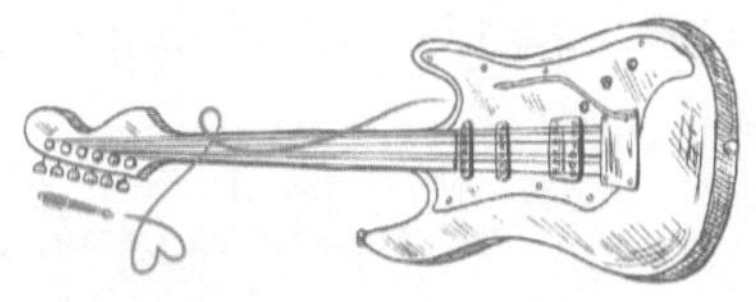

Twenty-Six
Layla-Five Months Later

Possibility-Lykke Li

Donovan was a good hook up for a while. I told him I just wanted sex, no strings, no emotions, and he was more than happy to oblige. But eventually he wanted more and I didn't. I couldn't. So I had to find other partners to meet my needs.

I've never been this girl before. The one who can't remember how many guys she's been with. The one who never repeats partners. But it's less complicated this way. I just need to get off to ease the tension. But I don't want feelings to weigh it down.

Lord knows I have enough of those already.

Tonight was the Grammys and instead of watching it live in my studio apartment, I'm watching the recordings on YouTube while the two guys I slept with are asleep in another room. I have a policy, no one in my apartment. I moved out to be closer to work a couple months ago. It made the most sense. There's nothing for me in Hawthorne anymore.

Besides McKenzie. I miss her like crazy, though. We talk occasionally but it's been a while as she's finishing school and still spending all her free time with the band.

Based on the photo I saw online, she went with the guys tonight. Pictures are one thing, but seeing her on the recordings walking with our guys without me hits harder for some reason.

I hold my breath as I listen to the announcer list the nominees for best new artist of the year. There's a fire in my soul when it comes to Atlas. But Chris and Cam? I miss them as much as McKenzie.

Who am I kidding? I miss Atlas too but I don't want to.

"And the winner for best new artist is…" stupid dramatic pause. "Broken Compass."

Every fiber in my being wants to shout loud enough for them to hear me downtown. I'm so proud of them, they've worked so hard to get here and if anyone deserves it, it's them.

My heart twinges when the camera pans to the band in their seats, hugging and celebrating together. McKenzie and Cameron share a beautiful kiss before the guys walk on stage with the session bassist who's become a permanent member of the band.

The committee on stage hands the award to Atlas so he takes the position in front of the microphone. Running his hand through his hair, he examines the prestigious trophy before finding the words to express what is probably a mix of racing thoughts.

"Wow," he exhales on a sigh, and I can hear the emotion welling in his throat. "Words can't describe how grateful we are for this honor. We want to thank everyone who has listened to our music and supported us through this wild journey. Without people showing our music love, we wouldn't be here." The audience applauds enthusiastically.

Another deep sigh and an averted gaze precedes the next half of his speech that tears my heart into tiny little pieces.

"The last person we want to thank isn't here anymore. He was a pivotal part of the group, our best friend, and instrumental in bringing Broken Compass to life. We wouldn't have made it this far without his steadying presence. So, Dallas," Atlas's voice chokes on our dear friend's name, "this one's for you."

Atlas lifts the award to the heavens along with his gaze. The rest of the guys each raise a hand to join the one holding the trophy in the air in a moment of appreciation for their fallen friend. There's not a dry eye on that stage as they all look toward the oasis we pray Dallas is in. Then the music and applause rings their cue to exit the stage.

I shut off my phone as tears begin to slide down my cheeks and throw the damn device into the couch–cause I can't afford a new one if I smash it across the room.

I hurt. I just hurt. It's a soul deep ache in my chest that cripples my mind. I just want the hurt to stop because as angry as I am, as much as I never want to speak to Atlas again, I miss them all so *so* much. I miss my family.

But I can't have them anymore. So I march back into the bedroom to fill the void with something else. It might be temporary, but at least it'll numb the chest-crushing agony weighing on me right now.

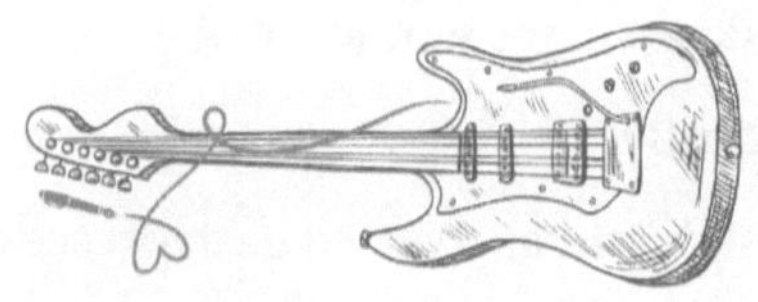

Twenty-Seven
Atlas

DON'T CRY-GUNS N' ROSES

She haunts me everywhere I go. I see her whenever I go into a new record store and wish she was there with me. I think I've caught a flash of her whenever I see a girl dressed in that retro 70s style she loves so much. I hear her whenever we play "Blood and Oxygen" because I wrote it thinking of her.

If only she knew how many of our songs were written about her, for her.

Including the one we're recording today.

On our European leg of the tour for our second album, we're partnering with a production company to record and film one of those acoustic performances in abandoned churches. The production company offered to hire a small choir to sing behind us, but the band decided—with approval from the label—that we wanted to showcase ourselves as musicians, not rockstars. All of us can sing so I designed an arrangement of our song "Leap" to be sung acapella by the four of us.

When I wrote the song for the second album, I wrote it with heartache and bitterness. I wanted it to sound angry with minor chords and heavy drums, a cathartic release of pent up resentment. But one day I heard Cameron mindlessly plucking out the notes on his guitar and realized I'd written a forlorn love ballad. I'd written a cry for help from one heart to another.

Still recovering from the jet lag I can never seem to get used to, I decided to go for a walk around the small town we're staying in. Of course I run the risk of someone recognizing me, but after being on a plane for sixteen hours and then trapped in a hotel room, I need fresh air to rejuvenate.

This little town is full of tiny shops you'd expect to see in a place that ends in *shire*: a bakery, a cafe, a bookshop, a—

I halt in my tracks, sure I must be hallucinating. I've seen people that resemble her over the years, similar hairstyles or facial features, but this is uncanny.

Reversing my strides until I'm standing in front of the bookshop again, I lock eyes with the most beautiful woman I've ever seen. She's just as breathtaking as the day I first laid eyes on her. Chestnut waves frame her round face. A smattering of freckles beneath a soft blush. But her smile doesn't quite reach her captivating eyes.

I've seen her photo attached to her articles countless times, because I'm a glutton for punishment and I continue to read every piece she writes.

So why is there a headshot of her I've never seen in the front window of a bookstore?

I guess the answer is in the poster.

#1 BESTSELLING AUTHOR LAYLA GRAYSON

Bestselling author?

The bookstore isn't closed yet so I hustle inside only to find a small round table bearing a banner with her photo front and center, as well as dozens of copies of the same book. *Her* book, apparently.

How did I not know she wrote a book?

We've been on the road for several weeks with little rest. I guess it is highly possible I missed this monumental step in her career, despite how obsessively I've tracked her.

Which is how I know that she's no longer with *Cadence* and took a job with *Rolling Stone*. That's a huge leap for her career. So why publish a book?

I pick up a hardcover copy entitled "Two Broken Hearts" and flip it over to read the summary on the back. Understanding is like a violent tsunami washing over me as I realize where the title came from.

Doomed from the start, two star crossed lovers who find love through art face the impending turmoil of young love. As the pair try to navigate stardom and connection, they are faced with the harsh reality that some loves don't survive the obstacles they face. But peace can still be found on the other side.

I've never been much of a reader but now is as good a time as any to start. I have to know what she wrote. I have to know if it's our story. She wouldn't write about us, would she? She wouldn't write about what I did. That's just not Rosie's style.

I take a copy to the front desk and pay for it, resigned to spend the rest of my sleepless night in the hotel consuming her words.

This is supposed to be one of those "we made it" moments. The fact that we're big enough to do special recordings like this should mean we are bonafide celebrities.

Yet I feel completely hollow as we stand in what once was an empty, ancient church that's now filled with recording equipment and lighting. The rest of the band is vibrating with excitement to start recording, but I can't seem to muster the same enthusiasm. I'm only three-quarters through Rosie's book but I don't like where it's headed. If the title "Two Broken Hearts" is any indication, there's no way this book has a happy ending.

The director moves into position. "Alright guys, let's get started."

I foolishly thought one day she'd hear this song and know it was for her. I thought it might give her the courage to reach out after all this time. I need her to know that if she called any one of us tomorrow, we'd welcome her back into the fold with open arms. We all miss her.

And now as we sing the lyrics to "Leap" I don't feel the same sense of hope. I feel determined.

It doesn't make sense
Maybe that's the way it's supposed to be
We've been pushing against the tide
Maybe if we start swimming we could thrive
So I'm diving head first into the water
Someone has to be the first to take the leap

I'll catch you when the fear hits harder
But I'm willing to see where this could lead

"Two Broken Hearts" is not our ending. I won't let it happen. I don't know how, but we will get her back. *I* will get her back. By whatever means necessary.

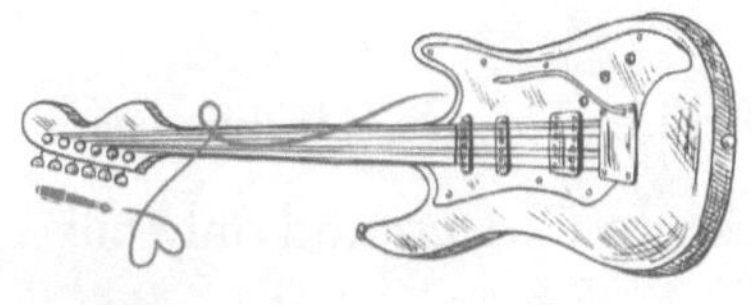

Twenty-Eight
Layla-Five Years Later

REHAB-AMY WINEHOUSE

"Forget it, Stan, I'm not doing it."

My boss at *Rolling Stone* drops his shoulder with an exhale that is always followed by a smoke break after these meetings. We've butt heads in the past but this is one I won't budge on. *Never.*

"I've known you long enough to know I can't make you do anything," he relents. "But without you this piece doesn't happen. They specifically said they would only agree if it was with you."

"It's freaking *Rolling Stone*!" Am I the only person who takes this magazine seriously? "They'd be insane to turn down a spread with us."

"They don't need us, though. They are insanely successful on their own, they don't need the exposure." The way Stan rubs his temples makes even my head hurt. "Their career began with you, and then it skyrocketed because of you. So they want to mark this milestone with you, as well."

That's a good line they've fed to my boss. But I know the real reason.

I haven't seen Broken Compass in five years. After our fall out, I moved to be closer to *Cadence* and only talked to McKenzie on occasion. But even that died out because of distance and life. She now represents the band in all legal matters. She's done a great job getting them to a place in business where they don't have to answer to the Dana's of the world anymore.

I saw on Instagram that Cam finally proposed to her after all these years. As soon as the photo of him on one knee in front of the Eiffel Tower popped up on my screen, I clicked the comment button to congratulate them...then hastily clicked out and kept scrolling, too cowardly to reach out after so long.

To this day, I still miss them all as if a limb had been amputated from my body. But despite that, I'm not sure I can face them again.

"Look, Layla." I know Stan is serious because he never uses my first name. "If you want me to get on my knees and beg, I will. We need this. And the only way it's going to happen is with your cooperation."

Arms folded across my chest, hip cocked to one side while my heeled foot taps the carpet, I consider what he's asking, consider what it could do for my career, and for the magazine.

God really does have a sense of humor. Why couldn't He have picked someone else to top the billboard over the last few years?

"Fine," I concede. Pointing a perfectly manicured nail at him I add, "But there are some details we need to adjust. I have my own demands."

"You always do. Thank you. Thank you, Layla."

I storm out of Stan's office, which isn't unusual, find my way back to my office, and collapse in my desk chair. Staring out the window across the cityscape, I let reality burden me with weight.

I have to be in the same room as Atlas Woods.

The last time we occupied the same space changed everything.

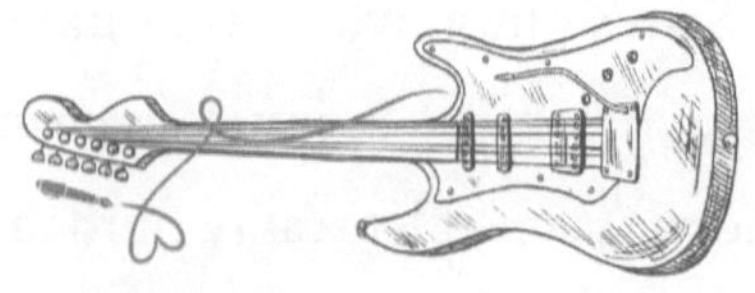

Twenty-Nine
Atlas

THE **W**INNER **T**AKES **I**T All-ABBA

I've performed in front of millions of people. I've performed at the Grammys. I've done things people could never dream of.

Yet this might be the most nervous I've ever been.

All four of us are in the conference room of our label, except instead of the oblong conference table that usually monopolizes the space, a smaller, more intimate table laden with snacks and beverages is centered between five chairs. Chris and Rob sit at the table fiddling with snacks. Cam is standing by the window watching cars go by. And I'm pacing a crater into the fucking floor.

I haven't seen her in five years. *Five years.* It's feels like it can't possibly have been that long while simultaneously feeling much longer since that day.

I've combed over what I'd say to Layla countless times over the years, if ever given the chance. Now that my chance is here, I don't have a clue what I'm going to say to her. I'm more worried about what she has to say to me.

Has she thought about me in the last five years?

I've never been able to escape her. She's everywhere. Every time I read about an upcoming band we're interested in, she's already written about them. I'll get to an event and someone will tell me I just missed Layla Grayson, the famous author.

And that book. I bought a copy the second her picture adorned the window of the bookstore. I could feel my heart crumble while reading her words. I could practically hear her speaking them in my mind. And that made it worse. Hearing her fictitious depiction of a doomed romance between a rockstar and an artist was heartbreaking, to say the least.

I just want the chance to own up to my mistakes.

My pity-party is cut short when a security guard opens the door to usher our guest inside.

My heart stops. My breath hitches in my lungs while my brain tries to take in every inch of the gorgeous woman in front of me. We're not old, but we've both aged over the years, and the evidence of how much we've grown as people is present in our appearances.

Layla struts into the conference room carrying a bag over one shoulder. The pencil skirt dress she's wearing amplifies curves I know and love so well. Back in the day, she used to let her hair run wild. Now, it's tamed into a messy bun at the back of her head, elongating her slender, kissable neck.

But traces of her personality can still be found, such as the hoop earrings and chunky rings she's wearing. That's all Rosie.

"It's been a long time, guys," she says by way of greeting. My heart stutters back into a functioning organ at the sound of her voice. But I don't miss how she's avoiding my gaze.

Chris leaps out of his chair and rushes Layla in the most unprofessional manner, though Layla doesn't seem to mind. Her face lights up when he wraps her in a bear hug, lifting her a couple inches off the floor. The faint sound of her laughter could inspire ballads.

"Girl, it's been way too long." Chris sets her back down but holds her hand out as he examines her form. "Look at you. So snazzy."

"Aww, don't stop." She beams. I don't know if anyone else picks up on it, but there's a rigid undertone to her posture that tells me she's just as nervous as I am, even though she's trying to sound poised.

Cam approaches her next, there's a moment where they share unspoken words and heavy looks before they embrace in a long-overdue hug. Cameron whispers something to her, but they're just far enough away I can't make out the words. Whatever it was, she looks taken aback by it.

"Congratulations are in order," Layla says as they break apart. She taps him on the arm as she adds, "I can't believe it took you this long to pop the question."

"I would have married her years ago," Cam defends himself. "She's the one who wanted to wait until law school was done. And then until the label was up and running. She's been a machine the past few years."

"I'd expect nothing less."

Finally, Layla looks over Cameron's shoulder to meet my gaze. There's so much emotion in those big eyes of hers. I want to dive into her mind to figure out what she's thinking, what feeling is the strongest. I'm sure she's furious but I want to know if she misses me more than she's angry at me.

"Atlas," she nods toward me. If that's all I get, then that'll have to do. I'm just glad she acknowledged me at all.

Then her gaze shifts to the last member of the band. "You must be Rob." Our bassist stands to shake hands politely with the woman he has no connection to. "Nice to meet you."

"And you," he replies, "I've heard only good things."

"Then they haven't told you everything," she teases.

Rob knows a lot, but not everything. Even Chris and Cameron don't know everything. They speculate, but I've never confirmed more than we had a falling out, I made a mistake, and we all had to pay for it.

"Well, gentleman," Rosie swings the bag off her shoulder, "why don't we get started?"

The interview starts with some basic questions about the upcoming tour and opening acts we have signed on. She likes to ease her interviewees into a sense of comfort before going into the heavier topics.

Which we entirely expected. However, that doesn't mean we are prepared for them.

The difference is that she has ties to these subject matters as well.

"Let's talk about Tattoo Records," she segways. "What motivated you to start your own label five years into the game?"

"It seemed like the smartest idea for us," Cameron answers professionally. We have no problem talking about the injustice of record labels taking advantage of younger artists. "Our first label held us under unfair contracts. We made little to no money in comparison to their royalties, not to mention a lot of restrictive conditions in the contract that we didn't think to look over."

Chris chimes in, "So now we offer lawyers fresh out of law school entry level jobs working with new artists we sign to discuss contracts and get some experience under their belt. We don't want anyone signing with us and resenting it one day."

"Sounds like you're reinventing the way business is handled in the music industry." Layla commends us.

Rob corrects her, "We like to think of it as giving a better chance to musicians than we had."

"Since you were a session bassist before joining the band, have you had a big part in designing contracts for session musicians and song-writers as well?"

"Absolutely," Rob says with pride. "I loved being a session bassist but there were always a couple things that bothered me. I'm glad I have a chance to make work easier for the people nobody hears about."

As Layla scribbles something on her notes, she asks, "And how was the transition from session bassist to full time touring member of the band?"

We all peer across the circular table to our friend with knowing smirks.

Rob chuckles with a hint of embarrassment as he answers, "Well, I had a rough time with the tour bus portion of it." We all snicker. "I got car sick pretty often. And it was weird having people know my name all of a sudden. I had to move after a girl got a hold of my address and showed up in lingerie on my front porch."

Even Layla laughs hearing that. We've all had our fair share of weird fan encounters. But it's different for a guy who never aspired to be anything more than a session bassist.

"How did you feel taking over for Dallas?" Layla cuts deep to the bone. As hard as it is to hear his name sometimes, I've gotten used to these kinds of questions.

Layla, however, visibly swallows a lump in her throat at the mention of his name.

Rob has always been incredibly respectful about the situation. That's one of the reasons we wanted him to take the position. He clicked well with us, which meant we could be friends without replacing who Dallas was to us.

"It's a tricky thing to navigate," he admits. "I'm extremely grateful for the career I have now. But I never want to take away from where the band started and how paramount Dallas was to them."

"Sounds like you're navigating it with a lot of grace and respect." Layla smiles softly toward Rob to offer some reassurance that she approves.

We gave Rob a heads up about her history with us, we had to explain why I was so adamant about her being the journalist to write our story. So I know he feels the importance of her approval on the matter. She was there too, after all, her emotions are just as important.

Switching gears, Layla jumps into another segment. "You guys have grown more than anyone could have imagined in the last five years. What are some things you wish you'd done differently?"

"Change our name," I laugh to myself. At Layla's raised eyebrows I realize I never told her that story. "The first time we performed and someone asked what our name was, I spaced. We hadn't thought that far ahead. So the girl I was seeing at the time yelled out '*Broken Compass*' thinking it was incredibly profound. After that, we were stuck with it."

The laughter that bursts from Layla could cure any disease, it's genuine and heart-felt. She holds a hand over her mouth as if that can stifle the melodic sound.

"I can't believe you've been stuck with this name for *years* all because of some girl. What else would you change? The label you signed with?"

"That's tricky," I answer for the band. "We had a lot of issues with the old label, but they also got us here. It's the butterfly effect. Would we still be this far in our careers if we hadn't jumped through the hoops the label put us through?"

Would she and I have had a chance if things had been different?

"I wouldn't change a thing," Chris interjects. "I think our mistakes made us who we are."

"Eternal sunshine leads to a desert," Cam says philosophically. "We need the heavy rainfall to grow."

"Did you get that out of a fortune cookie?" Rob teases him.

"No." Cam gets shy for a second. "A motivational playlist Kenzie listens to."

Us guys laugh at the thought of Cameron reciting motivational phrases in the car with his fiancée, but Layla clams up at the mention of her best friend.

I hope that with all the reconciliation that can be made through this process, she and McKenzie make up. They both need it.

The interview continues for a bit longer through questions that inspire reminiscence and insight to the band. It feels so natural having conversations with her again. I have to remind myself that we aren't in the cramped living room of that old apartment chatting like old friends. Time has passed, things have changed, and Layla is here to do a job.

But I have my own mission to accomplish.

At the conclusion of the interview, Layla stands gracefully as she packs her recording device and notes into her bag.

"Well, guys, I've had a lot of fun catching up," she says as if it's our annual lunch to chitchat. "I'm going to go back to my hotel and do some work, but I'll be at the photoshoot tomorrow."

The guys bid her adieu but I linger for a second as I watch her slip out the door. What's an appropriate amount of time to let the girl of your dreams walk away before you chase after here?

Now. Now is good.

I'm sure the guys aren't the least bit surprised when I rush out of the room to track her down.

Layla is almost to the lobby when I finally catch her attention. "Rosie." She halts in her tracks, I'm guessing no one has called her that in five years.

In a calculated moment, she slowly spins to face me with a mixture of emotions I don't want to dissect. "What do you want, Atlas?"

You. "To talk."

She closes her eyes as if that will help her calm her racing heart. "There's nothing to talk about. What's done is done. I'm here to do my job."

"You know exactly why we demanded to work with you." I hope that will keep her attention longer. "I saw an opportunity and I took it. A lot has changed in the last five years, Rosie. I think the universe wanted us to reunite."

"I think we just work in the same business."

Layla averts her gaze to the corridor that leads to the lobby. I can see her desire to bolt in every tense muscle of her body language.

"I don't want to talk about this, Atlas. Just let me do my job and we can move on with our lives."

"Impossible," I declare. "I've never moved on from you and I never will. You're a part of me." I drive the last point home by hammering a finger into my chest.

Layla turns her eyes back to me but there's too much confusion in them. She doesn't know what to think. I've spent my career learning how to describe the most intense emotions so I can write songs that speak to the heart. I see almost all of them linger in her beautiful brown eyes.

"You made your bed, Atlas." She doesn't even finish the colloquialism before walking away, heels tapping out of earshot.

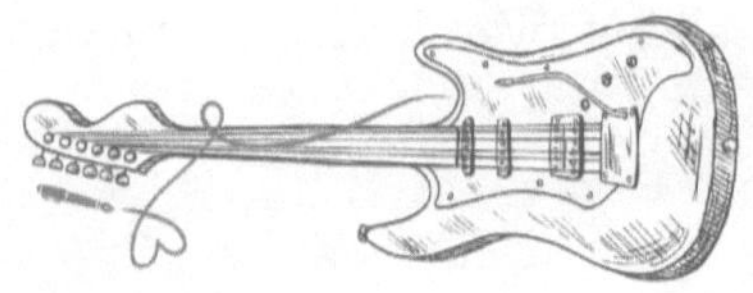

Thirty

Layla

COVER OF THE **R**OLLING Stone-Dr Hook and the Medicine Show

I can't focus on a damned thing. I prepared myself mentally to see Atlas again–to see all of them. Yet I still feel a shiver to my bones hours after the interview. It was all I could do to keep my shit together through the interview.

I'm trying to start the article but I'm too wound up to focus my energy properly. I have to be in the right headspace. The wrong headspace is how I wrote *Two Broken Hearts*, it was supposed to be a cathartic exercise to process my emotions after everything that happened with Atlas. Somehow, it turned into a book. One that should have never seen the light of day. And with one mistake it became a best-selling novel. I agonized over whether or not Atlas had ever read it. Fantasized that perhaps it never crossed his radar.

But it was a phenomenal storm I couldn't control and I profited off my misery.

Though I suppose Atlas did the same. Their second album was the perfect playlist for the broken-hearted from songs that captured grief to songs about the one that got away. I played it on repeat with a tub of ice cream and a box of tissues at my side for days, just letting myself feel what he intended listeners to feel: pain.

But one of the most excruciating things for me to fret over was whether or not Atlas told the band what happened. I had to walk into their conference room blind without knowing how much everyone else knew. If Atlas did tell them the truth, none of them let on.

Then Cameron had to go and rip my heart out when he hugged me. That alone made me emotional. But when he whispered in my ear, "she misses you." I almost lost it. Atlas's gaze over Cam's shoulder was the only sobering element that kept me from falling apart. I had to stay strong in front of him.

And the nerve of him. *Ugh.* I can't believe he has the gall to think we can fix this. Too much time has passed and too much hurt. He's not just messing with my head, he's messing with my career. Turning down this opportunity would have been the stupidest decision of my career.

It's still a toss up what the stupidest decision of my life would be. There's too many to pick from.

People love the behind the scenes element I bring to articles. A peek behind the curtain. They want to live the rockstar experience through my words. And that's exactly what *Rolling Stone* wants me to deliver with this spread. They want me to do a few tour stops with the band, live on the bus, and give their audience the *Almost Famous* experience.

It all starts with this initial interview to be released on the digital magazine before the full article is shared after the tour.

And tomorrow I have to monitor the photoshoot to make sure it lives up to *Rolling Stone* standards.

I've already spent too much time with them. I'm not sure how much more I can take.

Now that they're businessmen in addition to platinum record musicians, there's a tight schedule for this photoshoot. I showed up when the crew did to make sure everything was in order.

Paying homage to some of the greats, the design is simple. A black backdrop with dramatic lighting and photos of the band members from the shoulders up in various arrangements until we find the one that suits them best. The band isn't flashy and extravagant, even their shows use more lighting to tell the story than special effects. So it only makes sense to keep the pomp and circumstance to a minimum.

You can always learn a lot about the members of the band by the order in which they show up on time. I'll be honest, I expected Cam to be first, but Atlas glides into the studio fifteen minutes early in a professional sport coat and dark denim. It's out of the ordinary for him, like seeing Glinda the Good Witch in something besides pink.

Cameron and Rob are next to arrive and right on time. Meanwhile, Chris rolls in five minutes late. I'll give him credit though, I once had a musician arrive to their own photoshoot an hour late, no hair and makeup done, and we only had the studio booked for an hour and a half.

Pop stars are the worst.

The styling team worked their magic on the guys while I confirmed the concept with the photographer and her team.

Prompt as ever, the shoot starts right on time. All four band members followed the direction of the photographer to a T. Although they were arranged in various positions and poses throughout the photoshoot, the photographer doesn't seem sold on the photos quite yet. This is the reason we hired her, she's a perfectionist to a point of pain. Her meticulous attention to detail is always agitating in the moment but the end result is always worth it.

After examining the photos from the most recent arrangement, she looks from Atlas to the styling team with an idea twinkling in her eye.

"Could we change Atlas into a dark gray shirt?" She requests with a tone of authority. "The black makes him fade into the background too much."

The styling team rushes over with a dark gray button up flowing on the hanger as they usher him out of the identical black shirt in a hurry.

And that's when I see it.

Atlas had tattoos five years ago. He has even more now. All are black images depicting various themes from music to nature.

What I didn't know was that the only exception to his all black tattoo design is a red rose inked into his chest.

Right over his heart.

A rose. *A rose?*

I'm going to be sick. But I have a job to do. Personal feelings don't matter when you're on a time crunch. My acquired talent of concealing emotion proved to be useful over the years but now more than ever I have to keep it under wraps.

After the wardrobe change, the photographer's mood dramatically increases. She is buzzing with excitement as she snaps photos, bosses the guys around, and captures images that will go down in history as some of the best the magazine has ever seen.

Since the majority of the work is done, there is no more need for me.

The first chance I get, I duck out of the studio with my bag in hand, marching for the front door. That seems to be the only way I walk away from Broken Compass these days.

"Rosie." Atlas's voice is preceded by a door being shoved open and followed by the door slamming shut. "Where are you going?"

I don't even bother to turn around when I say, "I'm not needed here anymore. I have other work to do."

"Bullshit. You were fine earlier. What happened?"

"Nothing happened." I hope I sound more convincing out loud than I do in my head.

"Rosie, stop." I'm angry at myself for listening but the command in his voice halts my heels without a second thought. Too stubborn to keep going, I turn to face him to hide how cowardly I really feel.

"I saw something change in your eyes. What happened?"

You happened, I want to spit at him. So much happened. If I've learned anything from this week, it's that I haven't moved on from five years ago. I don't know how to navigate that field of backstory landmines in a working relationship.

Girding my loins and gearing up for a fight, I look Atlas dead in the eyes as I say, "I saw your tattoo."

He doesn't ask which one, he knows. And now he understands why I'm angry—no, not angry. Confused. I don't know whether to be flattered or frustrated.

"A rose, Atlas? Are you kidding me? Why did you get that tattoo?"

If he never meant for me to see it, he shouldn't have gotten it permanently engraved into his flesh. Downcast eyes tell me he wasn't ready to have this conversation but here we are.

When his gaze locks with mine again his full lips part a centimeter before he confesses his truth.

"You've always been a part of me, Rosie."

I'm sure he thought that would answer all my questions but it doesn't do shit. In fact, it raises more questions.

He had no guarantees he'd ever see me again, no promise I'd ever see that tattoo. So why did he get a crimson rose over his heart?

"This isn't the time or place for me to tell you the story. I want to tell you. God, I want to tell you everything. But I need more time and privacy to do it."

If he can't be straight with me, he doesn't deserve my time. I have a job to do and it doesn't entail digging at old wounds, no matter how infected they feel.

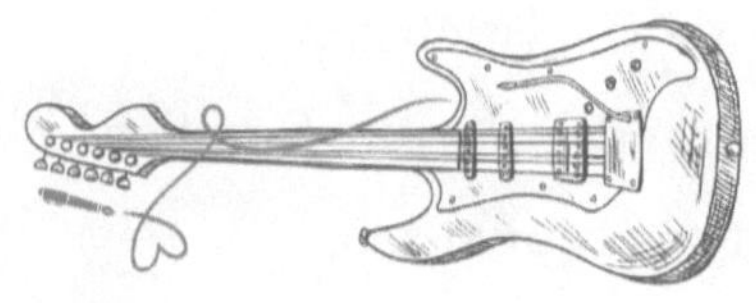

Thirty-One

Layla

HOLD ON-WILSON PHILLIPS

I've been putting this conversation off for way too long. I'm not normally someone who deals with task paralysis; if there's one item left on my to-do list, I can't go to sleep.

So I've been sleeping terribly for the past few years since I stopped making an effort with McKenzie.

McKenzie did nothing wrong. She was in love with Atlas's best friend and therefore too close to the source of all my angst. So I distanced myself from her as a self preservation method.

When my perspective changed a little over a year ago, I wanted to call her more than anyone else. My entire world had been flipped upside down and I didn't know what to do. The first person I wanted to call was her because I knew she'd have the right things to say. But my foolish pride and fear impeded reason. I know that if I had called her, she would have been there for me, and that made me feel the guilt even more keenly.

I'm a different woman now...or at least in a different situation now. Circumstance has brought us back into the same orbit so I need to abolish my reservations, put on my big girl pants, and take the first step.

I'm spending one last night at my small LA apartment before the tour begins. One last night of comfort and familiarity. Lounging on my sectional in what has become my safe haven, I hit the call button on McKenzie's contact. The ringing is like a countdown of intrusive thoughts.

What if she deleted my number?

What if she didn't and she ignores my call?

What if she answers only to call me every name I deserve?

What if she—

"Hello?" Her voice is hesitant like when you hear a bump in the night and call out for an apparition. But the softness hasn't changed.

"Kenzie?" *Does she know it's me?* "Hey, it's Layla."

"I know," she answers matter-of-factly. "I have caller ID. I just didn't believe it was really you."

"I deserve that. And more." I didn't think this far ahead as to how to approach this conversation. "Sooo, how are you?"

"I'm fine." Even though it's been years, I can picture McKenzie with arms crossed, intense stare drilling into my skull as she waits for a less cowardly approach.

It's never been this awkward between her and I, so I get to the point.

"I'll just cut to the chase. I'm sorry." I spill my guts before I chicken out. "I was a shitty friend who let go of years of friendship over something you weren't even involved in. You may never forgive me, but I wanted you to know."

I wish phones still had a crackle like old landlines so I didn't have to suffer in the excruciating silence of her pause. I can't even hear her breathing, my own thoughts are too loud.

"I've missed you, Layla."

Saying I sighed in relief isn't enough to describe the weight lifted off my shoulders. I'm not ignorant enough to think I don't have some serious groveling to do, but at least I'll have the chance to do it.

"I've missed you too, Kenz. I have so much to tell you and so much I want to know. But I want to say it again, I'm so, so sorry for ghosting you. I was hurting and didn't know how to handle it and you were a casualty of that."

"Aww, hun," the sympathy rings true in her voice. "I have so much I want to tell you too. And I hope one day you can tell me everything that happened between you and Atlas. Maybe it'll shed some light on some of his behavior the past few years."

Color me curious. "What do you mean?"

"Oh, just random, out-of-pocket behavior. Something will set him off and he'll get drunk then get a tattoo. Not often, but it happens."

Is that how he got the rose tattoo?

"I'll tell you one thing, whatever happened, he's never forgiven himself. I think he's been trying to make something of himself. I don't know if it's to earn your respect or your love or what. But he's been on a mission."

I'll have to unpack how I feel about all this later. I'm dying to know what's been going through his head for the past five years. Yet, I also don't think I'm ready to know.

Maybe this tour will be the opportunity we need to find closure. To move on so I don't have to cut my friends out of my life anymore.

But I'm not sure things with Atlas can ever be the same.

The importance of a best friend has been a heavy weight on my chest the past few years. The need for a girl friend to share my highs and lows with, my random thoughts. We are pack animals who desperately crave the companionship of fellow women who won't judge.

Being the amazing woman she is, Kenzie jumped right back into friendship with me. Even standing up for Atlas right from the get-go with concern for *us*. But I don't want to talk about him. I want to know about her. She shares all the great moments of the last couple years, right down to Cam getting down on one knee in front of the Eiffel Tower with a ring straight off her Pinterest board.

I told her how badly I wanted to call and congratulate them. She told me how much she wished I had, which broke my heart. And then we ended the night with promises of coffee dates and girl time whenever she joined the tour.

I can't wrap my brain around how quickly she's forgiven me but that's just who McKenzie is. She's the embodiment of sunshine and open-heartedness. Which makes her skills as a cutthroat lawyer that much more impressive.

And just like that, a small piece of me was repaired. The crack is still visible but at least I am one step closer to feeling whole.

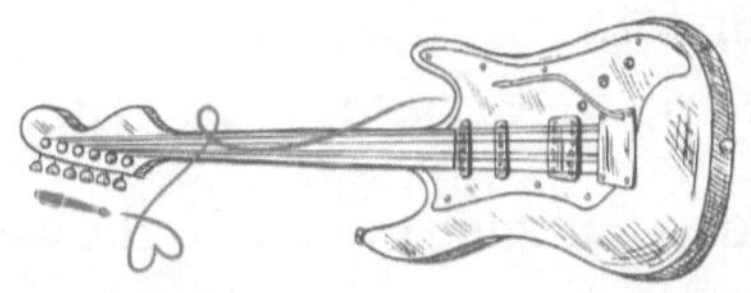

Thrity-Two
Layla

Options-Cameron Whitcomb

With the tour beginning on the East coast, we all take one flight on a private jet across the country. Tonight will be our first and only night in a hotel for at least a week. The tour manager tried to give everyone as much time in hotel rooms as possible while still including as many shows as necessary to reach fans and make the tour financially reasonable.

We all pile on to the small private jet at 8am sharp. Kenzie won't be joining us until the southern leg of the tour, so I'm stuck on the plane without a buffer. Then again, there's always Chris or Cam. We have a lot of time to catch up.

As much as I want to jump back into friendship with them, doubt wiggles its way into my brain to remind me I have a lot to make up for.

I've had years to think about the fact that cutting out everyone, when it was Atlas I couldn't stand to see, was a bitch move on my part. It felt easier to cut them all off. But perspective and distance have given me the opportunity to realize that I have some bad choices to make up for.

Prompt as ever, I think I'm the first one to the plane until I climb aboard and find Atlas lounging in a seat by the window. Effortlessly casual in his joggers and T-shirt, he raises his gaze to me with a spark of hope.

It would be weird not to greet him so I offer a polite "Good morning," as I take the seat across the aisle from him and start decorating the small table with my supplies. I might as well use this time to work.

"Morning. Have you ever flown private before?" Atlas asks before I can secure my headphones over my ears to block out the world.

Still clutching the headphones in front of me, I reply, "A couple times." I doubt he wants to know with whom.

My career has brought me to cross paths with a variety of people. Some of them were even in the same boat as me.

I guess it was too much to hope that would be the end of the awkward small talk because Atlas continues. "With who? For work?"

"Yeah, for work." Avoidance is my best friend right now.

"Does *Rolling Stone* have a private jet they loan out to employees? Or were you flying with other musicians?"

Stop fishing, Atlas.

"Other musicians."

I've busied myself on my laptop this whole time, trying to send the message that this is not a conversation he wants to have.

"Anyone I know?"

My exasperated breath is not for my sake but for his. "Um, probably. I flew with Damsels one time. Hitched a ride with Carl Pricket after a show since we both needed to go to Texas. And Donavan Gentry a couple times."

Five years apart and mentioning his name still raises the temperature of the air around us. I haven't the slightest clue if they've crossed paths over the years. Donovan is doing great in his solo career. He offers me tickets to his shows whenever he's in town or we catch up over coffee. But it's never been more than that. I took a step back from that friendship when he started dating a really sweet girl from his label, out of respect for her.

Now, our primary interactions are at music events. The polite hello and quick, friendly hug. There's no bad blood between us but I don't want to cross any lines with a girl in the picture. Even if neither of us are interested in rekindling our mutually beneficial relationship.

My constant salvation, Chris steps onto the plane looking a little groggy but full of spirit. With his presence, I'm saved from having to answer any further questions that Atlas may think he wants to know, but he doesn't.

Even if I was interested in making amends and seeing where we could go, I am a much more damaged shell of my former self. Atlas wants what we almost had, not what is available now.

Chris rubs the top of my head like a dog, rustling my wild waves in the process, before taking the seat opposite the table I'm occupying.

"Girl, I can't tell you how glad I am to see you. I missed you."

"Likewise, Chris," I shine a bright smile his way. "No one has been able to make me laugh like you."

"Good thing we've got a few weeks in cramped spaces for me to tell you every embarrassing story from your absence. Starting with the *real* story about that weekend in Miami. The press got it all wrong. I was not hooking up with two guys. It was three. And whoever gave me the pill said it was LSD, not Viagra."

"Dude, not the Viagra story again," Rob cuts Chris off as he joins the team with his bass in hand.

"I need to set the record straight," Chris insists with a light smack of his fist on the arm rest, "even if I have to tell everyone in the world individually."

"Don't trust the crew with your bass?" I point to the instrument as Rob settles onto the short sofa, stretching his legs across every cushion.

"Juliet doesn't leave my side." Rob strokes the neck lovingly like a gentle caress for a lover.

"Move over," Cam slides Rob's legs off the other half of the sofa as he boards the plane. "Ugh. I need coffee and a B12 shot."

"Long night?" I ask with a teasing tone.

"Yeah. Someone was chatting with Kenzie on the phone all night and I barely slept." Cam shoots me an appreciative, pleased wink from where he's leaning his head against the window.

I feel the bashful smile turn the corners of my mouth but I don't even try to hide it. I think that by making amends with McKenzie, I also made amends with Cameron.

"Finally!" Chris breaks the tension. Then to Cameron he asks, "By the way, when are you two going to finally tie the knot?"

"We'll start planning after the tour. I don't think either of us can muster the energy to plan a wedding right now."

"Then hire a wedding planner," Chris suggests. "Or better yet, I'll plan your wedding."

"I love you, man, but I would never give you that kind of power." Chris appropriately replies by sticking his tongue out.

"You already put me in charge of the bachelor party."

"Correction: you put yourself in charge of it. Not that I need one."

"The bachelor party isn't for the groom, it's for the groomsmen." Judging by the disgruntled moans of the other groomsmen, I'd say Chris is the only one looking forward to it. I suppose after several years on the road, being invited to the most glamorous Hollywood parties, and an endless supply of debauchery, the appeal of a wild boys night loses its shimmer.

"Whatever. We're still going big for my birthday party in Miami!" Chris adds a visual exclamation mark by pointing a finger at every single person, including me.

The funny thing is, this isn't a particularly big birthday, I believe he's turning thirty-two. But Chris is a birthday person with no reservations about enjoying the undivided attention.

The southern leg of the tour is only a couple weeks away. I guess we'll see what he has up his sleeve in no time.

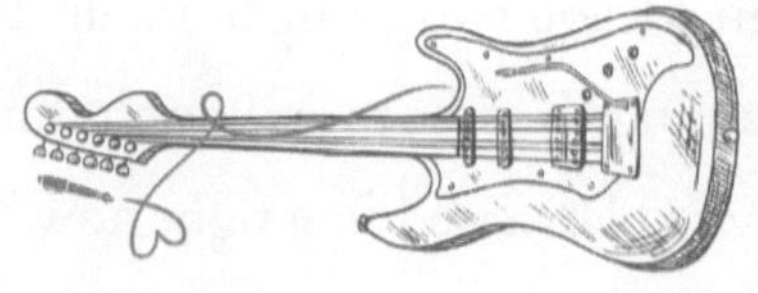

Thirty-Two
Layla

R OSE TATTOO-THE DROPKICK MURPHYS

The Boston Garden is booming. The opening band's music blares through the arena to the steady beat of encouragement from the audience. Playing the Garden for the first time is one sure-fire way to start the tour off with a bang. Back in the day, I saw the guys play countless times at various venues. It's hard not to be nostalgic about the times they played in smaller clubs on a raised platform instead of a grand stage. Look at them now.

I'd never admit it to them, but I attended one of their shows in Los Angeles as a regular spectator, I bought the ticket myself and hid in the back like a coward. Curiosity overpowered logic when it came to Atlas and Broken Compass. The performance was worth every penny, they played their hearts out for a hometown crowd that welcomed them back into their embrace.

Though, I'm not sure it was worth it for the extra pound of guilt I added to my conscience.

Being backstage at their first show of the tour was bound to dig up memories from their first tour, the night that changed everything.

Watching the guys pace back and forth, watching Chris tap his sticks nervously on any surface he can, reminds me of the night I took the picture of Atlas on the ground by equipment containers. That image was plastered all over social media. He even made it his profile picture for a while, even though we weren't speaking. I always wondered if that was his way of holding on to a piece of me.

I would give anything to jump in their heads right now, to hear their innermost thoughts. Are they the same as mine? Are they thinking about that night too? Or is it just because this is one of the biggest shows they've ever played?

I don't have a gauge other than the show five years ago to measure if this level of nervousness is normal for them?

When I spot Atlas sitting on the floor just like that first tour, a pit in my heart digs the buried empathy from within. So I extend an olive branch and join him on the floor. Outside of the office, I tend to dress a little more casual, even if I'm still technically working. A pair of jeans permits me the ability to sit crisscross-applesauce adjacent to Atlas on the cement floor.

"What cover are you doing tonight?" I ask to take his mind off things.

The guys have maintained their tradition of playing a cover for every performance. They reach across different genres and dabble in styles that wouldn't normally work. But they always manage to craft something uniquely their own every time. Their cover of

"Goodbye Yellow Brick Road" was so popular they even recorded it.

"We play a Dropkick Murphys song every time we're in Boston," Atlas informs me. Somewhere in the back of my mind I knew that, but managed to forget it until now.

"That doesn't answer my question." I try to add a hint of playfulness to my tone to lighten the mood.

My tactics must work because the left corner of Atlas's mouth turns up as if pulled by a string. His mischievous eyes connect with mine as he says, "You'll just have to wait and find out with everyone else."

In spite of myself, I shake my head with a repressed smile. "You Played 'Johnny, I Hardly Knew Ya' last time you were here, right? Isn't that a cover of a cover?"

"Technically. But I did bust out my bagpipe skills for that one. Made it our own."

"Did you bring the pipes with you tonight?" I don't see a random set of bagpipes lying around anywhere, so unless he's concealing them, the answer is probably not.

"Not for this song," Atlas confesses to my disappointment.

He's explored his instrumental talents over the years with original songs and covers, both for recordings and live performances. But the only other instrument I've seen him play is the banjo at that country western bar back in the day.

"Gear up, guys," the tour manager instructs the band. Atlas rises to his feet first then extends a hand to help me up as if it's the most natural thing in the world. We haven't touched in five years. This is the most air space we've shared in the same amount of time. I know he feels the zap between us when I gaze into his dark eyes and see the same memories circulating through his mind's-eye that are turning over in my head.

Frantic, frenzied touches.

Strong emotions.

Pounding hearts.

There's so much to unpack but I can't stomach the thought of dredging up the past right now.

The click-clack of Chris's drumsticks on a metal bar snap us out of our hypnosis and Atlas grabs his guitar before following the guys to their mark.

I remember this rush well, the bated breath and tense muscles before the guys step on stage to greet the adoring fans. The intense cheers of anticipation from the crowd that reverberate inside your skull the moment before they walk out.

And I remember McKenzie standing beside me for every second of it. So I pull out my phone and record the moment they walk out to their introduction and the riotous applause from the audience. I send the video off to McKenzie with no caption, just a fire emoji. After the guys finish their first song I receive a message back.

KENZIE: I LOVE THAT MOMENT.

KENZIE: Wish I was there to watch them with you.

LAYLA: Wish you were here too.

> KENZIE: Give Cam a smooch for me.

> LAYLA: How about I tell him you send your love.

> KENZIE: I guess that'll have to do. Let me know what cover they play.

The band puts on quite a performance, pulling out all the stops with fire displays and light work. Not to mention incredible musical skill. They even play a few fan favorite songs from previous albums.

But what everyone really waits for is the final song of the night which is always a cover. If I've learned anything about Bostanonians, it's that they're very proud of being Bostontonians. So the Dropkick Murphys covers are always a hit.

When Atlas trades his guitar for a mandolin, I'm on the edge of my seat. The crowd erupts when he plays the opening notes on the mandolin, apparently the whole arena is familiar with the Dropkick Murphys repertoire. Meanwhile, it takes me a moment to realize what song they're playing.

When the tune finally clicks in my brain, my heart plummets into my stomach. The lyrics for "Rose Tattoo" embed themselves in my chest like arrows fired from across the stage.

I completely forget to take notes as the words plow through me.

You'll always be there with me
Even if you're gone
You'll always have my love

Our memory will live on

What the fuck does this mean? Is Atlas trying to tell me something? It can't be pure coincidence.

I don't know what to do or say when the band takes their final bow and jaunts off stage. As soon as Atlas is in view, he searches my eyes but I don't know what for. He either thinks I'm going to kiss him or kill him.

But I remind myself–yet again–this is a working relationship. I have to compose myself like the professional, accomplished journalist I am and maintain sophistication. I can pace and ponder over this later.

"Great show, guys," I commend them with a steady tone as they pass me by.

And it's true. I loved almost every second of it. It felt like I was home for the first time in years.

"I'm going to Uber back to the hotel. See you guys in the morning."

No one bothers to stop me as I wave farewell with my back to Atlas.

Soon, I'll be in the privacy of my own hotel room where I can have a mental breakdown in peace.

LAYLA: They played Rose Tattoo

KENZIE: …oh boy.

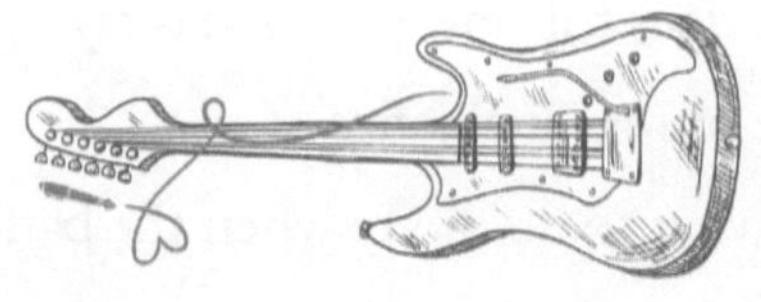

Thirty-Four

Layla

NEED YOU NOW-LADY A

After a plethora of tears, a good scream into a pile of pillows, and sufficient wallowing, I still can't sleep. It's nearly midnight but thankfully the hotel bar doesn't close for another hour so I don sweatpants and a plain white shirt to seek the old-fashioned remedy for anxious nerves.

The second the elevator doors slide open, I'm met with the melodic tone of a piano drifting through the lobby. The sweet music bounces off the marble floor, the high ceilings, and the gilded walls of this four star hotel. Apparently, the band is just boujee enough for a four star hotel, but not boujee enough to require a five star hotel.

It seems a little late for a hired pianist to still be working. Wondering if perhaps it's another guest, I follow the music that plays with the same effect as the Pied Piper toward the piano I saw at the front entrance when I arrived earlier this evening. Music is my entire life, I can't help the curiosity drawing me forward.

Just as I reach the top step that leads into the dropped lounge, the mysterious pianist effortlessly ends one song and begins the next. The hauntingly beautiful tune of "Need You Now" by Lady A cocoons me in a bubble of emotion. If the lyrics I recall didn't cut deep enough, the maestro behind the instrument plunges the knife even deeper.

Atlas hunches over the piano as his own connection to the song overtakes his senses. I've seen him lose control in his music countless times. He feels everything he plays so deeply. He walks around with a care-free swagger that people want in a rockstar, the mysterious one, the illusive one, the one that can't be phased. But If you pay close enough attention, you realize he feels emotions on a deeper level than the rest. I once believed that was what made him such a talented artist.

It's evident that is still the case.

It would be so easy to sneak away like a ghost in the night and pretend I never saw Atlas in what appeared to be a vulnerable moment. But I also can't pull myself away. I've desperately needed answers but refused to give him the opportunity to provide them. And he clearly needs closure. I'm not sure we can accomplish everything in one night, but perhaps we can begin.

Stalking over to the piano, I position myself in the curve of the grand piano beside the lid prop and study the crease between his brows. I see the flicker of recognition the moment he realizes I'm there but he refuses to cut the song short. Vibrations ricochet through my body as he plays through the final chorus and taps out the remaining notes of the song.

Only when the song is complete, and the echo of the final line filters through the air, does he acknowledge my presence.

Wordlessly, I seat myself beside him on the piano bench so we don't have to be face to face while we talk. Softer than before, Atlas begins a new song as background for our conversation, but the tune is unfamiliar.

"'Rose Tattoo.'" I say over the enchanting tune. A song title that carries more meaning for him than I realized. One that inspired his actions.

Atlas plucks softly at the black and white keys with eyes transfixed by the movement of his fingers. "About three years ago, we were playing in Boston. After the official show, we decided to go to a pub and unwind. It was a tiny hole-in-the-wall place with cheap beer and shitty food but at least no one recognized us."

Atlas shifts down an octave, twisting his torso away from me. "We felt a little nostalgic telling Rob about the Blue Room. This pub had karaoke too, so we drank a few beers and started taking turns. In the spirit of Boston, Rob picked 'Rose Tattoo' for me to sing without realizing it would be a reminder. I don't think any of them did. I have plenty of tattoos and most of them don't mean anything. I felt like a fraud. So I walked out of the bar and found the first open tattoo parlor and pointed at the first Americana rose on the wall. No one asked me about it and I didn't tell them. I'm sure they have their theories, but I think you'd be able to guess better than them."

I hold my breath as I listen until my chest is on fire. This is my chance to ask a question that has been nagging me since I stepped foot into the conference room at Tattoo Records.

"How much do they know?"

Atlas shifts his body back to the center of the piano as he climbs up the scale again, continuing the beautiful song as he goes.

"Not enough," he answers. "I wish I could make it all make sense for them. But I didn't know what to say. And besides, it feels like our story, not theirs. They've probably made assumptions, though."

Shame rings clear in his tone. Shame for how he treated me, shame for how we handled it. I feel ashamed that I abandoned everyone else. We both made mistakes that I pray the others can forgive me for.

"Can you ever find it in your heart to forgive me?" I wish I had an answer for him. But it's been five years of ignoring my problems with toxic coping mechanisms. I haven't fully faced the root of my issues until now. I haven't even begun to properly process what happened until this tour.

"I need time, Atlas." The song cuts off when Atlas drops his hands to his lap. Leaving only silence and regret for us to marinate in.

"What can I do, Rosie?" The plea in his voice cuts to the bone. I wish I could wave a magic wand and make the hurt we both suffer from disappear.

Peering down at my folded hands resting on my thighs, I utter the words I know he doesn't want to hear. "I don't know."

Atlas tips his head back with the release of a pent-up sigh. He's trying. He's trying so hard. But I'm not even sure what he wants.

"I know I messed up, Rosie. I know I hurt you. I know I need to atone for my sins. But I don't know what that looks like unless you tell me."

"Atlas." His name comes out quick and sharp. "I have been ignoring the past all these years. I've dealt with it in unhealthy ways and I haven't fully begun to work on it until now. Until *you* forced my hand." The accusation flies so easily from me. Is that really what's bothering me? Or am I just angry that I have to face the past?

"We need closure," he snaps back. "I saw an opportunity for us to work on that and I took it. I know I orchestrated this whole thing but we both deserve it."

"No, I deserve it. You're the one who used me." Lowering my voice to a harsh whisper I say, "You fucked me and then told me to leave. I didn't even get to come first." I scoff as I rise from the bench and march across the lounge back toward the elevator, nightcap be damned. Just as the elevator door is about to close, Atlas slips through the gap for the ride to the twentieth floor. If I remember correctly, we're all staying on the same level.

We ride in silence for two floors before I finally face him, arms crossed over my chest, and ask, "What is the end goal? Let's say I forgive you. Then what? Then we become besties? Then we pretend like nothing ever happened and pick up where we left off?"

"Then we have some semblance of a chance at exploring what could be." His words resonate in the cramped elevator, forcing us to share too much space so I can hear his every labored breath.

Something in his posture softens when Atlas speaks next. "Five years ago, I wanted us to be together. I wanted every piece of you to be mine and I wanted to pursue what could have been a great love story. Instead, I fucked it all up and I take every ounce of blame. But, Rosie," he steps closer to tuck a lock of hair behind my ear. It's such a shock I try to back away but he holds me in place. He doesn't understand, he doesn't know I haven't been touched by anyone in months. Not like this. "I will do everything I have to to make amends. Even if your forgiveness just leads to us never speaking again at least we will have that."

My racing heart could generate electricity at the rate it's going.

"Just don't cut the guys out again, if this all ends with us not speaking. You were family to them as much as you were to me. We all miss you."

Just when I felt like my shattered heart was piecing itself back together, it crumbles again.

The elevator finally comes to a smooth stop as a beep sounds, the doors opening. Atlas steps out before I do while I mull over everything he's told me until stepping off the elevator before the doors close again.

So much for trying to calm my nerves. Anxiety and I are two peas in a very claustrophobic pod, right now.

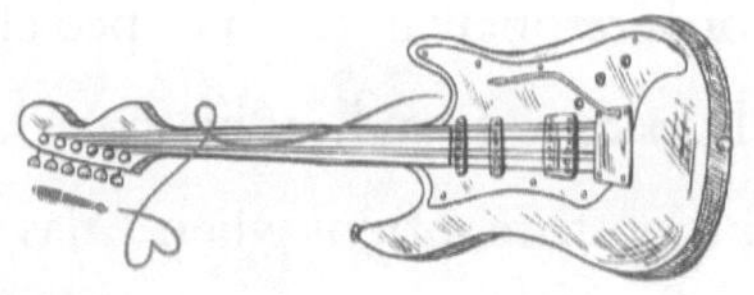

Thirty-Five

Layla

I'M NOT IN LOVE-10CC

After restless tossing and turning, two hours of fitful sleep, and frantic packing, I meet everyone in the lobby to load onto the tour bus for the next several days. Nothing like confined spaces to force people to face their issues.

Despite the lack of privacy on the bus, I'll gladly take the chance to make amends. Starting with arguably my biggest fan: Chris. Which is why I need to make him a priority.

It's been several years since I went on the road with a band and I can't say I miss the bunk beds. Regardless, Broken Compass is able to afford a tour bus with more wiggle room and a standard sized stall shower. There's less of a camper feel, more an apartment on wheels.

Instead of a tour bus with a double bed in the back, this one features a lounge area in the back, while the front section is more of a kitchenette with a small dining area.

Everyone finds their groove pretty quickly, where they spend most of their downtime and how they spend it. I've learned that Rob is more of an ebook kind of guy. Chris and Cam are both TV guys but argue over binging shows or devouring movies. I throw out the alternative of a documentary but that's shut down with quizzical stares.

No surprise here, Atlas spends the majority of his time working on new music whether it be jotting down lyrics or strumming his travel guitar to refine a beat. Occasionally, Cameron will jump in as an extra set of ears.

Cam may be one of the best guitar players of this generation, but Atlas has the ear for Grammy worthy music.

And that is how I find my first opportunity for a private talk with Chris. While Atlas and Cam work on music, and Rob takes a cat nap, Chris extends his feet onto the narrow sofa in the back, computer in his lap.

"Mind if I sit?" I point to the cushion Chris's feet are perched on.

"Not at all." Chris lifts his legs for me to sit down only to lay his slippered feet across my lap.

"What are you working on?" I'm stalling. He doesn't know it but I know it.

"Some stuff for the record label. We're setting up a meeting between one of our producers and a new artist to see if there's potential for more than just a one hit wonder."

Chris finishes typing something before the whoosh of a message flying into webspace precedes Chris closing his computer.

"What can I do for ya?" One of the things I love about Chris is the permanent smile on his handsome, bearded face. He's a big ball of love.

This is it. I need to woman up and do this. Rip off the bandaid, so to speak.

So I level my sorry gaze on Chris instead of avoiding his and say, "I owe you an apology." His eyebrows tip up in the center, compassion and sympathy written all over his face. "What happened with Atlas and I is...complicated. But in trying to protect my feelings, I abandoned the people I love, the people who accepted me into their family. For that, I'm sorry."

I didn't expect Chris to be mad, a selfish part of me felt easier having this conversation knowing he was the forgiving type.

"I really missed you, girl, we all did." Another knife to the chest that I deserve. "But I'm not here to judge you. We all make mistakes in the name of protecting ourselves. Can't tell you the number of times I ghosted a guy that would have given me the world cause I can't handle the distance when we're touring. That's my own cross to bear."

I want to reach over and hug this man who deserves all the love in the world, but his next words stop me. "As for you and Atlas. You guys need to work your shit out. But I think I have a pretty good idea of what happened." *Pause for dramatic affect.* "I read your book. We all did, in case you were wondering."

That stings.

Offering the truth, I tell him, "No one was ever supposed to read that book."

"Then why publish it?"

Bottling the rage I still haven't gotten over, I tell him the whole story.

"I was sending some finished articles to my old boss for proof and accidentally attached the book. It was just a way for me to process my feelings. My therapist says I tend to rewrite moments I wish I could change. Without my permission, he sent it to a publishing friend of his and the agent ate it up.

"I was furious with Travis, *furious* that he betrayed my trust when it was clearly an accident and he should have never read it. So I quit. But then I was in need of a paycheck with no job prospects. The publisher offered an advance if I signed with them so I did it. I was desperate. But I only agreed to the one. Novels are not where I want my career to be. I like journalism. I love music. And the income from that book set me up to hold out for a good opportunity instead of taking whatever I could get.

"That's when *Rolling Stone* reached out. They offered me a job without an interview, on the spot."

"Sounds like a dream come true," Chris smiles like a proud mama bear.

"It has been. Up until that asshole backed me into a corner so now I have to spend weeks on a tour bus with four stinky guys."

Chris brandishes a finger like a weapon. "Hey, say what you want about the rest. But I smell delightful."

Laughing, I pat the leg that's still draped across my lap and relish in this bit of normalcy.

Sensing my emotions, Chris assures me, "We're good, Layla. You don't have anything to worry about."

Click. Another piece of my heart fits back into place.

But my smile falters when Chris shifts gears. "I'm still rooting for you two, ya know. Always thought you and Atlas would be good together. Like I said, I don't know exactly what he did, but if you give him the chance to make it up to you, he'd do anything to win your heart again."

The problem is that he's never given it back. As much as I tried to find it in other men, Atlas has been the sole owner of my heart for longer than I even realized.

"I don't know, Chris," I say with a nod of my head as the weight of how this conversation turned rests on my conscience.

"There's been no one else, Layla." That confession brings relief to a worry I didn't even know I had. A worry I don't have the right to consider. "He hasn't said it, but he's been waiting for you."

Atlas has told me this, now Chris. Yet I can't bring myself to deal with that.

"Alright, I've said my piece. Let's watch Bruce Willis outsmart Alan Rickman."

Chris increases the volume on the TV, it doesn't quite drown out the sound of my raging thoughts, but it does feel natural. Just being around one another and doing normal things. It all feels like something you do with family.

And one person at a time, I'm getting mine back.

Thirty-Six

Layla

FOOLED AROUND AND FELL In Love-Elvin Bishop

Two weeks on a tour bus makes you appreciate the little things in life. A shower with no schedule, a full sized bed, privacy. Things we take for granted in our everyday life.

Every time we stepped off the bus to fuel up or for a show felt like escaping prison. Even the air at the gas station was sweeter than the same stale air we'd been breathing for days on end.

By the time we made it to Miami for two shows at Hard Rock Stadium, I didn't care if we stayed in the Bates Motel, I just wanted a room to myself for one night.

By skipping the last grocery stop and living on a bag of chips all day, we made it to the hotel early to settle in before the show tonight.

The bus pulls up to the back of the hotel so we can sneak in without the guys being spotted. Eagerly stepping off the bus I close my eyes and breath in the fresh air that doesn't suffocate my lungs only to be jolted out of my moment of peace by a squeal.

McKenzie bolts from the back door with the most adoring, gleeful smile on her angelic face. A warm smile stretches from cheek to cheek as I watch thinking she's about to tackle Cameron–her fiancé–so I'm unprepared when she plows straight into me at full speed. Bracing one leg behind me so we don't topple to the pavement, I fully immerse myself in the reunion by wrapping my arms around my best friend and giggling into her shoulder.

"Ohmygodohmygodohmygod," she shrieks into my ear. "I can't believe you're here."

Feeling a bit more sentimental than her, I utter through restrained emotion clogging my throat, "I missed you so much."

Kenzie pulls away to look me directly in the eyes and I see the same sheen of my eyes reflected in hers. How did I get so lucky as to find someone like her? Someone who offered forgiveness and friendship so easily.

"Babe!" Cam holds his hands out in disbelief. "You haven't seen me in weeks. I'm your *fiancé.*"

"Yeah, but I haven't seen my best friend in *five years.*" I giggle as McKenzie tips her head so our temples connect before she bounds across the space separating her and Cam before planting a chaste kiss on his lips. "I'll make it up to you later."

Cameron envelopes his girl in his arms with all the love in the world. There's never been a doubt in my mind their souls were meant for each other.

"Alright kids," Chris's boisterous voice breaks the tender moment as the guys file off the bus. "Get a nap, caffeinate, and get ready for an epic party tonight. I expect everyone to show up *on theme* for the party. Limo leaves an hour after the concert."

Chris's demand is met with a series of groans. I guess the novelty of glamorous parties wears off after a few years.

Regardless, Kenzie and I have been planning our outfits for a couple weeks. Chris organized a Studio 54 party at a club downtown and instructed everyone to dress for the occasion. I had my outfit ordered to McKenzie's place so she could bring it for me.

It's been a while since I attended a party that didn't involve networking of some kind. We'll see if my social anxiety can handle the pressure.

Holding my breath, I rap my knuckles on the door to the hotel room two doors down from mine. It's been 90 minutes so I assume the love birds have had adequate time to *reconnect* and it's safe to approach them.

Cam's head pops into the foot of space between the door and the door jam as he peers into the hallway. His knowing eyes scan my face for a moment before I hear McKenzie from the other side of the door ask, "Who is it, babe?"

Swinging the door open all the way, Cameron announces, "It's Layla."

"Eek," Kenzie bounces to the door. Grabbing my hand she drags me inside. "I assume you're here for your outfit, but I insist you bring your makeup over so we can get ready together."

She guides me to the little sitting area by the window where my outfit presumably resides in the plastic package on the table.

"That sounds awesome. But I wanted to talk to you guys first."

Bracing a hand on his fiance's lower back, Cam comes to stand by Kenzie, both wearing equally suspicious and concerned expressions.

Wringing my hands in front of my stomach, I do my best not to stare at the ground like my self-conscious self desperately wants to do, afraid of what I'll see on their faces as I speak.

"I owe you both an apology," I begin. Apparently, this is my new opening line. "I was a shitty friend when...everything happened. The drama with Atlas shouldn't have affected my friendship with either of you and I acted like a coward. And for that I'm sorry."

Breathe, Layla. Breath.

"Oh honey," McKenzie is the first to reach forward and cease my nervous habit by taking my hand in hers. But Cam still maintains physical contact with her, even as she takes half a step toward me. "I don't know what happened, but all is forgiven. Of course I was hurt that you cut us all out of your life but you came back to us. Despite whatever I can guess, I don't know exactly what happened between you two. And I trust you had your reasons."

You'd never guess that someone as sweet and compassionate as McKenzie was a shark in the courtroom.

I swivel my head so my gaze lands on Cameron. He looks considerably less convinced than Kenzie.

"I wish I could go back and change everything." If either of them notice the catch in my throat, they don't acknowledge it. I would change so *so much* in the week that changed everything.

Rubbing his free hand along his jawline, Cameron contemplates the sincerity of my words for a moment before he looks between me and my best friend.

"I'm not gonna lie. I was really mad at you for a while. Not for cutting us off, but for what it did to Kenzie." He loops his comforting arms around Kenzie's midriff. "But I also see that you're trying to make it right. I know Atlas put you in an impossible position and instead of backing down, you're making amends."

"Trying to," I mutter through the sob I'm trying to contain. I'll never fully forgive myself for the emotional turmoil I put the people I love through. But with their forgiveness, I'll get pretty damn close.

McKenzie beams. "Suspect as his actions may be, I'm glad Atlas pulled a dipshit move if it means you're back in our lives."

"Well, at least he did one thing right."

"My god, Layla," Cameron shakes his head, "if you gave that guy a chance he would do everything right–everything he could possibly think to win you back."

Groaning, I step away from Cam and Kenzie with a sigh. "Why is everyone so insistent on us being a thing."

"Because we've watched him love you from afar for five years," Cam announces. Until now, no one has mentioned the L word. Hearing it makes all of this feel too real, too heavy to bear.

"You deserve your happily ever after," McKenzie is practically vibrating with excitement over something that isn't even on the table.

"And you think my happily ever after is with Atlas?"

"Of course!" She says this like I'm ignorant. "He's your person."

"I thought you were my person."

"I am, but even Meredith had Derek." Good to see our years of *Grey's Anatomy* references are still in play.

Unprepared to deal with that load of baggage, I shift the topic. "Well, tonight is not the night to face that demon. So how about we get glammed for this shindig."

"You ladies have fun," Cam says as he grabs his phone off the bed before pecking a quick kiss from Kenzie. "I'll see you guys after the show."

"Knock 'em dead, sweetie."

Thirty-Seven
Atlas

SILVER SPRING-FLEETWOOD MAC

Running off the high from the first sold out show in Miami, the guys and I change in the green room for Chris's birthday celebration.

In true Chris fashion, he went all out. A floor length fur coat paired with reflective bell-bottoms–no shirt. And he teased his curly hair into a poof before wrapping a scarf over his forehead.

Since Cameron has Kenzie's help, he's in a respectable vintage beachy looking get-up that doesn't look too out of place in modern day, or in the disco club.

Rob really leaned into the theme with John Travolta's *Saturday Night Fever* suit, despite the fact he didn't bother to grease his hair in the same style as Travolta.

At a loss for what to wear, Chris offered to help me with my outfit. This process involved a lot of vetos before agreeing to the shimmering shirt that hangs open to dip between my pecs, and an uncomfortably tight pair of black pants that Chris swears will get me laid.

Not that that's on my agenda.

Unless one particular girl initiates.

The limo pulls onto the front drive of the hotel to pick up the girls and parks directly in front of the entrance so I get a clear view of the vision walking toward me.

I can recall the first time I saw Layla in that bar all those years ago. I didn't have a clue who she was but I was drawn to her aura. She's fucking beautiful but I sensed a spark in her I couldn't resist.

The woman walking toward me is clad tightly in a sequin jumpsuit thing that flares at her elbows and knees. The light reflects off her like a disco ball, highlighting the majestic beauty she is with every movement. Her eyes are dark, her lips glossy, and her hair a waterfall of voluminous curls. I couldn't take my eyes off her even if I tried.

Breathtaking doesn't even come close to describe how she looks, the way she makes me feel.

As the girls get closer to the open door of the limo, my soul sinks back into my body and I realize Kenzie is there too. Sneaking a peek at Cam, I see he's completely entranced by the velvet dress that plunges into a deep V over her chest, the fabric looping around behind her neck. Kenzie is also wearing one of the biggest pairs of bedazzled earrings I've ever seen.

"Hello, boys," Kenz greets us as she slides onto the seat beside Cameron. Layla follows, taking the empty seat as she shuts the door.

Surveying the occupants, Layla compliments us, "Well, don't you gentlemen clean up nice."

"Same to you, ladies," Chris winks in their direction. "I would like to thank all of you for committing to the theme. And further-more, I'd like to thank me for simply existing and giving us a reason to get dressed up tonight."

"Here here," McKenzie golf-claps.

"Now let's get this party started." Chris hits a button on the ceiling which triggers the music to switch from the local soft rock station to the bluetooth feature so his phone connects and "Le Freak" by CHIC fills the air.

Four disco songs later, we arrive outside the club Chris reserved for the evening. From the outside you wouldn't guess it was much if not for the never-ending line of people desperate to get in. No neon signs to indicate there's a wild club inside. Nothing remotely flashy and inviting about the gray stone wall and black door. Aside from the red rope and bouncer guarding the entrance like a dragon guards his lair.

A security team is already in position to usher us through the entrance past the crowd before it turns into a mob. But just a glimpse of us is enough for people to go wild with recognition. I remember the days when we could walk freely from place to place, we didn't have to make reservations days in advance and prepare a security team just to go out in public.

Would I trade the blessings I have now for that kind of freedom again? I don't know. I'd like to think the fame and fortune doesn't matter to me, but I also remember what it was like to live paycheck to paycheck. The strain of multiple jobs to make our dreams a reality.

I suppose we simply traded one set of problems for another.

"Don't Stop 'Til You Get Enough" welcomes us into the fold of the decked out club. I have no clue what the place looked like before Chris hired a professional team. But every inch is decked out in disco glamour. Silver and gold obscures my vision in every direction between disco balls, brassy fixtures, and flashing lights. It really is remarkable, even if not entirely my style.

As soon as Chris struts onto the platform overlooking the dance floor, he raises both hands in the hair with a simultaneous pelvic thrust of enthusiasm as he shouts, "Let's dance," like he's Kevin Bacon.

The party-goers reciprocate the energy with their own cheers as we make our way down the stairs to the main floor. Now that McKenzie is back at his side, Cameron loosens up a bit, the pair dancing to the beat of the music with each step. Rob, our resident golden retriever, smiles and bops along to the rhythm behind the waitress leading us to the VIP section behind sheer, shimmering curtains.

As for Rosie and I, we walk like normal people despite the chaos thriving around us. As she peers around the room taking in the glitz and glimmer, her eyes pass over me briefly. The moment she realizes I've barely taken my eyes off her, she flicks her gaze back to me.

Over the roar of the party in full swing, I tell her, "You look stunning."

A soft blush crawls across her nose and cheeks with an unsure smile that tugs the corners of her mouth.

"Thank you. You look…"

Filling in the words she's too shy to say, I supply, "Out of my element."

Shrugging one shoulder, Rosie laughs, "I mean, a little. I've never seen you wear anything so low cut. You're giving Cher a run for her money."

"Take one guess who dressed me."

Rosie looks toward Chris who already has a glass of bubbly in his hand, making himself comfortable on the crimson sofa in the lounge. "He certainly has style."

The six of us take seats around the oval table bearing flutes of champagne and an ice bucket with an extra bottle that I'm guessing will never run out.

I don't drink much these days but take the glass anyway. Even if it weren't for the fact one of my best friends was killed by a drunk driver, I'm also in my thirties. Hangovers last for days and I don't get energetic like I used to, I just get tired.

"A toast for the birthday boy," Rosie raises her glass with a delicate hand adorned by jeweled cuffs. "Cheers to another year around the sun and many more fabulous nights like this."

"I'll drink to that," Chris clinks his glass with the nearest one then downs the gold liquid in one gulp.

Through the comings and goings of people, plates of food, and endless beverages passed around, I never take my eyes off Rosie. Even as she lets loose with Kenzie on the dance floor, I absorb her aura like it's my own personal drug, getting high off the infectious joy.

She's been so reserved this entire tour, I felt like I didn't know the woman I was sharing a bathroom with for the past few weeks. But the woman on the dance floor right now is definitely one I remember. Carefree, impervious to criticism, confident in her bright personality. She used to be so without inhibitions. I feel like the woman I've been interacting with was simply a suit of armor to protect the woman I used to know.

Maybe with Kenzie back for a bit, the Rosie I fell in love with will stick around for a while.

At some point in the evening, Cam and Kenzie disappear because they've never grown out of that phase of their relationship. Chris accepted whatever pill was placed on his tongue thirty minutes ago so he's floating in his own little world. Rob found a couple girls to orbit him on the dance floor, so that leaves Rosie vibing to the music by herself.

Also leaving the perfect opening for anyone to sneak up behind her and grind all over her. Which is exactly what one guy decides to do. Some sleeze slinks up like a snake in the grass behind Rosie, taking her hips roughly in his grasp as he digs his boner into her ass. I try to tell myself that if this is what she wants I'll watch it happen. I don't have any right to her despite the emotional claim I want to place.

But the second her expression grows weary I leap to my feet and storm across the floor. Trying to avoid a scene, I push the guy out of the way with a shove to his shoulder as I take his place. My possessive touch replaces the invisible imprint of his hand on her round hips as I communicate with a glare that she isn't available.

"Woah, sorry man," the intruder surrenders with raised hands. Then walks away without causing any trouble.

This moment reminds me a lot of Rosie's graduation, when her asshole of an ex tried to stake his claim on her. I wonder if that's what Rosie is thinking about too when her eyes connect with mine.

I have two options here: I can walk away now that I've placed my mark over her. No one else will bother her.

Or…

I can continue exactly what I'm doing now. Of their own accord, I run my hands up her hips to the curve of her waist feeling every sensual dip and bend. We were both kids all those years ago. Now, she's a woman and she feels like it.

Every prior interaction leading to this leads me to believe she'll shoo me away. But when her head falls back against my shoulder, I take that as an invitation to keep going. Our bodies move in sync to the beat of "Heart of Glass" by Blondie, swaying and curving as one. All the while my own pelvis meets her perfect ass that I could take a bite out of in this enticing outfit. My skin is on fire everywhere we touch. Her breathing becomes shallow and I suddenly wish she was facing me so I could slip a knee between her legs while we dance and tease her more.

This moment is everything I've dreamed of and more. A moment where a crack in her walls lets me slip by. A moment where she lets me in just a little. A moment to remind her how synchronized we are.

And then the song ends and the moment shatters like glass. Something clicks in her brain and I feel the change take over her mind and body as reality sets in. I'm not sure what has her looking so freaked out, is she that afraid of me? It's like the moment in the elevator only amplified.

Rosie jerks out of my hold as if I electrocuted her with my touch, sparing only a glance before rushing away.

I can't let her walk away, though. Maybe I should, a better man would. But I'm a flawed addict desperate to understand, desperate to tell her this isn't something to fear.

Bypassing the VIP lounge, Rosie heads for the narrow corridor leading to the restrooms. That's where I finally get my hand around her elbow and stop her from continuing.

"Rosie," I plead. I don't know if it's the heartache in my voice that makes her halt or the spark of fear in her eyes when I touch her. But she takes the chance to rip her arm out of my grasp.

"I'm tired of chasing you," I confess. I'm tired of always running after her when she runs in fear. I'm tired of chasing what I know could be monumental.

"Then stop." My chest caves in at her words. "I can't keep doing this."

"I said I'm tired, I didn't say I'd ever stop. Because I know what you won't accept, you and I are meant for each other. Even if you didn't write our story that way."

Her furious gaze snaps to mine. I probably just shoved my foot in my mouth but it's been nagging at me for years.

"So that's what this is about," Rosie spits fire. "You can't let go of that stupid book and how I rewrote the story."

"No, that's not—."

"Sorry, Atlas. I don't care if your delicate male pride was damaged by my success or what I wrote. You just have to live with it."

Before I get a chance to explain what I meant, Rosie storms past me in a fit of rage back toward the dance floor. The closer I get to the VIP lounge, the more I recognize Chris's inebriated voice serenading us with Cher's "Believe" with surprising accuracy.

Apparently, someone set up Chris's favorite bar activity in our absence: karaoke.

Rosie already has her back to one of the support beams, arms crossed over her chest with barely dampened anger contorting her features.

When the song ends, Chris waves the microphone around calling, "Who's next?" No takers. Shocker. "Layla. You're up." He directs.

"I'm fine, Chris. Call on someone else."

With a pouty puppy dog face, Chris tilts his head toward Rosie. "Come on, Layla. You used to be fun."

A hush settles over our group. We all know sober Chris would have never said that. But his comment did the trick, because Rosie strides forward with assured steps as she takes the mic and enters a song into the computer.

I wait with bated breath in the back of the lounge, waiting to see what she picked. With Rosie's musical knowledge and skills, I'm sure she chose something to cut deep.

Sure enough, "Silver Spring" by Fleetwood Mac begins to play as the words appear on the screen.

I haven't heard her sing in five years, but Rosie's voice is just as hypnotic as I remember. Sultry in a way that captivates the listener. If only she'd pursued a musical career instead of a life of journalism.

Then again, if that were the case, we might have never met.

And I'd take the torture of her voice and this song combined over not knowing her any day.

Time cast a spell on you, but you won't forget me
I know I could've loved you, but you would not let me
I'll follow you down 'til the sound of my voice will haunt you
Give me just a chance
You'll never get away from the sound of the woman that loves you

The truth rings in the air: I'll never escape her. I owe more to her than I ever cared to admit in my youth.

And I've known for longer than I care to admit that I ruined what could have been the start of a great love. My own inability to process heavy emotions led to hurting the only girl I ever had a chance at loving.

I am in love with her. I'm in love with the woman she was and the woman she is now. I didn't realize how much I loved her until she was gone. That love has been the only thing holding me together.

As soon as the song ends, Rosie hands the microphone to Rob and stomps out of the VIP lounge, Kenzie on her tail.

It's time for the truth to come out. It's time for us to have the conversations we've been putting off.

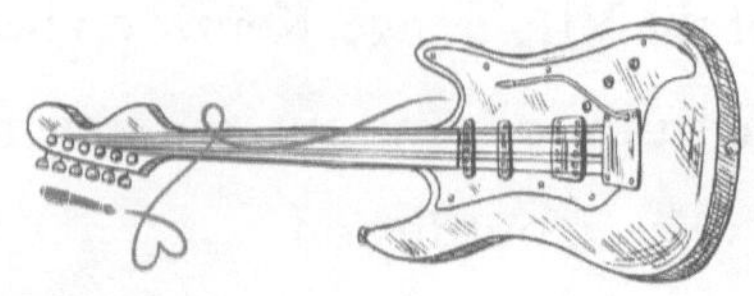

Thirty-Eight

Layla

NOTHING ELSE MATTERS-METALLICA

A very hungover Chris appeared at my door the next morning around 11am to apologize for his behavior. I'm guessing Cameron or McKenzie filled in the gaps in his memory.

It was easy to forgive him. That wasn't Chris, and he forgave me so easily when I came to him to apologize for my own behavior.

Then Kenzie was the next to show up with gummy bears and an ice cream bar from the hotel lobby. All I really wanted was to be alone but her time on the tour was so limited, I couldn't pass up the opportunity to spend some of it with her, just us girls.

Like the kind-hearted best friend she is, she didn't pry too much into the events of last night. She simply asked if I was ok and then proceeded to give me all the filthy details about her night with Cam.

It breaks my heart to hear how much she misses him when he's on the road. So much of their relationship has been spent apart, but they've also had the opportunities to pursue their careers. He doesn't get upset when she works late because he's on the road. And when he's on the road she loads her work schedule more.

Yet they've established a well oiled routine for when he's home so they can be present in each other's lives as much as possible.

Aside from my aversion to deep emotions and personal connections, I haven't allowed myself the luxury of a relationship in a very long time because I knew most people would want more than I could offer. My career has been my constant companion, the soul focus of my energy. There wasn't enough room for another human being.

But seeing how well Cameron and McKenzie balance their time, relationship, and careers is rather inspiring. Maybe one day, with the right partner, I could find someone to coexist with.

Two more weeks on the road did nothing to lessen the tension between Atlas and I. By the time we reach Texas, I'm ready for more privacy and distance from him. We haven't interacted more than "excuse me" as we passed each other on the bus or "pass the salt."

While no one has confirmed it, I believe with every fiber of my being that the tour manager planned the Texas shows for this day in particular.

Five years since Dallas's death and the guys are playing in his hometown, his namesake.

We all give each other the space we need after two weeks of bunk beds and meal rotations on the bus. No one comes to my door in the hotel and we all meet in the lobby in time for the security team to transfer us to the venue.

Though I have a feeling that the low energy and lack of conversation has more to do with the anniversary of Dallas's death than with our need for space.

No one speaks in the SUV on the way to the venue, no one communicates more than necessary backstage as they gear up and finish sound check. The crowd is just as ecstatic as usual but the guys are too weighed down by their thoughts to feed off the energy.

"Hey," Atlas finds me standing against an extra speaker working on my tablet. "Come here for a sec." It's the most we've spoken since Miami, but the tone in his voice has me following with rampant curiosity.

Atlas leads me to two people standing near the stage entrance, something about them becomes increasingly more familiar with each foot I cross to close the gap between us. The older woman looks at me with kind eyes I can't place until her husband turns my way and the resemblance shocks my system.

I haven't seen Dallas's parents since his memorial. And even then, I didn't speak to them. I kept my distance.

The first and last time I spoke to them was when I called to notify them their son had died in a car accident. That kind of memory haunts you forever. The minute Dallas's mother speaks, her voice takes me back to the shrieks that echoed through the phone when I gave her the morbid news.

"Layla," she says softly. "It's so good to see you again." For a moment I fear this gentle woman is about to pull me in for a motherly hug I won't be able to stomach, but all she does is run a hand up and down my arm in a soothing manner.

"It's good to see you two. Both of you." I don't actually mean that, it hurts too much to see them. But it's the polite thing to say. The sting of my lie is soothed by the gentle smile she and her husband give me.

Turning to Atlas, Dallas's father says, "Thank you so much for inviting us. We're glad we could be here today."

"We're honored to have you," Atlas replies. "It's the first time we've performed on this day since our first tour. So we have a little tribute planned for him."

"That's so thoughtful of you." There are no tears in the woman's eyes, but I hear the sob caught in her throat. I make a mental note not to look at her whenever this tribute occurs otherwise I'll lose it.

The concert goes according to plan, everything on schedule, and the crowd goes crazy for the set list.

Then it comes time for the cover song of the night, the final song. I'm as much in the dark as everyone else as to what they have planned for tonight. Which is why I'm surprised to see the screen behind the guys illuminate with more than just their logo which usually presides behind the band during the concert.

Broken Compass is known for their music and ability to transcend the audience during live performances. They don't do flashy set designs or dance numbers because they want the music to speak for itself. So I'm unprepared for the moment photos of Dallas and the band from years ago start popping up on screen starting from a time before I knew them.

"Five years ago today, we lost a great man," Atlas speaks into the microphone while Cam strums a subtle melody on the guitar. "He helped make Broken Compass what it is today. So—in the city he called home—we'd like to honor him in our own special way." Atlas raises his guitar pick to the heavens. "Dallas, this one's for you. We miss you every day, brother."

To accompany the slideshow of memories, the band begins to play "Nothing Else Matters" by Metallica and my heart physically cracks down the center. It's such a simple tribute but it speaks volumes if you know your music history.

The song grows more tense with each verse, each note, and my chest begins to feel like an anvil is pressing in further after each chorus. I can barely take it when photos *I* took of Dallas begin to appear on the screen. Polaroids, digital, film. I can't recall if I gave them to the guys or if they went far enough back on social media to find them. Either way, I'm grateful now more than ever that I captured those little moments.

Once upon a time, I was teased for lugging a camera around with me and taking photos of the most mundane moments. But it's times such as this that remind me—remind others—why these memories captured in time are so valuable.

In so many ways, this is a beautiful tribute to their fallen friend, to someone who was taken far too soon from this world. Yet simultaneously it cuts deep. Every moment is another reminder that Dallas should be here but a drunk idiot stole him from us.

My therapist said I never fully dealt with his death and the connected emotions because of the events that followed it. And she's right. I haven't dealt with it.

I wonder if this is how the guys have dealt with it. Through music.

"Dallas always said you put them on the map," his mother leans into my side, offering her comfort. "He would be so proud to see how far they've come. To see that they never gave up. And he'd be glad you're here to witness it."

She's right, Dallas had the same kind spirit and gentle love for everyone his mother does. But hearing her say it only drives the blade deeper into my chest.

There are days I wonder what would have happened if Kenzie and I hadn't left early. Would one of us have offered to drive? Would we have hurried the guys along so no one would have been in that intersection when the driver ran the red light?

I've done enough research on deaths in the music industry to know that's survivors guilt eating away at me. But it's hard not to fixate on the *what-ifs* when they might have changed everything.

I know the band would have blown up regardless, they were on track while Dallas was still alive to reach this level of fame and success. But what would have been different if he was still here, playing with the band?

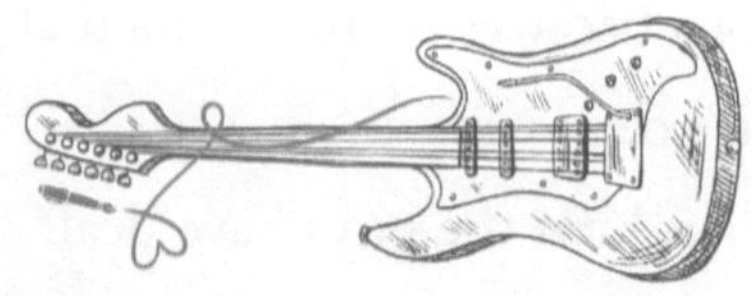

Thirty-Nine
Layla

CHANGES-**B**LACK **S**ABBATH

A hot shower barely burns away some of the pent up emotion from the concert. I feel like I could drown in fire and it still wouldn't be enough.

Just after climbing into my sleep shorts and t-shirt, a knock reverberates at my door. I have a pretty good idea of who it is, but I open the door anyway to see Atlas's somber expression staring back at me.

Everything about his body language is different than I've ever seen. He looks vulnerable, defeated, desperate.

"Can we call a truce?" The plea in his voice ignites a need to comfort him that I can't shake. So I nod my head once and step aside to let him in. After closing the door he informs me in a hushed tone, "I don't want to be alone."

I didn't realize I needed company tonight either until he walked in. I thought all I ever needed was solitude to cope in private. But there is so much we've been putting off, maybe tonight is the night to call a truce and heal some old wounds. Until now, we've been tense, I've been hostile, and that isn't an effective way to communicate. There's no better day than today to work on things.

It's what Dallas would have wanted.

I curl my legs beneath me on the bed, leaning back against the mound of pillows, while Atlas takes a seat in one of the armchairs in the little sitting area. We just sit like that for a while, occupying the same space and letting the silence speak for us. Or maybe we're just getting comfortable since we haven't really spent this much time in private together since reuniting.

Finally, I extend the first olive branch and break the silence. "The tribute you guys performed was beautiful."

Atlas finally looks at me so I can see the sheen coating his eyes. "It seemed fitting, although nothing ever really feels like enough for him."

"I know what you mean." My hands ache so I massage the palms in my lap, one after the other. "Sometimes I feel guilty that I'm still here. I wonder what would have changed if Kenzie and I had stayed instead of leaving before you guys."

A beat of weighted silence passes before Atlas utters, "I always wonder what would have happened if I had driven that night." My breath stops at that. "I was in the passenger seat. I watched it all happen. My mind plays tricks on me sometimes and slows it down so I see every excruciating moment of it."

Air clogged in my chest, pulse racing, heart crumbling. I listen because there's nothing else I can do.

"I saw the headlights coming for us and shouted his name...but it was too late."

"You know it's not your fault, right?" I need him to know that. I need him to relinquish that burden. "The guy responsible is still in jail."

"Logically, I do. But we drew picks for who had to drive home. If one of so many things had gone differently that night, maybe he'd still be here. Maybe I wouldn't have to feel guilty every time one of our songs makes the top ten, or we hit another milestone in our careers, I feel guilty that he's not here to share in it with us."

"He's credited on the first album, do his parents get his royalties?"

A real smile—however faint—graces Atlas's face. "Yeah. They keep donating it to different charities, though. So the guys and I paid off their house after that first year. They're simple people who don't want a fancy life. They just want the house they raised their son in and to honor him in whatever way they can."

Tears well in the corner of my eyes. "They sound like the kind of people who raised Dallas to be the compassionate guy he was."

"Yeah." Atlas smiles again as his mind wanders to a memory or thought that takes him out of the present. Atlas knew him longer, they shared a lot. But I like to think that I still got to see the best parts of Dallas. Only because he was gracious enough to show them to everyone. He didn't reserve kindness for his closest friends. He offered it freely to anyone he met, including me.

Seemingly out of nowhere, Atlas rises from the chair and slowly approaches the bed, keeping his eyes fixated on the opposite side of the bed where he lands. He sits on the edge, bending one knee to balance himself as he turns slightly to face me.

"I owe you the truth, Layla." If it weren't for the severity of the conversation, his use of my first name would have clued me in that this was an important conversation.

"I was a mess after Dallas died. You know that better than anyone. And I had to keep it all together. I put the pressure of our success on myself because I didn't want to be a one hit wonder. If we didn't make it, then what was the point of it all? It almost would have been like Dallas died in vain."

I wait with baited breath for whatever he has to say next. I can see the anxiety rolling around in his eyes as he figures out how to word whatever it is he has to tell me.

"Do you remember Dana Bohem?"

Involuntarily, my eyes roll to the back of my head at the mention of that insidious woman. While I can appreciate a woman putting her career first and establishing her place in power, I've never orchestrated people like puppets to get to where I am.

"What about her?"

The pressure in Atlas's chest loosens with a sigh. "I've never told anyone this, not even the guys. But she was coercing me to sleep with her."

"*What?*" The expletive leaves my mouth before I can think better of it.

Atlas nods once, eyes turning away in shame. "In negotiation meetings to establish our contract, she was always very polite and professional. Then, one day, she cornered me after a meeting and asked me to come back to the office later that evening and she gave me an ultimatum. Come to her beck and call or she wouldn't sign us."

Without thinking, I scoot closer to Atlas on the bed, resting my hand atop his to offer whatever comfort I can.

"Atlas," his name escapes on a whisper. "How long did this go on for?"

"Years. I put my foot down after Dallas died but she said that with one member of the band gone, she had every right to terminate the contract, or at least renegotiate which would mean canceling the tour. And I couldn't do that to the guys. I couldn't do that to Dallas. What would be the point if we lost our chance after he was gone?"

From this close, I can see the tear streaks on his tan face tracing random patterns down his cheek. The air grows heavy with the weight of his confession lifting from his shoulders. All these years, he's been harboring this secret. All that time that he gave up his dignity and his body for the sake of a dream. If it was just him, I know Atlas would have never agreed to Dana's terms. But he wasn't sacrificing himself for selfish reasons, he didn't want to take away what might have been their only chance at success.

"Do you want to know the last thing Dallas said to me in the car?" I don't think I do because I know it will wreck me. But I need to know at the same time.

A shaking breath leaves Atlas in a staccato pattern. "He said 'This is the best night of my life.' And I knew it was all worth it to see the happiness in one of my best friends. Two seconds before his life ended."

Trying to hold back my cries only leads to my chest caving in on itself. So I do something I haven't in a very long time and initiate contact as I wrap myself around Atlas and hold him. Without hesitation, he embraces me with both arms, silently sobbing into my hair. We just hold one another for a lifetime in an attempt to heal the wounds that have been festering so deeply beneath the surface.

Weaving his fingers into my hair, Atlas holds me close as he says, "I'm so sorry for what I did to you. I wanted to run after you the second it was over and grovel at your feet. But I was broken and tainted and I didn't know what to do. So I let you go, thinking that was best for everyone.

"But it wasn't, Rosie. We need each other. Maybe I'm a selfish man for expecting you to forgive me because I can't let you go. But I don't care. I've known you were mine before I ever got the chance to be the man you deserve."

As much as we needed this—as much as I needed to hear it—I'm crushed with the knowledge that all of the events that transpired could have been avoided. Broken Compass could have been a massive success with Dallas still alive and Atlas and I could have fallen in love a million times over by now.

But I guess no success story is without skeletons. No love is uncomplicated.

And while I may not ever understand it, everything has led us here for a reason.

I see things with more clarity than before. His confession leads me toward forgiveness for Atlas. But I still have my own secrets to share if we are ever to move forward.

It's been a long night and I'm sure Atlas isn't ready for more confessions.

"Do you want to spend the night here?" Asking Atlas to spend the night feels the same as asking the girls in my second grade class to come to my birthday party. "Nothing too...intimate. But if you don't want to sleep alone tonight, you don't have to."

A crack forms in his controlled exterior, letting the soft light of his broken heart through. With a sweet smile he nods. "Yeah. I'd like that."

As we crawl under the covers and drift to sleep, his hand finds mine beneath the blankets.

He's still holding my hand when I wake in the morning.

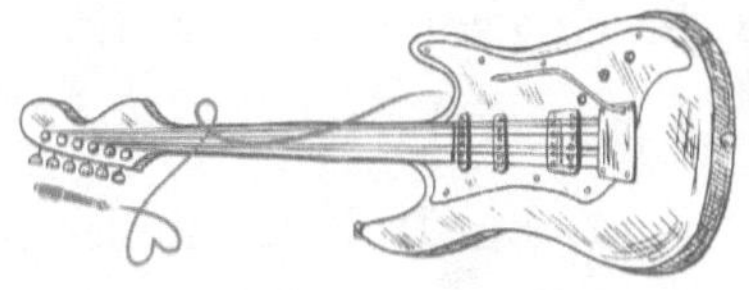

Forty
Layla

STAY-RHIANNA

Atlas doesn't rise when I wake or shower *or* get dressed. He must have needed sleep more than I realized. I can't imagine the burden that's been lifted from his conscience after last night's revelations.

I leave him tucked in bed as I venture down to the lounge of the hotel in search of food. I'm seated at a table by myself consuming the omelet I ordered and answering emails on my phone when Rob pulls a chair out for himself to join me.

"Morning, Layla," he says in a bright voice.

"Good morning," I return the cheerful tone even if I feel an emotional hangover from last night. "Sleep well?"

Rob shrugs one shoulder. "Eh, it was kind of an emotional night. Hard to fall asleep after all that."

I thought about that last night, how hard it must be for Rob to play in a tribute to Dallas, to see the love the fans have for him even though Rob has spent more time in the spotlight. Anyone who pours their heart into their work knows that comparison can be a fickle bitch, never allowing you to feel satisfied.

"Do you mind if I ask you about last night? On the record?" He has every right to say no. But Rob just smiles politely and agrees. "What was it like for you to play a tribute for the guy you replaced? To see the way the fans reacted to it?"

Considering my question for a moment, Rob runs his hands over the day old stubble on his cheek. "One of the reasons I was willing to transition from being a session bassist to a permanent member of a touring band is because of the fans. Not like I wanted the fame and adoration. But because I saw how much the audience valued the *music* and the band themselves. Some fan bases feel hollow, ya know. Like they only care about the radio hits or the trends. These fans care about the music. And that's been kind of rare in the music industry lately."

It warms my heart to hear that Rob sees what I see. Broken Compass is more than just a one hit wonder. They speak to people on a deeper level which incites a connection between them and every person who is invested in their music.

"I guess, all that's to say, I'm glad I got to honor a guy who inspired some of that passion in the fans. This band wouldn't be what it is without him."

All I can think to offer is a smile. Words have evaded me more times on this tour than any other time in my life.

"There you are." I peer over Rob's shoulder to see Atlas approach in a fresh set of clothes. I suppose he went back to his room to change after sleeping in jeans all night.

"Hey man," Rob greets his friend as Atlas claps him in a brotherly manner on the shoulder. "Good timing, I was about to go order food from the kitchen and take it to my room. You can keep Layla company."

"You don't have to leave," Atlas assures him.

"Nah, I'm going to try and get some more sleep before the next show tonight. I'll see you guys later."

Atlas takes Rob's place in the chair adjacent to me. Now that he's closer to me, I can see the exhaustion lining his features despite the hours of sleep he got. He never slept that long on the bus. Either because we were on a fucking tour bus with a bunch of people making noise. Or because he needed to release some of his demons to find rest.

I fly home after the next show to start writing up the final article for *Rolling Stone*. There's no need for me to complete the entire tour. Which means I don't have much time to give Atlas some of the backstory he deserves. He wants to fall madly in love with a woman who doesn't exist anymore.

"Hey, do you want to go somewhere with me?"

Curious, Atlas scrunches his brows as he asks, "Like where?"

"I don't know. On a walk or to the park or something. Just out of a hotel room. Do you think you can look inconspicuous enough to get out of here?" He's too easily recognizable these days, especially when his face is plastered all over the local news and media detailing *Broken Compass's heart wrenching tribute to their fallen member.*

"Yeah, I think I can do that."

"Great. Let's sneak out the back."

After retrieving a hat and lightweight hoodie from his room, Atlas meets me at the back entrance of the hotel to sneak away. He still looks like himself, but unless you know to look for him, he blends into the crowd. Despite the fact that it's autumn in the rest of the country, Texas has yet to receive the memo from Mother Nature. The hoodie might seem out of the ordinary, but no one seems to pay attention as we walk down the street.

"I appreciate how honest and vulnerable you were with me last night," I begin. I don't really know how to explain how I spent my time over the last five years. Part of me doesn't want to tell him because I see how guilty he already feels. Knowing Atlas, he'll just blame himself for what I put myself through.

"I want you to know I forgive you," his steps falter hearing the words he's been so desperate for. But his pace resumes as he takes a chance and laces his fingers with mine. It feels so normal to walk like a couple down the street, holding hands. Only there's nothing normal about this.

"I could never put myself in your shoes and the impossible situations you were in. I think we both made mistakes. I should have spoken up. I shouldn't have let it get so far when I knew you were in pain. And instead of coping with it in a mature, rational way, I internalized everything."

We round a corner lined with towering bushes and come across a grassy lawn split down the center by a winding cement path.

"I handled my own emotions poorly, as I'm sure you're aware. But you don't know all of it." *Deep breath.* "I felt so used when I left you. I felt tainted, in a way. And looking back I know that was entirely wrong. But in an effort to bury all those feelings, I tried to find validation in other ways."

Atlas's hand tightens in my grasp, tensing in preparation as he listens patiently. I can only imagine the scenarios he's conjuring in his head. I doubt any of them are close to the truth.

"I spent the better part of the last five years sleeping around. *A lot.* I know you don't want to hear that but I need to explain. I was so lost. I was looking at everything all wrong and I didn't handle any of it right. I thought that through sex there was power. *I* got to choose who was inside me. I thought there was power in deciding what to do with my body, deciding who I did it with. But it always felt hollow."

Spotting an empty bench off the path, I tug Atlas toward it and ask, "Mind if we sit?" He doesn't speak, he just lets me lead him along so we sit side by side, thighs touching, hands still clasped, but I can't stand to look him in the eye as I confess this next part of the story.

"And then I got pregnant." I've never told a soul that, not even McKenzie. Dropping that bomb is a weight off my chest, though.

"Rosie." My name leaves his mouth on a whispered breath. "Do you have a kid?"

Swallowing my emotion I answer plainly, "No." I still don't know how to feel about this next part. "I was scared, I was focused on my career. I felt completely alone. My parents don't live close by so I wouldn't have any help. I was convinced I wasn't meant to be a mother and this was all a mistake. I was going to get an abortion but nature decided I wasn't ready to be a mom and I miscarried instead. It was…a traumatizing experience, to say the least. No one tells you what you'll have to go through when your body rejects a baby."

That's when Atlas maneuvers toward me, keeping my hands cocooned in his, as he looks longingly into my eyes with all the guilt I knew he'd place on himself.

"I am so sorry, Layla." He presses soft lips to the back of my hand. "I'm so sorry for everything I put you through."

"I don't blame you, Atlas. I need you to know that. There was a time when I hated you but it's taken a lot of therapy to work through it.

"The fucked up thing is that, after the miscarriage, I went right back to mindless sex with strangers only to realize I was an idiot. I spent too much time trying to find my worth in others when I should have been looking internally. That's when I started therapy and my therapist recommended I go one year without sex or relationships, one year of celibacy, to discover who I am past the trauma and the heartache and the physical attributes. It's been eleven months since I've been with anyone. Eleven months since I've been this close to another human being." I gesture with a hand between our chests. "And I've learned so much. I'm going to stick it out another month. So if you're willing to wait, then we can explore things further. But I owe it to myself to see this through."

"Layla Rose Grayson," he says with complete devotion, "I would wait a thousand lifetimes for you."

When his hand releases mine to brush his thumb over my cheekbone, I feel how much he wants to kiss me, I feel the charge between us. And I want so badly to give in. The first few months of this celibacy thing felt excruciating, like going through withdrawals. Gradually I started to see the value in it, felt the power in valuing my body and autonomy over short-term satisfaction.

But this moment with Atlas feels just as agonizing. I wish I could press my lips to his and seal this moment but I owe it to myself to continue. I've come too far to give up.

And if he's a man of his word, he'll wait for me.

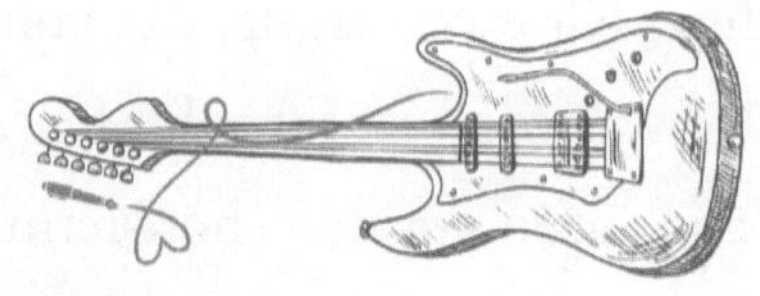

Forty-One
Layla

I Found—Amber Run

With the burdens of our secrets off the table, interacting with Atlas feels more like the dance we used to waltz through all those years ago. Flirtatious, playful, full of sexual tension. Which makes this no sex thing that much harder. Even being back in New York while the guys finish the second half of their tour.

I'm still pinching myself thinking I'll wake up from this fantasy that he so easily forgot about my past. Once the aching need to relapse and find someone to sleep with subsided, I was left with the sickening pit in my stomach that feeling defiled embeds there. I did this to myself, I made my own choices. But I still feel the acute layer of filth coating my skin from every single person who ever touched me when I should not have given them that right. I felt sullied, yet that didn't stop Atlas from telling me he still wanted me as much as he did five years ago.

The first thing I do in the morning now is check my phone, because I know there will be a "Good morning" text waiting for me from Atlas. But this morning the text reads differently.

> **ATLAS: Go open your door.**

Three minutes after sending he sends another text.

> **ATLAS: And good morning.**

Anxious excitement springs me out of bed. I throw a robe over myself and rush to the front door of my apartment. I swing the door open to find a beautiful bouquet of mixed flowers all in various hues of orange, red, and yellow, complete with roses that bare a sunset pattern. As I carry the vase inside, I pluck the card planted at the center of the bouquet from the plastic holder.

Before opening the card, I snap an artsy looking photo of me holding the flowers so my eyes peek over the top but the rest of my face is concealed and send it to Atlas. Then I tear into the envelope expecting to find a card with something sweet written inside. Instead, I find a plane ticket to Vegas for tomorrow afternoon, landing just in time for their next show.

I tap the little phone icon beside Atlas's name on my phone and set it to speaker as I wait for him to answer.

"I miss you," he says upon answering.

"Vegas? Tomorrow?" I reply. "And I miss you too."

"You can work on the plane and then take twenty-four hours away from answering emails to relax. Then we can fly back to LA like we planned."

In just a few days, I will have reached one year of celibacy. I didn't know how I'd feel about this milestone but I also didn't think I would have Atlas Woods back in my life. The first few months, I couldn't wait for this day so I could finally have sex again. But as time passed and I started to reevaluate my outlook on life, I thought that I would just treat myself to a spa day instead. I'd made the decision months ago that I didn't want to have sex again unless it was meaningful, unless it was with the right partner. I never imagined the man I've subconsciously been wanting all along would be waiting for me on the other side of this journey.

So after a lot of talking about it, we decided to take the week he and the band have off to feel out our relationship, spend time together without the rest of the guys and see where things lead. He's made it abundantly clear that if I'm not ready, he's willing to wait as long as I need.

But if I am, then—in his words—he'll "show me all the respect and love I deserve." A little jolt of electricity shot to my clit when he told me that over the phone. Even now I can hear the sultry, sleepy tone of his voice, the confidence in our relationship.

I've been making work my priority as a way to fill the void of human connection for too long. So it's an easy answer when I tell him, "I'll see you tomorrow night."

"Good. I can't wait." Even without seeing him on FaceTime, I can hear the smile in his voice.

"Where are you guys now? You left Colorado this morning, right?"

"Yeah. We should reach Vegas by midday tomorrow."

"Hey," Chris's voice sounds far away but I can hear his words over the phone. "It's getting cramped up there. You can't hog the lounge all morning. You'll have to go back to subtle sexting like the rest of us, dude."

Even though that's not what we're doing, I still giggle a little hearing Chris be Chris.

"I'll call you tonight," Atlas starts the process of saying goodbye.

"Alright, I'll talk to you then." There's that awkward space of time where I know we both want to fill the void with the three big words we've avoided. But instead we finish with our usual farewell: "Miss you."

"Miss you too, Rosie." Then the line goes dead.

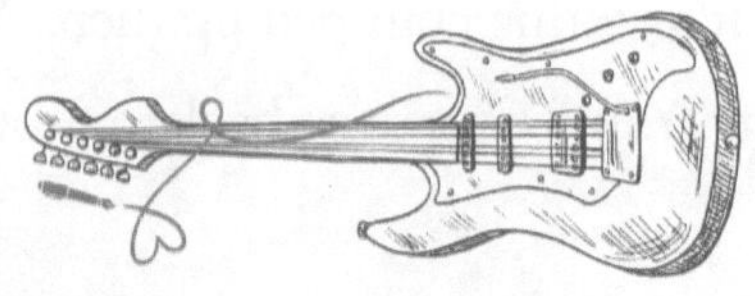

Forty-Two

Layla

IRIS-THE GOO GOO DOLLS

"We're getting married!" Kenzie greets me at the airport as soon as I walk into baggage claim toting my carry-on over one shoulder. I brace just in time for her to collide with me, arms cutting off my air supply by lassoing my neck.

Talking through a clenched jaw because she's hugging me so tight, I say, "Honey, I love you and all, but I think Cam would be pretty upset if I married you first."

Releasing me, McKenzie holds my shoulders with the biggest smile plastered across her face. "As much as you'd make a great wife, not today. Today, I'm marrying Cameron."

"As in...marrying him *today*? Like this will be your anniversary every year after?"

"Exactly!" I don't think I've ever seen my best friend this happy before. "I got in last night and we were talking about the wedding and realized neither one of us wants to plan a whole big bad wedding. And we don't want to wait anymore. All we want is a party with our best friends. So as much as I know Atlas is dying to see you, I'm stealing you away to go dress shopping before the show. Then after the show, *it's wedding time!*" She sing-songs the last bit with a little shimmy.

I just laugh, because what else is there to do besides get excited for my best friend to marry the love of her life.

And find her the perfect Vegas Wedding dress.

By the time I make it to the hotel, the guys are already at the venue for the concert. Though I realize checking in that I don't know the nuances of this arrangement. Are Atlas and I sharing a room? Or did he get me my own? How far ahead did he plan this?

Standing in the lobby with my bag over my shoulder and my suitcase propped beside me, I dial Atlas.

"Hey," he answers immediately. I hear a bit of the hustle and bustle behind him as people finish setting up all the equipment. "Are you here?"

"I'm dropping my stuff off at the hotel." I explain. "Um, did you get me a room or are we sharing one?" Why does this feel so awkward to ask?

I'm preparing what probably would have been a rambling speech about being able to roll with whatever his plan is, but Atlas saves me the embarrassment with a well thought out answer.

"I was hoping you'd spend it with me, obviously with a safe distance and boundaries already established. But if you aren't comfortable with that, the front desk has our card information so you can order a room for yourself. Whatever makes you most comfortable."

His respect for me makes the decision that much easier.

"Thank you," I say with genuine appreciation. And just to leave him hanging a bit I finish the conversation with, "I'll see you in a bit."

Then I walk over to the front desk and ask for a key to the room for Atlas's alias name. "Hi, I'm the second party checking into the room for Art Vandelay."

I don't think I've ever seen Atlas smile as broadly as he does during the drudgery walk to close the distance between us backstage. It's bright and effervescent, filled with more delight than I even see when he's on stage. As soon as I'm within reach, he pulls me into a hug full of promise and comfort.

"I missed you," I inhale his scent as I nuzzle my nose into his neck.

"I missed you too." I swear he does the same, committing every ounce of this interaction to memory. Pulling away from me but keeping an arm slung over my shoulders, we walk toward the rest of the band. "I'm glad you came."

Narrowing suspicious eyes on him, I ask Atlas, "How long have you been keeping the wedding secret from me?"

Glancing at an imaginary watch on his wrist, Atlas replies, "Oh, about thirty-six hours. Surprised?"

Taking my eyes off him to observe Cam laying with his head in McKenzie's lap while she runs nimble fingers through his hair, my answer is simple. "Not really. This makes sense for them."

"Couldn't agree more."

After the concert is over and the guys tip the crew extra since they have to bail early, we all change into our Vegas chapel wedding attire in the green rooms (except Kenzie who is waiting to surprise Cameron with her look) and pile into the security vehicles bound for the Las Vegas strip. Even the security team must be excited since they put a bottle of champagne in the car for us. But without flutes to pour it in, we pass it around like the pack of wild animals we are.

In truth, we don't need alcohol to feel the intoxicating effects of this monumental occasion. The beautiful thing about soul deep friendships is their happy moments become your happy moments. I can't think of a time I've been more excited than right now, seeing people I call family celebrate the love of two incredible human beings.

Forgoing the Elvis impersonator officiant, a woman in a feminine gray suit stands at the front of the chapel waiting for her cue to begin. Cam managed to find a deep burgundy suit last minute that fits his tall, lean frame. He stands at the altar with the officiant, chatting with Chris and Rob who sit on the groom's side (even though we are all here for both of them) while Atlas and I sit on the bride's side to balance the space out. An assistant waits in the back with a camera to capture the service.

But my best friend deserves more, so I brought my Polaroid camera and gave it to the assistant to snap a photo of the newlyweds walking back up the aisle.

After a knock sounds on the door, the assistant hits a button on her phone to queue the music before pressing a button on the wall to automatically open both baby pink doors, revealing the glowing bride behind them.

McKenzie stands tall and proud in the satin mini dress that hugs her bust while the tulip skirt gives her a feminine figure. The ensemble is complete with white gloves, red heels, and a bouquet of red and white silk roses held just in front of her belly button. A short—albeit tacky but cute—veil sits nestled at the back of her head. She's Vegas wedding chic.

As the music progresses, McKenzie ascends the aisle with all the grace and poise of a model until she comes to stand at the altar where she passes her bouquet to me, freeing her hands to hold Cam's.

It's a short, simple service, no eloquent filigree about love or reciting poetry. Just the bare minimum to make this shindig legal. As the Officiant begins to ask, "Cameron, do you take McKenzie to be your lawfully wedded wife?" I reach for Atlas's hand beside me and squeeze.

"I do."

"And do you McKenzie take Cameron to be your lawfully wedded husband?"

"I do." She's practically vibrating with giddy anticipation.

"Then by the power vested in me by the state of Nevada, I now pronounce you husband and wife. You may kiss the bride."

Cameron and McKenzie don't waste any time as they eagerly reach for one another, falling face first into a passionate kiss before Cam dips his new bride for the camera.

The four of us erupt in applause and hollers, I'm bouncing up and down with excitement. And just as planned, Cam and Kenzie jaunt back up the aisle, hands bound, with the brightest smiles on their elated faces. The flash of the camera goes off before I hear it print out the Polaroid and the assistant hands it to me while the newly married couple kiss again, completely incapable of separating.

Happiness looks different for every person. Some people look forward to the elaborate weddings with a bouquet toss, a large crowd, and lots of dancing. But for Kenzie and Cam, it looks like a first dance under the moonlight while Atlas plays "Iris" by the Goo Goo Dolls on an acoustic guitar.

And it couldn't be more perfect.

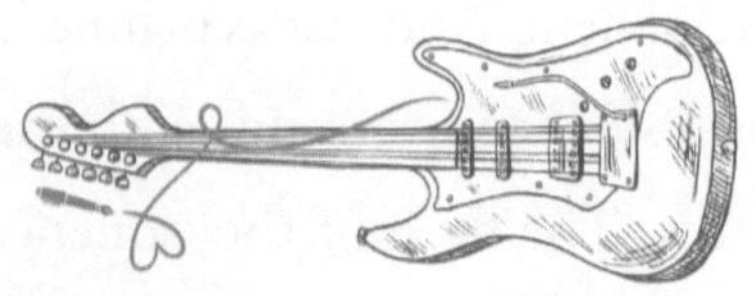

Forty-Three
Layla

THEN CAME THE MORNING-THE LONE BELLOW

We don't make it back to the hotel until 3am but no one is complaining. The memories made tonight celebrating our friends are worth every hour of missed sleep.

It helps that the band has a week off before their next show which means everyone gets to sleep in.

As Atlas and I ride the elevator to the top floor, he keeps his hands securely in his pockets.

"So," he angles his body off the wall of the elevator toward me, "what did you decide."

I know exactly what he's asking. Part of me wants to toy with him a bit longer, but instead I smile and say, "We've spent enough time apart. I don't want to miss any more nights with you."

The ding alerts us we've arrived at the top floor as the doors peel open. Taking the first step forward, Atlas extends a hand for me that I gladly take as we walk forward. Tomorrow is one year of celibacy. And I'll be damned if I break my streak before accomplishing my goal.

We walk hand in hand toward the room. Once we're inside, Atlas makes himself comfortable by tugging his wallet and phone from his back pocket to discard on the little table by the door. Then he slips his black Vans off.

This is uncharted territory for us. The night he stayed in my hotel room, I was already showered and changed. And he just slept in the clothes he was wearing. This feels far more domestic. What's the routine? Does he shower before bed? I know I do. What does he sleep in? I brought shorts and an oversized t-shirt for the sake of keeping things PG.

Wait, what side of the bed does he sleep on?

As if reading my thoughts, Atlas asks, "Do you have a side of the bed?"

I look at the king size bed made with crisp edges and the fluffiest pillows known to man. "The left," I answer.

"Fine by me. I'll take the right."

Atlas starts digging through his bag so nonchalantly, so carefree.

"Do you normally sleep on the right?" I ask.

He laughs. "I normally sleep on a tour bus. At this point, I can sleep anywhere."

He has a fair point.

"Do you want to use the bathroom first?" I should have known he'd be a gentleman about all of this. If there's one thing Atlas has fought the hardest to prove, it's his respect for me.

"Yes, please. I won't be too long."

I overthink everything in regards to if I should wear my hair in the braid I always do which isn't sexy, or down which means it will get in my face. Should I break out my silk pillowcase or is it too soon to appear that extra?

As for the t-shirt I packed, it took ages for me to decide. I went back and forth wondering if he'd read into it, but I prefer to sleep in my Broken Compass shirt that I got at the first concert of theirs I attended. I hope he finds it endearing instead of groupie behavior.

I emerge from the bathroom acting as if I'll be going to sleep by myself, unattractive hairstyle and all, with the exception of using the good body wash and lotion I packed so I smell decadent.

"All yours," I tell Atlas who's lounging on the bed looking at his phone.

When he peers up and takes in my appearance, a reminiscent smile graces his face.

"Wow, I haven't seen one of those shirts in a long time."

Toying with the hem I respond, "I've had it for years. It's by far the most comfortable."

Atlas walks over to me as though he's about to pass me but stops to massage the material of the sleeve between his fingers. Then his knuckles graze my arm, sending goose flesh down to my toes.

"It looks good on you." Then he disappears into the bathroom.

I'm relieved when he returns later in a pair of boxers and a gray t-shirt. If he'd been shirtless, I might have lost all self control. But I should have known he'd keep things modest for me.

I'm already laying in bed when he slips under the covers on his side, keeping three feet of space between us like no man's land.

As if extending a life preserver, he slides a hand into the open space while turned on his side toward me. I don't give myself time to think about it before reaching my hand out for his. Our fingers lace together and I watch as his thumb gently strokes my own.

What now?

"So," he breaks the awkward silence, even though we should probably be sleeping. "What have you learned over the past year?"

Sighing, I reply, "Do you really want to know?" This conversation could get very deep.

"I wouldn't ask if I didn't want to know."

I can't see his face in the dark but I can see our hands between us, his thumb now tracing circles over the edge of my palm.

"I've learned quite a bit about myself. I've learned that it's important to feel your feelings and burying them only creates more problems. I've learned to value my time and energy more. As well as the genuine connections I make with people.

"And I've learned I don't trust easily. Which can be good and bad. But ultimately, it's a survival tactic."

"What do you mean?" I picture his brows pinching together in the darkness.

"Aside from not trusting people to form those genuine connections with them, my therapist pointed out I never put myself in what could be considered dangerous situations with men. I never spent the night. Never gave my full name. Never let any of them restrain me..." that last admission hangs between us like a grenade without a pin. "I never trusted anyone enough to try it."

"Is that something you'd want to do?"

Are we really having this conversation? I guess it makes sense. "I've been curious. But every time I thought I'd want to try it, I didn't feel comfortable." A beat of silence passes before I ask, "Have you ever tied a girl up?"

"Can't say I have," he answers. I don't know if I'm relieved or not to hear that.

"What about you? Do you have any fantasies? Anything you want to try one day?" I don't want to be the only one confessing intimate details.

"Rosie, I've thought about you for the last five years and a million ways I want to make you come. So yes, I've got fantasies. But we have plenty of time to explore them later."

Well fuck if that doesn't make this final night of celibacy even more excruciating.

"You wanna know what I think?"

I don't know, do I? "Hmm?"

"I think you've proven yourself to be capable of healing and growing, and not a lot of people are. I think you're strong for making the tough decisions. I also think you've been dimming yourself to protect your heart. But you have us back, Rosie. I'll treat your heart with the gentlest care. I promise. And so will your friends."

I think that heart might be melting at his words. I never imagined I'd find love like this. Tonight, lying near Atlas while our hands are joined and my heart is flayed open for him, I realize that's what this is.

Love.

Using every ounce of that strength he mentioned, I scoot to his side of the bed and curl into his chest as his arms instinctively wrap around me.

I've also learned that intimacy isn't just sexual, it's emotional. The two are not mutually exclusive.

Falling asleep in Atlas's warm embrace—no sex—might be one of the most intimate experiences of my life.

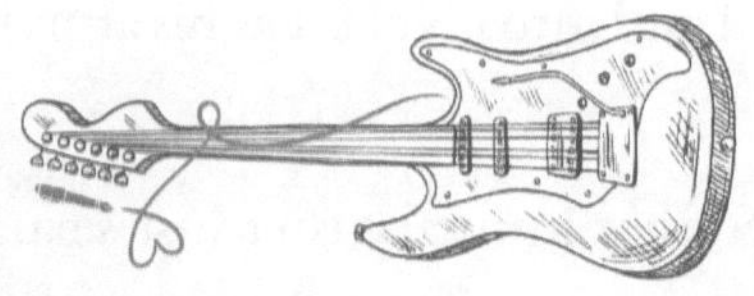

Forty-Four
Layla

Like A Virgin-Madonna

I'm scrolling through the collage of photos from Kenzie and Cam's Vegas wedding on the Broken Compass social media page when the security vehicle comes to a stop.

The PR team waited until the newlyweds were safely out of the country for their short honeymoon before announcing to the world that Cameron Carmichael was officially off the market. While the happy couple jetted off to Bora Bora for a week of secluded bliss, the rest of us parted ways for some respective downtime. In the words of Rob, "After this long on a bus together, I can't wait to not see your faces for a week."

The sentiment was shared, except when Atlas and I slid into the car together, he pressed a quick peck to my cheek and said, "I can't wait for a week with just you." And that was the extent of our physical contact aside from holding hands on the drive to his house.

Said house sits right outside this car. Atlas told me he bought this house after the first tour and never bothered to upgrade to something fancier since it was just him living here. Since property sale records are public information, and intense fans have access to the internet, he's had to upgrade the security. But other than that it remains remotely the same as when he bought it.

In the midst of mansions and private beach access, a quaint classic style beach house sits before me. Complete with a manicured lawn, native plant life, and a deep almost black shade of gray to make it feel slightly more masculine. I even spot a tower on the second floor that stands taller than the roof. It's not what I ever would have pictured for Atlas, I would have expected something more modern and simplistic. But somehow, I can see it now. I can see him sitting on the balcony of the master bedroom playing guitar and writing music for the wind.

The man in question slips his hand into mine as he leads me toward the front entrance, rolling my suitcase behind him.

The inside isn't beachy and airy like most of the houses in this neighborhood, it's cozy and welcoming. The style of decor is somewhere between mid century modern and cottage chic. Warm tones add an inviting aura to the space making me feel at home already. I can't put my finger on it but something about the house feels distinctly *Atlas.*

All the records the band has released so far are framed on the wall of the foyer so there is no doubt in your mind who's house you just entered.

"Come on, there's something I want to show you." Atlas leads the way as we pass a luxurious sitting room, a dining room set for twelve, and a spectacular kitchen on our way to a wide set of stairs leading to the second level. Atlas doesn't bother to show me the bedrooms or point out the bathrooms as he pulls me along to the door at the end of the hall. The second I step into the octagonal space, I know we're in the tower I saw from the outside. If the tall ceiling didn't give it away, the bay windows would.

But what I'm most struck by is the impressive collection of vinyl records stored on shelves lining every wall that doesn't contain a window. It appears Atlas had custom shelving units built to not only perfectly store vinyl records in an upright position, but also to cover every part of the walls a window doesn't occupy. Not an inch goes unused.

The room is complete with a vintage record player set into a small table beside a plush olive sofa that looks like it would envelop you like a cloud. It's the perfect space to get lost in music and find yourself.

"Atlas," his name escapes on a breath. "This is..."

"My favorite place in the world." He finishes for me. "I've wanted to show you this room since I bought the house."

"It's perfect."

Leisurely, I stroll the perimeter of the room examining the organized shelves, admiring how much his collection has grown. He's come a long way since the cube shelves in the living room of the tiny apartment the guys shared.

I make a point to stop in the L section and stroke my finger along the spine of the Led Zeppelin IV record, relieved he still hasn't found Led Zeppelin II.

"With all of our traveling, I've had a lot of opportunities to visit small record shops all over the world." Watching Atlas gaze at his collection with a sense of appreciation is remarkable. "As you can see, I've added a lot to the collection over the years."

"If you're not careful, I might spend the whole week in here," I tease. Although, something tells me Atlas wouldn't mind that.

As his gaze settles on me, I see the moment his mind turns from his record collection to the reminder of why we're here in the first place. He takes calculated steps toward me like a predator cornering its prey. And I welcome it, I'll gladly stay ensnared in Atlas's trap.

But instead of caging me against the wall of records like I expected, he shows a massive amount of self control as he stays one foot away from me. Close enough to hear the pounding of my heart, but not close enough to feel the rise and fall of my chest.

Tauntingly slow, Atlas pulls a small velvet box from his pocket. Any other girl would assume it's a diamond ring based on the size of the box, but I know better. I know he wouldn't wait all this time just to rush things.

And I know he doesn't want to scare me away.

"What's this?" I ask as the box transfers from Atlas to me in the small space between us.

Not waiting for him to reply, I tip the lid back on the jewelry box to find an engraved guitar pick on a silver chain. Two triangles with one side together almost in the shape of a diamond.

"Happy one year of celibacy, Rosie." If I didn't already think it was a sentimental gift, I would after hearing his explanation. "Through your highs and your lows," he points at the triangles pointing in opposite directions, "I'll be with you every step of the way."

Blinking back the mist coating my eyes, I look into the dark, soulful gaze of the man I love before pushing onto my toes, leaning into his chest, and pressing my trembling lips to his.

This man loves me, there's no doubt in my mind about it. Even if we haven't exchanged the words yet, they aren't needed to feel what his actions are saying. He'll be with me until the very end, loving me every step of the way.

With so much build up toward this moment, I was worried it wouldn't feel natural, I was worried I'd feel uncomfortable being intimate with someone again. But that couldn't be farther from the truth. I feel like I'm home. Atlas is the harbor I've been searching for, even if he's the one who also sent me into rough waters.

Tenderly, his hands cradle my jaw until one slips to the nape of my neck, tangling with my wavy hair. Meanwhile, the other skims down my side to my hip, keeping me steady as he finally walks me back against the wall so my body is pressed into his. I feel the passion in every taut line of his body, the tension of years waiting for this moment.

This moment is something we've never had. We've had an orchestrated kiss in front of thousands of people. We've shared our grief in a carnal way. But we've never had a kiss like this that felt untainted, pure, magical. It feels like we've been drowning and we finally breach the surface to breathe one another in. He's my oxygen, and I'm his blood. We need one another to survive.

Breathless and desperate, Atlas pulls away first with a sigh as though it's agony to do so.

"I don't want to rush this." Even though it makes perfect sense and I should be grateful for the consideration, a twinge of disappointment deflates my chest. "I want you more than anything, but only at your own speed. I want to make you dinner first. I want to spend time with you without four other people in the same room." We both chuckle at that. "And I want you to tell me what you're comfortable with."

I dip my head to his chest with a rush of air leaving my lungs and reply, "That sounds lovely." Then my head snaps up with a quizzical expression. "You can cook?"

Atlas laughs. "I can make pasta. And that's about it. The rest of the week I have a meal service set up."

"You really have thought of everything."

"I've had a lot of time to plan this."

And there goes my racing heart again.

"And this is my room." Atlas finishes the tour of his house in the master bedroom beside the music room.

Keeping the same decorative style as the rest of the house, it's chic but inviting, a balanced blend of dark neutrals and warmth.

The room isn't excessively large but there is enough room for a few pieces of furniture. But my eyes immediately fixate on the king sized bed and the solid metal frame. I didn't think much about where I would break my celibacy, or how. I considered finding a random stranger at the beginning of this journey.

But now that I'm standing in Atlas's bedroom facing the very place we're going to have sex, it feels like my first time all over again.

Would Madonna's "Like A Virgin" be too inappropriate at a time like this? Because that's how I feel.

"The closet's in there," he points to a closed sliding door on the right. "And the bathroom is through here." The open door on the left reveals a massive walk-in shower with multiple shower heads that spray in every direction.

"I have something for you as well." Digging through my suitcase I find the record I've been holding onto for three years cushioned between all my clothes. Thankfully it didn't suffer any damage in transit.

It's not wrapped, but I hand the Led Zeppelin II album to Atlas feeling awfully pleased with myself. This is a full circle moment. I'm thanking my past self for deciding to purchase the record when I came across it even though there was no promise of seeing Atlas again.

Maybe I understood what he meant by the records choose him. Because I couldn't physically leave that record store without it.

"Rosie," he stares at the album with bewilderment. "When did you get this? Where?"

It's cute how he wants to know the stories behind all his albums.

"I found it in a record store outside of Austin about three years ago. I can't explain it, but I knew I had to get it. I didn't think I'd ever see you again or even *want* to give this to you, but the record had other ideas and insisted on going home with me that day."

Atlas sets the record on his dresser, out of the way, before facing me head on, leaving too much space for my liking.

If he expects me to be the one to make the first move, he's mistaken. I feel like a virgin navigating the complex dance of initiation with another person despite my experience. The bold, desperate girl of the past is gone. What's left is just a self-conscious woman in need of some guidance.

Whether he sensed my discomfort or he's just that kind of guy, Atlas steps into my bubble of worried air with hands on my arms, bringing his comforting presence with him.

"Just say the word and we'll go right to sleep," he offers politely. I know that would make his blue balls fall off, so the magnitude of his offer isn't lost on me.

I may have been waiting a year to have sex again, but he's been waiting five years for this moment.

And in a lot of ways, I think I have too.

Looking up into his sincere expression, I tell Atlas, "I want you. We've waited long enough."

With a smile that's somewhere between ravenous and overjoyed, Atlas slips his hands beneath my ass and hoists me into the air so he can carry me to the dresser against the wall. The moment my ass touches the surface, he devours me in an all-consuming kiss.

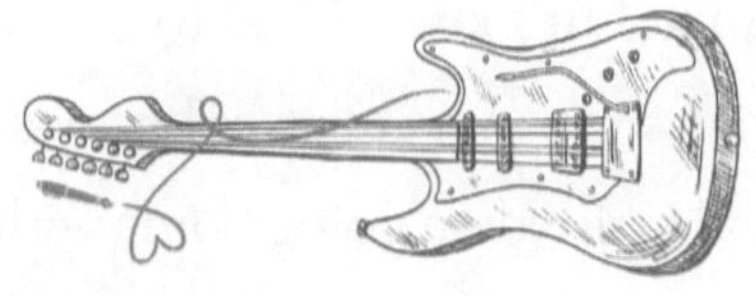

Forty-Five
Layla

JUST **P**RETEND-**B**AD **O**MENS

His enlarged erection fights against the confines of his jeans as he grinds himself into my center, swiftly reminding me how good it feels to be captured in his embrace. My core is throbbing at the first touch. Three hundred and sixty-five fucking days since the last time someone touched me this way. Since the last time I knew carnal pleasure with another person.

But none of those meant anything. Something tells me this interaction will be far and beyond anything I've ever experienced. With the right person, I know it will be transcendent.

"Tell me what you want, Rosie." Atlas whispers into my ear as his mouth trails my jawline to the artery in my neck. "Tell me how you want it."

Atlas is perfectly capable of pleasuring a woman, that much I'm sure of. Asking me how I want it has nothing to do with performance and everything to do with gauging my comfort level.

Taking a quick nip of his ear lobe, I answer, "Don't hold back." I'm not fragile, I'm not broken. I'm stronger than ever before because of what I went through.

And I crave this man and all he has to offer like the most potent drug on earth.

Without needing further instruction, Atlas rips the plain gray t-shirt I'm wearing over my head, leaving the necklaces in place. I follow suit by pushing the unbuttoned shirt off his shoulders then lifting the hem of the black t-shirt beneath so we are chest to chest, skin to skin, even if my bra is still on.

To my surprise, he leaves that alone as he picks me up and swings me toward the bed in a few strides, laying me down with a bit of force. Moving as one cohesive mind, I prop myself on my elbows to lift my butt in the air so he can slide the wide legged pants over the globes of my ass and down my legs. Now, I'm in nothing but my lace bra and panties, waiting expectantly to see what he'll do next.

The ferocity in his gaze morphs into barely restrained lust as the tension in the air softens. Atlas helps me to stand in a moment of tenderness, so we are face to face, chest to chest, nose to nose. He places a soft kiss on the corner of my mouth as one hand slips to my back to unclasp the bra, letting the structured material fall to the floor. But despite my breasts being on full display, Atlas doesn't look down, not initially. He lowers to his knees in front of me, letting his lips trail my body with feather-light kisses as he grips the waistband of my panties and lowers them over my hips, down my legs, gently placing them on the floor.

Only once I'm completely bare does Atlas stand, back up, and admire my naked form with appreciative lust. Only now does it don on me that Atlas and I have never seen each other naked before. The one time we had sex we were both clothed. The closest we've come to this is in swimsuits at the beach.

The vulnerable realization sends goose flesh prickling down my arms but I try to maintain an unfazed confidence.

Atlas returns to stand directly in front of me, bringing his sturdy hands to my waist so they can freely explore my body.

"You are a vision, Layla." My chest rises into his with my heavy inhale. "You're beautiful." He's not trying to win me over with pretty words, he's stating how he feels, simple as that.

There's no need for me to respond as he lowers his mouth to my nipple and sucks it between his lips, trailing his tongue around the hard peak. Hands firmly against my back, he holds me in place as his mouth takes a turn exploring me.

Operating with a mind of their own, my hands weave into his dark locks, tugging and toying with the soft strands as my body gives in to the pleasure. My head tips back without thinking which arches my breast into him more as Atlas switches back and forth, leaving kisses everywhere.

Although I think I could come from this alone, I'm pleased when Atlas maneuvers me back to the bed so I lay with my legs hanging off the end. He stands above me, between my legs, staring down at me like a feast laid out for him to consume. And I desperately want to be consumed by him.

"I've always wondered what you taste like," he says as he lowers to his knees between my legs. "And now I finally get to find out."

Before finding my core, Atlas gently nibbles my inner thigh, a tease through and through, until his nose brushes my clit. Then his tongue slides through me, one languid stroke through my center, up to meet the spot that's begging for his attention. A low rumble rises from his chest before he descends upon me like a starved man.

Instinctively, my body responds to every touch as he eats me alive, devouring me with a tongue so wicked it's sang the most beautiful words, but it's just as talented at driving me wild. My back arches off the bed, I grip his hair so tight in my fist I'm sure it stings. But I can't find it in me to care when this torture is so enticing.

"Atlas." My voice comes out raspy. "*Fuck.*" I'm so close but there's no need to tell him, he knows.

I've longed for this for a year, longed for him even longer. I'm a writhing mess on the verge of explosion I can hardly stand—

He pulls away. He fucking stops. *Why did he stop?*

Like a lion cornering its next meal, Atlas scales up my body, hungry eyes fixed on mine the entire time.

"I was close," I tell him, hoping he didn't think me uttering his name was his cue that I'd finished.

"I know," he informs me with a malicious grin. "I've been waiting for this for too long, and so have you. So I'm going to make it worth the wait."

As he presses a devious kiss to my lips I wonder *is he edging me?*

I crave the return of his body heat the moment he lifts off the bed and strides into the bathroom. He returns a moment later with a package in hand that he's ripping into to extract a pair of padded handcuffs connected by an adjustable chain. Suddenly his intention settles over me and I can't tell if the butterflies in my stomach are from excitement or trepidation. Maybe both.

"You said you'd never trusted anyone to do this before." With a forceful pull, Atlas yanks me into a standing position at the foot of the bed so our bodies are pressed together. Staring into my soul with all the love in the world he asks, "Do you trust me?"

I've never seen this primal side of Atlas before, but I never want it to end. As much as I fell for his sweet, sentimental side, the part of him that got me such a thoughtful gift in honor of my year of celibacy and the growth I had, I like this side of him more.

One word and my fate is sealed. "Yes."

A smirk that tells me I'm in for a wild night stretches across his handsome face before Atlas grabs my wrist and locks it in one cuff. He then tosses the free cuff over the metal frame of the bed so my arms are in the air before confining my free wrist. Calculating every second of this night, he adjusts the chain so I can comfortably stand on the balls of my feet, but not flat footed.

The anticipation is killing me. I'm dying to know what he has in store.

Standing back to admire his handiwork, Atlas gives me an appreciative once over with hungry eyes before twirling a finger in the air and commanding, "Turn."

I do as I'm told, spinning on my toes so my back is to him. I hear him open and close a drawer behind me before his hand smacks my asscheek and his warmth covers me. One hand reaches around to grope my breast while his face nuzzles into my neck, kissing me hard enough to leave a mark. I tip my head to the side to provide as much access as he requires, loving the feel of his mouth on me in any capacity.

Then a buzzing sound fills the space, knocking me out of my trance so my eyes shoot open just before a vibrator circles my nipple. I gasp at the contact, relishing the blissful torment and wishing the toy was between my legs instead.

Atlas takes his time playing with me, whispering dirty words into my ear. "I can't wait to bury myself inside you."

Neither can I.

"I've dreamed up all the filthy ways I can play with this pretty pussy and make you scream."

Yes, that's exactly what I want. Now!

"But I want to have a little fun first."

Oh shit.

The vibrator sinks to my core where Atlas swirls it between my legs before letting the concentrated tip meet my clit. Already tender and swollen, my clit is famished for a release. I lean my head back against his collarbone as the pleasure begins to build again, aching and wanton.

"You make the most beautiful sounds." His warm breath whispers over my neck. "I've thought about how you'd sound countless times, every time I fucked my fist wishing it was you."

"Ohmygod." My words come out as one as I chase the orgasm I feel coming on, hoping he'll let me have this one.

"But I think the first time I make you come—the first time I hear you scream my name—I want it to be on my cock."

Then he pulls the vibrator away leaving me panting for more.

I grunt my frustration as Atlas spins me back so the chain is unbound. My hands are wrapped around the cool metal so tight, every muscle in my body begging for release.

Once I open my eyes I realize it's my turn for a show as Atlas unbuttons his dark jeans without removing his gaze from my own. Painfully slow, he tugs each pant leg off to reveal thick thighs and a trim waist. Then—finally—he slides his briefs down his legs until he matches me in complete nudity.

And my god, I thought I remembered his size but seeing him now, unhurried and standing like a bronzed Grecian statue before me, I'm salivating at the thought of him inside me.

Digging into a drawer once again, Atlas retrieves a condom and rolls it down his length before tossing the wrapper.

I need him so much it's painful. I've stood on the precipice of two orgasms without falling over the edge and I don't know how much longer I can wait.

Thankfully, He doesn't leave me hanging for long before lifting me by the ass to wrap my legs around his waist. I'm tempted to chase whatever orgasm I can get by grinding into him, but decide whatever he has in store will probably be so much more satisfying.

My nipples press into his chest, a light sheen of sweat coats our skin, the air is humid with desire.

Then inch by blissful inch, Atlas stretches me as he sinks into my heat. We share a mutual groan of satisfaction until he's perfectly seated inside me, supporting me with hands under my rear.

"Fuck, Rosie," he grits through his teeth as he pulls out again. "You feel like heaven."

All I can manage to say is "Atlas," as he slams back into me.

Every inch of me is on fire as Atlas repeats the process over and over, picking up speed with each thrust.

"Yes, Atlas please. Yes."

"You're perfect, Rosie," he says through clenched teeth. "I never want this to end." I can feel how much he enjoyed playing with me in every jolt of his hips, every time he sinks to the base of his shaft. I can see it in his furrowed brows and taut lines of his body. He's holding out as long as he can, dangling me over the promise of an orgasm in the process.

Just when I think I can't take much more of this torture, Atlas reaches behind me to the bed and retrieves the vibrator, flicking the device on once more before positioning it between our bodies so the vibrations send shots of electricity through my veins. With one hand keeping me steady as my legs bind us together, Atlas drives into me with wild abandon, a crazed animal finally unleashing his fury in the most delicious way.

"Oh fuck, *Atlas*."

With every part of me being stimulated, the pent up orgasms finally crash over me like a wave of euphoria. One after the other, it's like the orgasms I was denied earlier course through me in perfect succession until I'm a shaking mess of riled ecstasy.

"That's it, Rosie. You take it so well."

I'm lost in a world of orgasmic bliss until the final thrusts from Atlas trigger his own release and a growl that reverberates through the room, through my body.

I can barely feel my limbs when he finally reaches up to unlock one wrist before draping my arms over his shoulders and hoisting me into the air. One arm beneath my back, one beneath my knees, he carries me into the bathroom and uses one foot to turn the bath water on as we sink into the tub and let the hot water smooth our aching muscles, cleansing us of the past.

Atlas keeps me cradled between his legs as he unlocks my other wrist. I relax into him, savoring every moment of this night and the connection we strengthened.

"I love you," Atlas whispers into my hair as fatigue takes over.

But I'm not too tired to return the sentiment. "I love you too."

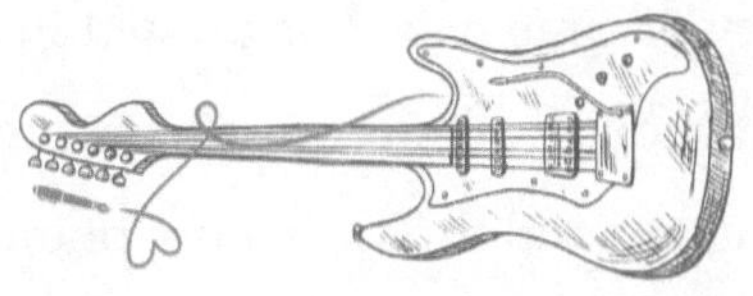

Forty-Six

Layla

You Put A Spell On Me-Austin Giorgio

It's been three days of nonstop sex, late night talks, and more love than I ever thought possible. We've learned a great deal about each other along the way.

For example: Atlas is one of those people who takes showers in boiling hot water.

And I'm the kind of person who tries to stop the microwave on the last second so I don't have to listen to the incessant beeping.

This is what our relationship needed, uninhibited time to see how we do without the chaos of the rockstar lifestyle. Without other people weighing in. There's no buffer between us in this perfect isolation.

I was worried we'd find out it was always just chemical attraction, that we couldn't spend time together that didn't involve work or music. But it turns out we've needed each other to survive. The final piece of the puzzle has been set in place and I feel whole again.

I brought an entire suitcase of clothes for this week but I've spent the majority of time naked or dressed in one of his shirts. When I was looking for a fresh shirt to put on, I found a crisp white button-up in his closet and threw that on, prancing back into the bedroom asking, "When have you ever worn white?"

Darkened eyes told me Atlas liked the look of his clothing on me. Then he answered. "I've never worn it. I had someone buy some business professional clothing for me and she threw that one in 'just in case the need ever arose.'"

"And has the need arisen?"

"It has now." Although the material is high quality, the white is not opaque enough to conceal the slight hue of my nipples. The shirt did not stay on long, but I returned it to my frame the next time we left the bedroom.

We've spent a great deal of time in the music room as well. Atlas has shown me all his prized possessions, the random records he's found over the years, the artists no one has ever heard of before. He's positively luminescent when he talks about music. I think one of the reasons he's been so successful in his career is because he doesn't see it as work. I'm sure the paperwork and corporate details of owning a record label are tedious. But music in any form inspires him to continue to create, to explore, to never be satisfied.

We've spent the last hour listening to an undiscovered Swedish band. Atlas lounges on the olive sofa in a pair of black sweat pants and nothing more, refined muscles on display as he drapes one arm over the back of the sofa.

I'm examining his collection for the hundredth time in nothing but the white shirt, finding a new record every time I scan the shelves. I brought my film camera with me in case we went anywhere worth documenting. But as I let my eyes fall on the man watching me across the room, I decide this moment is more than worthy of documentation. So I lift the camera, position him in the bottom right corner of the frame so the bay window occupies the top left, and snap a photo of him. The light of the window illuminates one side of his face while the other is cast into shadow. It'll look amazing in black and white, even if no one other than he and I ever see it.

"It's nice seeing you take pictures again."

"I've been taking pictures the entire tour," I remind him.

"No, you've been doing your job and documenting it. You didn't start taking pictures for fun until Cam and Kenzie's wedding." I guess that's true. "I like the way you smile when you take photos of things that actually bring you joy. You're coming back to life."

I narrow my eyes. "What do you mean?"

Atlas runs flexed fingers through his tousled hair, tilting his head with a smile. "I hope this doesn't offend you, but when you walked into that conference room at the record label, I felt like you were dulled, somehow. Like you lost your spark. And over the past couple of months, I think you got it back. You're coming back to life."

He's right, but I don't know how I feel about him noticing my depressive state so early on. Was I that transparent?

Leaning against the wall opposite the sofa, I stare at the ever-changing ocean beyond the window. "I guess you're right. I really lost myself without my family. I had no one. And I know I made the choice to cut everyone off, but I didn't know who to be without you guys."

"You're not alone anymore."

I watch Atlas from across the room unabashedly. He's beautiful, in the way that some men are. Smooth lines, tan skin, and high cheekbones. His posture is that of a man who's comfortable in his own skin. I've spent years trying to replicate that kind of confidence in public, only to cower in private. But being with him makes me feel like none of it matters. With the right person, you simply feel alive.

A light bulb shines above my head when an idea sparks to life. Lips twitching into a mischievous smile, I ask, "Do you know what boudoir photos are?"

With pinched brows Atlas asks, "Like dirty photos?"

"Common misconception. They're more artistic than just a dick pic."

"So what are you asking, Rosie? Use your words."

A subtle thrill shoots down my spine. "I want to take some of you. Just for our eyes, of course."

"You're the professional." Atlas leans forward to brace his elbows on his knees, chin balanced on a fist. "Tell me what to do."

Those are dangerous words.

"Lean back," I instruct. "And rub yourself over the sweatpants."

Atlas keeps his dark eyes fixed on me as he follows my instructions. A cloud of lust coats his vision as he keeps me in his sights while one prominent hand begins to massage himself through the jersey material.

"Like this?"

I nod as I lift the camera to look through the viewfinder and snap a photo. The little flash brightens the room for a split second, highlighting the tightness of his jaw.

"Now pull your cock out," I tell him next. I rub my thighs together as the excitement builds between my legs. This private show was crafted in my wildest fantasies, yet here it is coming to life.

Muscles flexing, Atlas reaches beneath the loose waistband of his pants to free his already hard erection. It's become abundantly apparent that when it comes to me, Atlas is always ready for more.

"What now, Rosie?" *He's such a tease.*

"Now stroke yourself, slowly."

A firm grasp on his cock, Atlas glides his fist up and down along the shaft, smearing his thumb over the tip when he reaches the top. The heat in his gaze ignites a fire in my core. I almost forget the reason we're doing this—almost. So I lift the camera again, taking a step closer to him, and taking another photo.

"Now let go." I don't mean literally, and he knows that. So as his speed increases, Atlas drops his head to the back of the sofa as his pleasure expands through his body. Tight muscles and a face twisted in agonized bliss, he's the sexiest thing I've ever seen. The rose tattoo over his heart flex's with every stroke.

This will likely be my favorite photo of the bunch.

"Come here, Rosie." Atlas slows his pace and lifts his head so our eyes connect again.

Since he was so good at following directions, I reciprocate by climbing onto the sofa. One knee on either side of his leg, balancing so I hover over him while he continues to torture himself with leisurely strokes.

Atlas's free hand caresses my thigh as he moves up my leg, beneath the white shirt, and tenderly—just barely—glides through my center. I sigh, raising my camera to capture this angle from above, looking down at the majestic sight before me.

After I take the photo, Atlas tells me, "Give me the camera." Not willing to back down from this match, I do as he demands, removing the strap from around my neck and looping it around his. Once I've done as I was asked, Atlas's hand finds my core and effortlessly slips two fingers inside. Humming in delight he says, "Mmm, you like this don't you."

A breathy, "Yes," is my only response as those skilled fingers curl inside me. The same hands that play remarkable music strum my inner walls exactly where I need them to. Atlas has spent the better part of three days becoming well acquainted with my body, studying every response I provide.

As his precise ministrations elicit moans from me, he can add my body to the extensive list of instruments he plays.

His thumb joins the mix as he bends his hand to rub my clit in tiny circles while his index and middle finger continue to pump in and out of me. Losing my control over my body, I send a hand flying to his shoulder to find balance as the orgasm builds in the pit of my stomach. He sends me higher and higher, the noises I make reflecting the elation.

"Oh shit," I rasp as I feel the orgasm within reach.

"That's it, Rosie," Atlas's husky, lust-filled voice heats my skin. "I want to hear it. I want to see it."

Lost to wild abandon, I give myself over to the orgasm while screaming his name until my body is quaking with each ripple of pleasure. Atlas doesn't release me until the clenching ceases. Somewhere in the back of my mind, I register the sound of the camera clicking and the subtle flash of a photo being taken. Only once every ounce of ecstasy has been coaxed from my body do I open my eyes and look down to find the man of my dreams beaming at me, a post orgasmic glimmer in his eyes, and evidence of it on his stomach.

"You're better than my wildest dreams," he tells me through a breathless sigh of relief.

I collapse onto the sofa beside him, anxious to develop these photos and relive the experience.

Keeping in mind that his semen is on his stomach, I curl into his side to avoid touching it while still sharing the rush of oxytocin surging between us. His heavy breaths draw my eyes to that damned tattoo, the one I was so angry about. But looking back, I think I just didn't know how to cope with his devotion, with his certainty. Years of feeling inadequate make it hard to accept love when it's right in front of you. I once heard the line "we accept the love we think we deserve" and it wrecked me. I'd been accepting half-assed affection and empty promises for too long. But I also didn't think I deserved everything Atlas was offering me.

Until now.

I trace a lazy finger over the perfect lines. Noticing how his heartbeat makes the rose pulse with life.

"You were so certain we'd find our way back," I expel my thoughts out loud.

Atlas's hand gently wraps around mine, not stopping my pattern, just connecting to it.

"Nothing has been the same since I met you," he confesses. "You're my everything. It took me too damn long to see it and then I lost you. Now that I have you back, I won't let anything ever come between us."

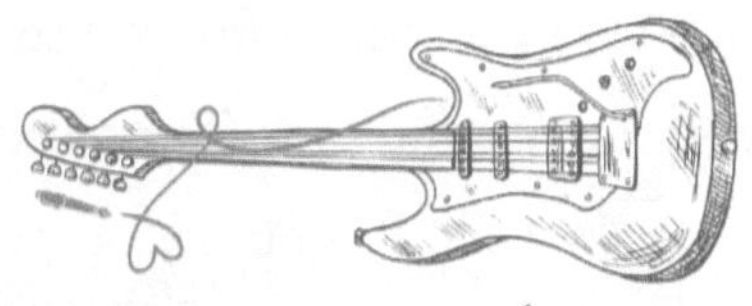

Forty-Seven

Layla

SOMEBODY **T**HAT **I** **U**SED **T**O Know-Gotye

After five days of perfection, being parted from Atlas is like losing a limb.

The good news is that with the Dodgers in the World Series, Broken Compass has been asked to perform before the game for their hometown crowd. Which means I get to see him sooner than their week off before the European leg of the tour.

With the magazine feature coming out and a few more months of touring, we decided to keep the relationship a secret from the outside world until things settle down a bit. I'm not sure how my boss would feel about the implications of the journalist for the feature sleeping with the lead singer. While Atlas has worked tirelessly to remake his "bad boy" image the original label wanted him to carry, this story has been told before. And no one comes out looking good in it. The last thing we want is for Atlas to look like a womanizer and for me to look like a fame chaser.

I walk into the stadium with a little surprise for Atlas in my purse. He meets me at the player's entrance so we can avoid the public attention as he escorts me back. The second I see his relaxed frame leaning against the wall, I jump into a sprint the rest of the way, crashing into him less than gracefully. I pictured this reunion going a little smoother in my head.

Although, Atlas doesn't seem to mind as he takes the brunt of my weight and folds me into him with the warmth of a hug only he can provide. One second I'm breathing in his distinct scent, the next his lips are on mine and I'm aching for a repeat of our week in isolation.

"Hey, gorgeous," he says by way of greeting, creases forming around his mouth and eyes with his bright smile.

"Hey, handsome," I return the compliment.

Still in the honeymoon phase of this relationship, we stand suspended in time basking in the affection our hearts are incapable of ignoring.

"I have something for you." I let my cheeky grin clue him in to what's coming before extracting the developed photos from our spontaneous boudoir session so he can peek through them. I've already made copies for myself to tide me over while he's on the road. It's hard to have phone sex or send dirty pictures when he's sharing a bus with three other guys.

Atlas gives me an appreciative glance as he scans through the photos of him enjoying himself. I point out my favorite which happens to be when he's lost to the sensations and I managed to catch his eyes rolling back as his head dips toward the back of the sofa. It's so sultry it makes me wet just looking at it.

When he comes to the photos he took of me he stops to absorb them to memory as if he wasn't there to witness it. As if he wasn't the one to take the photos in the first place.

"If your goal was to make me hard before I play in front of thousands of people, you've succeeded." He nuzzles into my neck, tickling the sensitive skin behind my ear with his nose so I release an involuntary giggle.

"At the risk of sounding like a creep, I will definitely be jerking off to this over the next couple months." He holds up a photo of me with breasts bared, mouth agape on a moan, and his hand buried inside me. The only tell that it's him is the tattoos on his wrist.

I rise onto my tippy-toes to take a quick nibble of his ear lobe before saying, "Likewise." As I lower I remind him, "But I still expect some dirty FaceTimes when you're in hotel rooms."

Reaching one hand behind me to squeeze my ass cheek, he whispers in a sultry voice, "Nothing beats the real thing. But I'll take what I can get."

I feel like a lovesick preteen giggling at his hot-and-heavy flirtation but I can't help it. A small part of me is still grasping the reality that Atlas Woods is my secret boyfriend. It sounds so high school until I remember we are fully grown adults who do very adult things to each other.

"Come on. The band's this way." Atlas tugs me along by the hand through the wide halls of the private entrance, tucking the photos back into their envelope before slipping it into his back pocket.

I admire some of the Dodgers memorabilia on the wall as we walk side by side, hand in hand, in search of the rest of the band. Kenzie texted me thirty minutes ago she was already here, but I had work to finish before I could slip away.

We skitter along when an unwelcome reunion stops me in my tracks.

"Isn't this a surprise." I never thought I'd hear that voice again. I thought I'd scrubbed it from my memory but it comes grating back to me as Jack steps out of a connecting hallway.

Atlas must recognize him too, based on the tick in his jaw at the sight of my ex-boyfriend.

"Jack." I level my voice so I don't sound as caught off guard as I am. "What are you doing here?"

"I work here," he answers in a snide tone, a tone of entitlement. "The question is what are *you* doing here? The last I checked, you can't get to the press boxes this way."

"She's with the band," Atlas informs him. He probably should have dropped my hand the second we heard Jack's voice. But he only tightened his possessive hold on me. It's too late, anyway, I guess. Knowing how spiteful Jack is, he'll probably go to the media with some outlandish story about finding us banging in a closet by morning.

Jack's cold gaze slithers down to our clasped hands then back up with a knowing smirk. "I thought you'd outgrown the groupie thing, Layla. I guess some people never change."

"Now that I can agree on." His smirk dies with that remark, replaced by a frosty hatred. As a man who's never been denied anything in his privileged life, he doesn't take criticism well. Clearly he hasn't changed.

I remind myself I'm not the same girl he knew in college. I'm not the same girl he manipulated and emotionally abused. I have to say it over and over in my head so I don't submit to his cruelty.

Thank goodness for steadfast Atlas at my side, my constant rock.

Knowing the severity of his words, he fires them like bullets across the hall so they land directly in my chest. "I see you're still screwing around. You should feel honored, rockstar, I heard she doesn't do repeats."

My bones freeze down to their marrow. *Is he referring to what I think he is?*

"Watch your mouth, rich boy." Atlas takes half a step forward.

A wicked grin curls Jack's features into a menacing smirk. "I heard one of the players a few years ago saying he met this hot journalist at a Hollywood party who sucked his brains out before he screwed her senseless. Said she worked for Rolling Stone but he couldn't remember her name. And I thought, what are the odds it's the same slut I knew in college? Guess this answers my question."

Atlas closes in on Jack in the span of one heartbeat, his thick forearm braced against Jack's delicate neck, pinning him to the wall. With utter vehemence I've never heard in his voice before, Atlas growls in Jack's face. "Don't ever speak about her like that again, you entitled prick. You think you're untouchable? You're not. One word about harassment toward me and your sorry assistant-to-the-assistant-coach-ass will be fired in a flash."

Fury burns in Jack's eyes as Atlas's threat settles over him. If we didn't already have an enemy in Jack, we sure do now.

"Hey there you are," Rob's voice causes Atlas to step back to my side, but not without one last harsh stare of hatred in Jack's direction.

Rob slows to a cautious waddle like someone trying to talk a jumper off a ledge. "Everything ok, man?"

"Yeah, man, everything's fine. Let's get ready to go on."

Atlas places a protective arm around my shoulders to guide me toward the rest of the band. It feels good to be claimed by him, even if it is a detriment to our reputation.

My career could very well be on the line after this. The media cycle will plaster whatever story Jack tells them everywhere for a couple days, then the wind will die down and his career will live on.

I, on the other hand, may not have a job in the morning.

When we reach everyone else, McKenzie notices my spooked expression immediately and comes to my side.

"Are you alright?"

I nod unconvincingly. "Yeah, I'm fine."

Atlas tucks me into his side, kissing the top of my head before the guys walk out as their name is announced to the thunderous applause of Dodger Stadium. It's the fifth night of the World Series. They've won three out of the four games so far, and the hope is that they win the whole thing tonight in front of the home crowd.

Broken Compass plays two of their lesser known songs for the audience. They're cult favorite songs but not broadcast on the radio often. Then they perform the national anthem before the game commences and Los Angeles explodes with fireworks and celebration as the Dodgers win the World Series.

I wish I was in the celebrating mood, I wish I could jump up and down with uninhibited excitement for the LA team that has worked so hard to get here. But my mind is bogged down by a guillotine dangling over my head.

After making the appropriate appearances at celebration parties with the rest of the band, Atlas usher's me back to his place. The car ride lacks the enthusiasm of the after parties. We both feel the weight of whatever is about to happen, knowing too well that Jack won't let go of an opportunity to hurt either one of us. That man can carry a grudge.

As soon as we walk in the door, I unload all my fears.

"What are we going to do, Atlas?"

Choosing this moment to comfort me with his actions first, he cocoons me in a soothing hug to calm my nerves.

"We'll weather the storm," he answers simply, as if it's that easy.

Taking the lead since I'm too wrapped up in my own thoughts to function, he leads me to the couch where he pulls me into his lap, rubbing soft circles over my back as he holds me.

"I could lose my job, Atlas."

"You won't. You're too valuable."

"Or too much of a liability." I can already hear Stan scolding me for bringing this kind of heat on the magazine. "This would be damaging to the magazine's credibility. They might be pressed to take action if it gets out of hand."

"We have a *history*, Rosie, we are together. It wasn't a one time fling."

"I know. But I've seen innocent stories get blown out of proportion. We take ourselves very seriously and try not to give into the rumor mill, but sometimes it spirals so much it's all we can do."

"So we get a handle on it before the media does." I hear a plan brewing in his tone. "We announce our relationship as soon as possible, imply the severity of it, and then Jack's story falls on deaf ears."

"It might work." I run over all the possible outcomes in my heavy head. "But I could still get fired."

"We have a shit show on our hands," Atlas declares, plain and simple. "So let's try to limit the number of worst case scenarios possible. I know your job is still at risk but at least we'd have control over the narrative. We can tell people exactly what this is, a love story that's been a long time coming."

I lift my head to gaze into the eyes that have brought me so much peace, finding solidarity and support within them.

Running my fingers through Atlas's dark locks I tell him, "I love you. So much."

With a hand cupping my jaw, Atlas brings me in for a soulful kiss that promises everything and more. "No matter what happens, we'll overcome it together." A charming smile lifts one corner of his mouth. "And I gotta say, I'm glad I'll finally be able to claim you in public as mine."

Laughing into his next kiss I say, "Hey now, I might have a few kinks but exhibitionism isn't one of them."

With a teasing lilt Atlas replies, "What a shame."

Forty-Eight
Atlas

GIVE **M**E **L**OVE-**E**D **S**HEERAN

There's more than just the fear of losing her job weighing on Rosie. It doesn't matter how much time we spent apart, when you love someone, you pick up on all of their cues. I can tell by how resigned she is, the way her shoulders slouch forward, and the way she's closed off her thoughts to me, that something else is bothering her.

I have a feeling I know what it is, but I need her to talk to me if we are going to make this work. She's my partner. This isn't casual. I want her to know I'm here for her without judgement.

She's been in the shower for fifteen minutes now, I figure that's enough time alone with her thoughts that I can join her.

I push the door open to the bathroom engulfed in steam. The fogged glass of the walk-in shower obscures her naked form with condensation but I can make out the curves of her luscious body. And although I know she needs emotional support right now, I can't wait to get my hands on the woman I'm obsessed with. The past couple weeks have been excruciating without her.

I strip out of the clothes from the game, tossing them in the hamper by the linen closet before opening the shower door to step in behind her. If Rosie hears me, she doesn't turn to acknowledge my presence.

As much as I want to make her come over and over again right now, she needs me, not my needy dick. So I pull her back to my chest beneath one of the shower heads and let the warm water wash away her fears, her demons.

I once read about all the science behind a hug. That putting pressure on the central nervous system helps to calm it. That seven seconds of contact with another human being releases oxytocin in the brain. I even read that hugs have been proven to temporarily reduce chronic pain.

So I pour all the love I can into this one interaction with the hope it will lessen her worries.

"What's really on your mind, Rosie?" I speak softly into her ear from behind, keeping pressure with my arms over her chest.

Her breathing is shallow when she answers, "I'm ashamed." Realizing she probably thinks I think she's ashamed of me, she remedies, "Not of you. Of who I used to be."

"I'm not judging you," I remind her. And I never have. We all dealt with the loss of Dallas in different ways. She never knew that Chris got fucked up on a hallucinogenic on Dallas's first birthday in heaven. She'd never know that Cam tried to drink away the pain until Kenzie put a stop to it before it became a problem.

And I had my own demons to wrestle with. I got tattoos and wrote depressing music that never saw the light of day. We all grieve in different ways. And even though people say grieving is healthy, it's not. Not until you come out the other side.

"I wish I could say he was lying, that I never slept with someone from the team. But I don't know. It was all a blur. I didn't care how I was used because I was using them to numb the pain."

I did some research after our talk in Texas and found out that hyper-sexualization is actually a really common coping mechanism for people. They bury their worries in feelings of pleasure much the same way people use drugs and alcohol as a temporary fix. But the pain always comes back in the morning.

"Why would you want me Atlas?" My heart breaks a little hearing a question like that fall past her lips. How could I want anyone but her?

"Why would you want someone who's probably fucked hundreds of guys? Doesn't that bother you? Why would you want someone who's damaged and used up? Why would you want me?"

Before this self-deprivation can go any further, I squeeze her shoulder with reassurance, locking her against me. "Because that's not how I see you." I don't care how many guys she's been with. She's mine. She's my Rosie. She's so much more than her mistakes.

"You spent the last year of your life becoming the woman you want to be. You found a sense of purpose within yourself instead of in another person." And then she let me love her.

No matter how many times I can tell her I'm proud of her for changing her life and seeing the value that I see in her, I know it all has to be an internal choice.

All I can do is love her and remind her she's whole.

She may very well push me away, but I follow my instincts and remind her in the best way I know how: with my actions.

I've written more songs about Rosie than she will ever know, but as my hands glide over her smooth skin, silky under the water, a new one takes form in my mind. I can hear the melody, I can hear the piano accompaniment to the acoustic guitar. The words start to form lyrics in my mind as her breathing deepens with every touch.

Treading carefully, I slide my hand down her stomach, inching between her legs so I can stroke her sweet pussy in languid, soothing motions. Meanwhile, my other hand tightens her against my chest so she's fully caged against me, feeling my swollen cock rut against her perfect ass.

"I love you." I remind her. And I'll keep reminding her until it sinks in and replaces the negative thoughts that invade her mind. "I love you. I love you. I love you. I love you."

When she tips her head back against my shoulder, I walk her back a few steps so I can reach the detachable shower head on the wall and change the setting. Just as I press into her so I feel her stretch gloriously around me, I lower the strong stream of water so the blast assaults her clit while I fuck her slowly from behind.

Easing her out of her agitated mind, I let the shower head do the work of bringing her to her first orgasm while I savor the clench of her pussy around my cock. She doesn't say my name, she doesn't swear, she just moans through the orgasm. That's how I know she needs more.

As I angle the spray of water away from her body, I increase my speed and pressure.

"You are everything I ever wanted, Layla." I speak over the wet sound of my pelvis slapping into her voluptuous ass. "I love all of you, not parts of you."

Her body begins to tighten again like a knot being pulled beneath my hands.

"We are two imperfect people who create something beautiful when we come together."

"*Oh fuck,*" she sighs as my thrusts get deeper with each word.

"I ask myself how I got so lucky every single day. How did I get so lucky that you chose me? That you forgave me? That you willingly give your heart to me?"

The familiar tingle builds at the base of my spine. My body wants to come but I need to hold onto my girl just a bit longer. I need her to feel worshiped before I even think about my own release.

"So don't for one second think that you're anything less than the girl of my dreams. We may not be perfect people, but you're perfect for me."

I lower the shower stream back to her throbbing center just as I start to feel her body prepare for an orgasm so the sensations collide to give her the release she needs. She utters my name like she's desperate for air as her entire being convulses around me. Only then do I fall over the edge with her, cherishing every moment I never thought I'd have with her.

We come down from the high our bodies created together to finish showering before I carry her to bed, letting her fall asleep in the crook of my arm before I sneak out of bed to chase the song she inspired in me.

It takes me most of the night, but by morning I have a new favorite song.

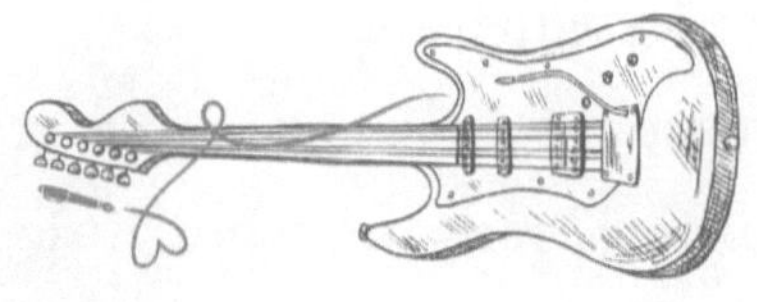

Forty-Nine

Layla

WORKING GIRL-CHER

"Remember, tell them we are going public and stand your ground. As soon as you give me the go-ahead, I'll make my post."

Taking a deep breath of the stale New York air, I nod despite the fact that Atlas can't see me to agree to the plan. I head up to Stan's office to come clean before Jack has the opportunity to take this right from us. He may have already gone to the press, for all we know, but I'll be damned if we don't try to control our love story for once.

I have one particular pair of heels I wear when I need a boost of confidence. I found them at a vintage shop a few years ago. A pair of 70s Charles Jourdain mustard yellow open toe heels. I imagined a fashionable business woman owned them at one time and I let the imaginary strength of the boss babe fuel my spirit as I strut into Stan's office to tell him that not only are Atlas Woods and I together, but I'll be relocating to Los Angeles. I pray to God and all of the women who came before me in a man's world that he accepts my terms.

Stan's assistant waves me past her desk as soon as I exit the elevator. "You can go right in. He's expecting you." As he should be since I set the meeting.

I offer one courtesy knock before pressing on the door handle to let myself in to the grand office. It's spacious and unencumbered by excess furniture. A wall of windows backlights Stan at his desk only adding to the air of importance around him.

I've never been intimidated by him, it might actually be the other way around. But I feel like the walls are closing in on me as I muster the courage to state my piece.

"Layla, nice to see you." Stan gives a few more final taps to his keyboard before providing his full attention. "What can I do for you?"

I don't take a seat, standing reminds me to keep my posture elevated. The chairs across from his desk are deep which always encourage the occupant to curl in on themselves. I will not be perceived as weak.

Time to rip off the bandaid.

"Well, Stan, I'm here to tell you that Atlas Woods and I are in a relationship and we will be going public with it as soon as I leave your office." Widened eyes reveal that his brain is already turning over how to spin this story, how to talk me out of this, how to handle the PR shitstorm coming his way. "Oh, and I'm relocating to the Los Angeles office."

Now I'm met with utter disbelief.

Since Stan is in a comatose state of shock, I take that as my sign to leave. "Good chat. I'll head to my desk and start the transfer paperwork."

"Wait wait wait." He elevates a hand like a crossing guard stopping cars. "Just a second, here. Let me wrap my brain around this. You're telling me you slept with the lead singer of the band we're featuring, and you're chasing him back to California? Do you realize the nightmare this could bring down on the magazine?"

"No, Stan," I say with an exasperated sigh. "I'm telling you I knew Atlas Woods and Broken Compass long before I ever worked here, as you know. And we had a lot of history. Things have changed over the past few months and we are giving this relationship our all. And I'm telling you you'll have a new asset in California, where a lot of the Hollywood buzz takes place. Less traveling on my part."

"Layla, this has the potential to look very, very bad—"

"I'll be straight with you, Stan," I school my body language so he can see that I'm serious. "My ex-boyfriend saw Atlas and I at the Dodgers game and he has a grudge against us. This story is already going to break, so we have to get ahead of it and give the world the romantic love story they'll swoon over, instead of letting a scandal break. There won't be any fodder for the press if we show them a united couple in love. *Which is what we are.*" The inflection in my voice is enough to convince Stan.

Rubbing his temples, Stan asks, "Ok. How are you planning to announce this grand love story to the world?"

"Atlas is going to post a soft launch to his social media accounts as soon as I leave this office. You and I both know the hits will start rolling in after that. Instead of letting this be a crisis, we're going to use it to everyone's advantage."

"Well, I guess thanks for giving me a heads up." The sarcasm in his voice is not lost on me as Stan reaches into the top drawer of his desk, taking a bottle of antacids from it and popping a couple into his mouth. Poor guy, I do not envy his job.

"Thanks for your understanding, Stan."

"It's not like you're giving me much of a choice."

"You could always fire me."

My boss levels me with a disdainful, unamused glare. "I'd rather deal with the transfer paperwork than the termination paperwork."

As I walk out the door he gets in one last remark. "Don't come crying to me if this doesn't work out."

"We'll send you an invite to the wedding," I reply just to drive his cortisol levels up a notch.

"Wait, *you're engaged?*"

No. And we definitely won't be any time soon. But the stress in his voice is worth the rumors.

I step into the restroom before leaving to call Atlas. As soon as he picks up I say, "All systems go."

A light chuckle greets me, caressing my mind that misses him terribly. "Already done, Red One. Go take a look."

"You already posted it?"

"I knew he wouldn't fire you, but even on the off chance he did, we still would have had to go public. So I took some preemptive measures."

"Hanging up, now." Even though my voice sounds irritated, we both know I won't be perturbed with him for long.

Especially after I see the selfie we took in his house the morning I left for New York. It's a soft launch mirror selfie of us hugging, his arm banded around my back so my face is away from the camera, but his face is in full view. Now everyone knows that Atlas Woods, the infamous bad boy who isn't anything like the image he's been portrayed as, is off the market.

What I didn't expect was for a song to be attached to it. There's no title or artist, but I'd recognize Atlas's style of playing anywhere. And When his voice comes through my speaker next, I almost lose it.

A slow, steady melody with a soft piano in the background as he sings lyrics I've never heard before.

You're everything, everything

I hold heaven in my hands

I'll hold you through all the years

That we've yet to plan

Who knew two imperfect people

Would be so right

I don't care how much time we've missed

we've got the rest of our lives

Blinking back tears, I dial Atlas once more.

"Did you like the song?"

"Like it? I loved it. Atlas, it was beautiful. When did you write that?"

"The last night you were here." If it's possible to hear a smile, I hear it course through his voice through the phone, warming me to my bones. "The words just came to me. I couldn't help myself. I had to record it for this."

I don't even know what to say. The fact that he wrote a song for me is one of the most romantic gestures he could have done. Atlas speaks his heart through music. I've listened over the years as he poured his heart into every album, knit-picking the small details others may not notice for hints about what he's feeling, what he's going through. Writing a song for me is one of the greatest professions of love he could give.

"Are you familiar with the myth of Atlas?" He draws me out of my thoughts.

"He's the god that holds the world, right?"

"Actually, he's a titan, sentenced to support the weight of the heavens for the rest of time for his part in the Titanomachy." Ok, Where is this leading, Atlas? "You are my heaven and earth, Layla Rose Grayson. But it's not a punishment for me to support you, it's a blessing. I can't wait to spend the rest of my life with you, at whatever pace you want to take it."

How dare he make me cry when I have this much makeup on.

"I love you, Atlas. You're my world." My voice starts to crackle with emotion. "Thank you for keeping me afloat."

"Always, Rosie."

With that, I head down stairs only to be stopped by one of the security guards a the door.

"Did you order a car, Miss Grayson?"

"Yeah..." There's a question in my voice. "Why?"

"There's a ton of paparazzi outside. Not sure who they're waiting for, but you might want to wait until your ride gets here."

I have a sinking suspicion who they might be trying to catch off guard.

The second I get the notification that my ride is here, I turn to the security guard with a little salute and say, "Wish me luck, Mark."

With a polite smile he pulls the glass door open. "Best of luck, Miss Grayson."

I'm going to need it.

Stepping out into the busy entryway is what I imagine gladiators facing a pack of lions in an arena felt like. Except in my case there's flashing lights and parasites trying to leech anything they can from me.

I get it, I'm in the journalism business too. But my work doesn't rely on gossip and harassment.

"Layla, Layla over here."

"Miss Granyson, care to comment on Atlas Woods' post?"

"How long have you and Mr. Woods been seeing each other?"

"How did you tame the notorious playboy?"

If they stopped listening to their own gossip, maybe they'd see the man I do.

As soon as I'm secure in the car, I snap a quick photo of the mob and send it off to the man responsible.

> LAYLA: You better have a good way to make this up to me.

His reply returns instantly.

> ATLAS: Hurry back to LA and I'll spend hours making it up to you;)

I spend the car ride back to my New York apartment considering all the ways my life is about to change. It feels surreal when I let myself examine everything that's happened, all the changes my life has endured. There was a time I never thought I'd overcome the demons haunting me yet here I am, on my way home to the love of my life, the man who's made it all seem like a fever dream.

I guess once you find the right person, all the struggles you faced seem worth it if it leads to this kind of love.

Because as much as I used to wish I could go back and alter the mistakes I made, I wouldn't change the things that brought Atlas and I back together. It wouldn't be our story without the hard work we put in to get here.

Epilogue
Layla

L AYLA-DEREK AND THE DOMINOS

"So what do you think?"

This is my fifth time pacing the floor plan of this house and the feeling of belonging is still there. The dark wood features and cream walls feel like home. The dining room that fits a table for twenty so we can host our music family feels like home. The balcony in the master bedroom overlooking the private beach feels like home.

But most of all, the room with the vaulted ceiling Atlas designated as the record room facing the sunset feels like home.

"I think it's perfect," I answer while staring at the built-in shelves surrounding the entertainment center. I can already picture the awards, nick-knacks, and memorabilia we're going to display there. Mementos from all of our adventures together.

After three years of living together, Atlas and I decided it was time to buy a home together. We have a future, we have forever, but we wanted a home to spend it in that felt like *us*.

Strong, affectionate arms wrap around my abdomen from behind as Atlas's warm scent envelops me, triggering countless memories. Some people associate perfumes with certain memories. If I could bottle Atlas, I would, just so I could revisit those feelings and thoughts whenever he's away.

The band certainly travels less now that the label is well established and Kenzie is expecting in a couple months. But any day apart is still too much for me. I travel with them as often as I can but I have my own career to care for, which keeps me in LA for long stretches of time. Thank goodness for vacation days.

"This is our house, Rosie. It was meant for us, I'm sure of it." Whenever Atlas gets that feeling deep in his gut, it's never wrong. He knew I was meant for him as much as this house is meant for us. Whatever our future together looks like, it'll be made here.

"Just think of all the music you'll make here." I tilt my head into Atlas's, savoring this moment of calm before the chaos ensues.

"Just think of all the places I can make you come," he whispers in return, rustling my hair. My spine stiffens remembering that our realtor is meandering about somewhere. The last thing I want is for her to overhear a comment like that.

"Are we ready to sign the paperwork?" Said realtor interrupts our moment, striking a mild panic attack in me. Amused, Atlas softly chuckles into my neck, the bastard loves making me uncomfortable.

If she did overhear Atlas's flirtation, she doesn't let on to it. With a wink she adds, "I understand you guys have a commitment later today."

"You could say that," my teasing voice is directed at Atlas who insisted we close on the house as soon as possible, despite the opportunity the band has been waiting for their entire career taking place later tonight.

The realtor gestures to the kitchen island where the paperwork is neatly laid out, a ballpoint pen for each of us, so we can spend the next twenty minutes going over the fine details before jetting off to the stadium.

Today marks a big moment in our lives for more reasons than one.

Standing in one of the suites overlooking the entire football field with McKenzie and her robust belly beside me, I still can't believe we're here.

The band has had a lot of "we finally made it" moments in their career. But playing the Super Bowl halftime show is probably one of the biggest nights of their lives.

"I can't believe our guys are playing the Super Bowl!" I say to no one in particular. "Remember when they were just playing little venues followed by karaoke at The Blue Room?"

Kenzie grumbles a reply, "I can't believe I'm freaking pregnant and I'm going to have to pee through the whole game."

"Hey, they have TVs in there. You can still watch." A scathing look of disapproval is all I get in return.

This baby was not exactly planned but she and Cam are more than excited to start their parenthood era. That being said, pregnancy has not been easy on her and she's ready to pop this kiddo out, which will be celebrated with several margaritas.

The two of us could care less about the actual Super Bowl, we're just here for the concert. Though I have to admit, the energy in the stadium is infectious, the consistent roar of the crowd, the secret chants I didn't know teams had, it has a way of sucking you into the excitement.

Fortunate enough to spend the game in the suite instead of in the stands, we have unlimited access to food and drinks. I heard pregnant women eat for two but holy crap, Kenzie can put away the sliders when she's pregnant.

Finally, halftime arrives and the field clears of all football related personnel as the stage and lighting equipment is moved into place. I've seen a lot of grand performances over my career, but never anything quite like a Super Bowl halftime show.

The remaining lights in the stadium dim before a burst of fire signals the start of the performance. First one, then three, then the entire stage lights up with the spotlights surrounding the band. They're met with more noise than I've ever heard in one stadium before as the music slowly grows to a crescendo. Naturally, the band has to start with their first hit, "Blood and Oxygen." But gradually they move into more of their popular songs from the past decade of their career. It's amazing what they've accomplished over the years.

Seamlessly, the band maneuvers through each song with smooth transitions. And in true Broken Compass fashion, they planned to end the performance with a cover song to pay tribute to the greats. But Atlas (and the rest of the guys) refused to tell anyone what the cover would be. It's not unlike Atlas to keep the cover songs a secret from time to time, but the mischief in his eyes leading up to this night clued me into his playful intent.

However, when the opening riff to "Layla" by Derek and the Dominos echoes through the stadium and Atlas's sultry voice sings my name for the world to hear, I melt into a puddle of emotion.

Layla

You've got me on my knees

Layla

I'm begging, darling, please

Layla

Darling, won't you ease my worried mind?

I know the song is more about pining for a lover, but part of me wonders if this is his reminder that he knew we were meant to be, long before I did. A reminder that he never gave up.

This is my life: in love with a rockstar and a family of friends I couldn't imagine living life without. The Layla of many moons ago would never believe the healing we've done, the relationships we've mended, and the life we built. I'll never be able to thank Atlas enough for being a stubborn ass who knew this is where our life was headed. If not for him, we wouldn't be this blissfully happy.

Watching him live out his dream has been one of the biggest joys of my life. But being his partner through it all has been worth every struggle to get to this point. Cam once said that eternal sunshine only produces a desert. After years in the rain, I think I'm finally enjoying the garden.

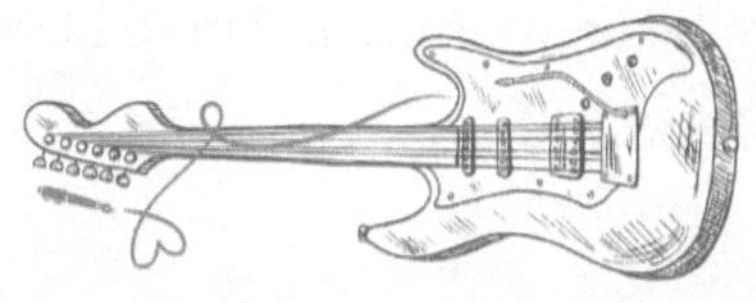

Acknowledgements

I ALMOST GAVE UP on this book, whether it be imposter syndrome, seasonal depression, or the fact that I wrote the majority of it with a heavy dose of pregnancy brain fog.

But with an amazing community like Booktok who inspire me daily, I've made friends who encouraged me to continue this piece and share it with the world. All I can hope is that one person connects to this story the way I have.

As always, I first want to thank my husband for all his unconditional support and believing in my dream. You're book husband material.

Thank you so much to my beta readers Jenna, Lisa, Jess, and Ashli. Your notes, reactions, and encouragement meant more to me than I can say! Without you, I might not have published this story.

Thank you to you, the reader. Without you, I wouldn't be able to achieve my childhood dream of being an author and sharing the stories my wild imagination comes up with.

Finally, thank you to my children for being my purpose. Being a writer is second to being your mom. I'm so blessed to live out my dream of motherhood with you.

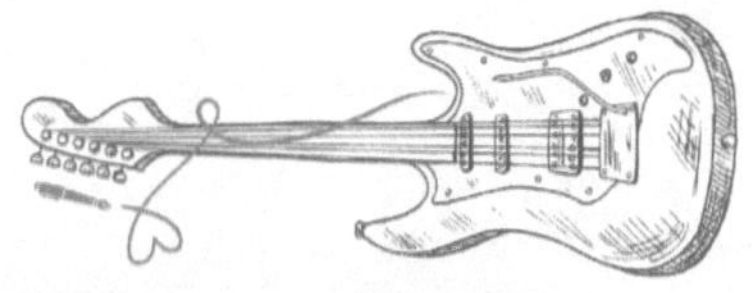

About the Author

Marisa Haartz is an independent author. An Oregonian transplanted in Arkansas, she lives with her family. She holds a degree in psychology which looks very sophisticated on her wall while she writes steamy books about lovable unlovable characters.

When she's not writing, she's hallucinating while reading ink on pages, or playing adult dress up. AKA cosplay.

Find her on social media as @marisahaartzauthor

9 798218 669935